TRIUMPH

TRIUMPH

A Novel

Judge Clarence Jones

Library of Congress Control Number: 2014918856
ISBN: Hardcover   978-1-4990-8515-0
                    Softcover   978-1-4990-8516-7
                    eBook   978-1-4990-8517-4

Rev. date: 02/24/2015

To order additional copies of this book, contact:
Xlibris
1-888-795-4274
www.Xlibris.com
Orders@Xlibris.com
636555

CONTENTS

Dedication

This book is dedicated to my amazingly devoted wife, Maureen. Her support for my 21 years of work as a judge, and patience over the years while I wrote this fictionalized account of certain real events made this novel possible.

I also wish to thank Jim and Barbara Maggio of Sarasota, Florida, and Rita Gould of Killingworth, Connecticut, for editing my manuscript.

PROLOGUE

5:14 AM

The deserted hospital halls are silent and white. A fluorescent bulb flickers behind its plastic cover. The midnight shift nurse examines a chart at her station. A young woman slips out of bed, lifts an infant from the bassinet, and walks into the bathroom. The infant near her breast whimpers and suckles, jerking her head back and forth under her mother's palm. The woman's index finger covers one tiny nostril, her thumb the other.

"Sh-h-h Katie, . . . I'll let go in a minute. Everything's gonna be alright."

Standing in the dark bathroom, away from her hospital bed and out of view of the ceiling camera, she thinks nothing is wrong. The doctors will take care of everything.

5:30 AM- Police Station

At any other time Mark would have admired his new pewter thermos, but now he just fills it with lukewarm left-over coffee and fastens his jacket without much thought. Adjusting his holster, he shuffled to the unmarked, standard-issue black police vehicle—car 22- and sat down with a sigh.

"Morning," Juan shouted with inappropriate cheerfulness, "Here we go again, affidavits to finish, court to get to, a judge to persuade, and children to rescue before their mother has them selling drugs, or themselves. Just another day in paradise."

"Never say the word 'affidavit' before seven a.m." Mark groaned, unscrewing the cap from his thermos. "It makes me nauseous."

Mark was tired from more than just the early hour. It didn't show in his body—there wasn't a hint of gray in his dark brown hair, or any slumping of his six-foot frame. The weariness was deeper, and it made him feel old. Car 22 reluctantly came to life and joined the few other vehicles on the road at daybreak. Mark pointed beneath the dashboard to the black lettering coming across a bluish yellow computer screen.

> . . . message from social worker at hospital states a mother demands to take daughter home against advice of hospital personnel. Hospital: infant daughter at high risk if released. Child underweight, periodic breathing problems. Child Protection has custody of sibling. Mother suspicious and hostile. Police assistance needed immediately. Car 22 report.

On the job ten years—not long enough to question its effect on his once wrinkle-free face—Juan had just celebrated his 32nd birthday. Mark looked at him and had a vision of his young partner's future. Young for the moment, with two children at home, the lines on Juan's face would deepen and darken. The voice would slip from crackling to scratchy. The weariness would become a part of him. Small prices to pay for a roof over a family's head, Mark thought, small price to pay for a safe city.

Car 22 sped up Chapel Street, passing Temple Street and the Lilly Baptist Church on its corner. Near the lower green of the University Campus, Juan angled a sharp left onto College Street, past the Shubert Theatre where the University Players were putting on something by Eugene O'Neil. A minute later, Car 22 screeched to a halt at the Hospital's Emergency Entrance. Juan glanced at the clock on the dashboard.

5:45 AM, Hospital Entrance

New Haven police detective Jill Smith, standing under a canopy, her eyes dark from a long night duty, beckoned Mark and Juan to the automatic doors. "What's the problem?" Mark asked, eschewing pleasantries.

"Don't know. Something about a woman trying to kill her baby. I was told to send you upstairs as soon as you got here. Fifth floor."

Mark and Juan rushed into the staff elevator, heavy with the smell of bleach and coffee. A muffled ding and the fifth floor doors opened, revealing two of the city's super-sized police officers. Something funny and intelligent tries to work its way from Mark's brain to his tongue, a comment about Nordic types and Roman fear, but he only mustered, "So serious that they have to send you guys?"

The taller of the two—at least six-foot-seven, Mark guesses— answers. "Nah, it's just that we were near the hospital when the call came in. You two experts are requested in the baby's room, down the hall, where the doctors are standing, looking lost."

"When did we become experts?" Mark wondered aloud while walking quickly toward the huddled medical staff. "And in what?" Juan questioned, then smiled and reached into his pocket.

A white-coated man and woman turned as Mark and Juan approached, their faces anxious. Juan flashed his badge. "What's the story?"

"We've got an erupting volcano. The woman is hysterical, desperate to take her daughter home. She tried to walk out with her earlier. When we tried to reason with her, she started screaming. That was ten minutes ago. Now the whole hospital is awake. Our social workers are talking with her now. Sorry you guys had to get up for us."

"No problem, we're already awake. What's your name?" Mark asked.

"Dr. Carter, Maureen Carter," she said, reaching to shake his hand, but Mark busily scratched her name in his notebook, and Juan took her hand instead. "I'm the chief resident on this ward. This is Dr. Barry Winston, a resident."

"Lieutenant Mark Jones. Juan Castile is my partner." Mark responded, without looking up. "Do you mind if we speak to her?" Juan asked.

"Go ahead," Dr. Carter responded, opening the door to Room 11-02. As the officers entered with detective badges on display, two social workers make a speedy exit.

Mark approached slowly, speaking as softly as Juan has ever heard him. "Ma'am, we're from the police department—"

"You can't have my baby!"

"I know. I don't want your baby. What's your name?"

Dorothy casted suspicious eyes at the two men. She pulled the quilted bedspread up to her chest, covering the infant in her arms, and ran her fingers through her hair, puffing it up.

She looks insane, Mark is thinking. *How long has it been since she's slept?*

With lips twisting she began speaking.

"I told these doctors it's not my fault. She's always sick so I bring her here; I didn't hurt her or anything. They are threatening to keep her! Who the hell do they think they are! I'm taking my daughter home!"

"Dorothy, we're going to step outside for a moment, okay?"

"I'm taking my goddam . . ."

Mark shut the door behind him.

"She hasn't done anything that we see to warrant arrest," Juan stated.

"No. But we can't let her leave here. Her other daughter has been taken by the Department, and the dispatch said this child has serious breathing problems."

A nurse slipped past him and opened the door. Juan started to stop her, but Mark grabbed his arm.

"It's okay. Estelle knows what she's doing," a doctor, in the hallway, replied. The door left ajar invites Juan to listen to the conversation inside.

"Why you doing this to me, Estelle! What I done?" Dorothy implored, her voice rising. "You've been a good nurse to me. What happened?"

"Honey, you know we're just worried about your little ones. Maria's so thin! Her birth weight was normal, but now she's well below the standard. Way below. And now we've got to be watching Katie too."

"But I didn't do nothing wrong! Maria won't eat! They just took her 'cause she don't like lots of food? I went to the classes. I took her to the clinic. I need my Maria back!" Dorothy is wailing now. "God, if they take my Katie—"

"Dorothy, you need to get some sleep."

"I DON'T NEED NO SLEEP! It's a trick to take my baby!" Dorothy leaned half off the bed, holding Katie in one arm, and reached for

Estelle with the other. "Estelle—please don't let them take my baby! Where's Henry?"

"No one's going to take Katie anywhere." Estelle replied. "But she does need to stay here for observation. Here, take these little pills."

Estelle held a cup to Dorothy's lips prompting her to swallow two green pills.

"Lay back now," she said.

"But what about the police? Bet they're just waiting—"

Estelle gently ran her right hand up and down Dorothy's right forearm. "Just breathe, darling. Just breathe."

A few minutes pass. Dorothy's eyes became too heavy, and Estelle emerged from the room with Katie in her arms.

Mark and Estelle look at each for a moment.

"The two investigators from Child Protection are in the office. They have a 96 hour hold on this little one," Mark said slowly, as though Estelle were the mother.

"I heard."

"You did good, Estelle."

What you have just read is a scene that is happening far too often in these United States, over-stressed mothers trying to cope with the needs and responsibilities of raising children. You will decide whether or not Dorothy is a bad mother.

But I'm getting ahead of myself. Allow me to introduce myself. My name is Sam Hughes, Judge Sam Hughes, if you will. I'm a judge in Juvenile Court and, sadly I will play a significant role in the fate of Dorothy's babies.

Also allow me to allay any of your fears that this is going to be a sad tale of woe. On the contrary, it's a story of triumph—triumph of the human spirit, triumph of good over evil. There are times when I will narrate this book, and times when the characters and action will proceed without my voice. Please allow the narration, characters and action to blend.

There are several characters that drive this story. Of course there is Katie, the protagonist; her biological parents and foster parents; myself, the judge who appears at significant times in her life; a Governor; the child welfare Commissioner; and a prominent attorney among others—all of whom you will know and judge. The first character is Dorothy—young Katie's mother.

CHAPTER 1

Dorothy, the early years

Montgomery, Alabama, 1980

Montgomery, Alabama is the capital of the state of Alabama, and can probably be considered the birthplace of the modern civil rights movement. On December 1, 1955, Rosa Parks was arrested for refusing to give up her bus seat, sparking the Montgomery Bus Boycott. Martin Luther King, Jr., then pastor of the Dexter Avenue Baptist Church, was one of the boycott organizers.

Dorothy lived in what was called an annex neighborhood of Montgomery. The annex neighborhood was one of the eccentricities of Southern cities, and the strange residential patterns were a topic of conversation among residents and visitors. Dorothy could walk from the colored section—about eight blocks square of unpaved roads and small front-porch houses on diminutive lots—through the white residential section of paved roads and wrap-around porches on larger lots, and then into the eastern part of downtown. Tall buildings, restaurants, clothing stores, a central outdoor bus terminal, a Woolworths, all appeared like adjacent neighbors lining Jefferson Davis Boulevard, a three mile ribbon of a road stretching East to West, ending at the Antebellum State Capitol Building.

If one were to keep walking, he or she would pass the Capitol building, then through another white residential section and emerge into another colored section. Back and forth, black and white, white and black.

Born in the colored section, Dorothy grew up in what was commonly called a shotgun house on a dirt and gravel street lined with other shotgun houses. They were called shotgun houses because if the front and rear doors of these small houses were left open, the buckshot of a shotgun fired through the front door would go right through the back door, hitting no walls in-between. Some people say this as if it's legend.

Girls in the neighborhood were envious of Dorothy's good looks. Entering puberty she was only about 4'5" tall but by the time she reached her late teens, she was 5'6"—taller than all of her girlfriends. A caramel complexion spread evenly over her petite picturesque frame from her toes to that face of hers—that alluring face. That face with those eyes people were afraid to look directly into for fear of being mesmerized. Those eyes also held the shadowed sadness of a futureless future.

Dorothy attended Faith Baptist Church on most Sundays and taught Sunday School. Her mother, Mary, was proud of the way Dorothy taught the seven and eight-year olds in Sunday School Class. She watched Dorothy get their attention by holding up a drawing of a large whale, illustrating how Jonah was converted to Christianity after being swallowed by this great creature. She properly cited Jonah, Chapter 2, Verse 2 of the Holy Bible as the authentic source of this story. The kids were transfixed.

One Sunday, during the grown-up service, Dorothy overheard a strange sound. An old man, sitting in the congregation, started moaning a song in a low, guttural voice. Soon other old and middle-aged men joined in the moaning, repeating what the first man had started.

Dorothy wondered where these sounds came from and what they meant. Her mother said the slavery days. Dorothy couldn't imagine the pain of those days. One by one several men came and kneeled on the floor in the front pews, the front of their bodies now visible to the congregants.

"You woke me up this morning, and made a way out of no way," the first man prayed aloud from his kneeled position, his right thumb and middle finger holding his bowed head.

"Amen" members of the congregation shouted amid the discordant moaning.

"And I thank you, God" the first man emoted.

Then another shouted: "You brought me from a mighty long way—thank you."

"Can I get a witness?" a loud voice pleaded, evoking "Amen," "Amen" and "Amen" from the congregation.

The deep ritual of the service, and warm feeling emanating from it, comforted Dorothy, though she did not know from what or how dark the shadow would be that would carry her away, where the moans of this moment would be forgotten. Mary was deeply affected by the service. "Baptist born, Baptist bred, Baptist 'till I die," she told everyone who listened and some who didn't.

There was one Easter Sunday, somewhere between the preacher yelling and the passing of the collection plate that she spied a tall dark brown-skinned kid other children called Henry.

Chapter 2

Henry, the early years

Well, when John was a little baby sitting at his Mama's knee, she said . . . someday he'll be a steel driving man, LORD, LORD, someday he'll be a steel driving man.

Strong lungs proclaimed his arrival via midwife late one night in his mother's bed. As he grew, his birth name Melvin gave way to a new one more fitting to such a big, fast, and tall boy. He was twelve when the song "John Henry" was popular on the radio, and that's how Melvin became the neighborhood's Henry. He was a superb athlete and everyone admired his athletic prowess, but it didn't make Henry feel superior.

Henry and his parents lived on an unpaved road in Montgomery, Alabama. Kids didn't mind the dirt. On this brown gravel and pebbled road bare feet raced at the end of the school day. Kids knew which part of the dirt to run on—avoid the sand that gave way and twisted ankles, avoid the rocks that brought blood, stick to the packed earth and leap over the ruts. Henry always won the races, pulling away from the other boys and girls and leaving them still pounding the dust at least a half block from the finish line. He was the fastest runner on the middle school track team, and won most of the meets.

Henry didn't know he was poor. Poverty to him and his friends was a name with no reference. They gathered at twilight near the street light pole: twelve of them, ages five to eleven, under watchful eyes of their parents, and played games like "London Bridge is Falling Down" though they didn't know what a London Bridge was. They

watched for the blinking yellow, blue/green and turquoise colors
of lightening bugs flickering in the night, and later counted to see
which child's jars contained the most fireflies.

Henry got up at 5:00 one chilly morning, loaded the wood in
the stove, and watched its belly change from black to crimson. It
was a nice fire in mid-winter. The house would be warm soon, and
returning to bed, he pulled the heavy quilt up over his shoulders.

Sizzling sausages awakened him. "Henry! Food's ready!" His
mother called from the kitchen.

"Be right there, Ma." He was already up, tugging on his favorite
blue jeans. Entering the kitchen, Henry saw his father's empty chair
at the head of the table. "Where's Dad?"

"Had to leave early. Take your seat, son. Would you like another
biscuit?"

"Thanks, Ma. I would like some more of those grits."

"I hear you've been taking up with a girl across town" his mother
said while ladling heaping buttery mounds of grits onto his plate.
"What's her name?"

"Where did you hear that?"

His mother looked up from her plate into the grinning face of
her precious boy. He blushed.

"It's a small town, son. Word gets around. When are we going to
meet her?"

"I dunno."

"Well, you got to tell me all about her. What's her name?"

"Dorothy."

"Where'd you meet her? When'd you see her?"

"One question at a time, Ma."

"Okay. Well, where and when did you meet her?"

"First spied her at Church. Couple months ago."

"So, what's she like, son?"

"Nice."

"Nice looking?"

"That too."

"Tall? Short? And when will we get a chance to meet her?"

"Got biology lab this morning."

"You avoiding my questions?"

"Yep. Gotta go."

Henry put his plate in the kitchen sink, kissed his mother on the cheek, picked up his book bag and sprinted out the front door on his three-mile trek to school. He didn't mind the trek as long as it wasn't raining. The red brick, two-story school building faced the Boulevard, but because he was a little late, he entered through the rear door and was the only student in the hallway.

The hallway clock showed 8:10, but Henry knew it was four minutes fast. He turned the corner and reached the classroom door. Teacher Shirley Lane stood frowning.

"Better take your place, Henry. Everyone else has started."

Henry didn't mind. This was biology, his favorite class. The book part of the class was not his favorite, but he liked examining the big dead cats. Henry and the others in the class took their position alongside aluminum examining tables. He opened a long plastic bag, and restraining his excitement, removed the grey cat covered in liquid.

"Smell doesn't bother you, Henry?" Teacher Lane asked.

"No ma'am, but what is it?"

Ms. Lane moved closer to observe his work on the long grey cat.

"It's formaldehyde, an embalming fluid—it keeps the tissues moist."

"Where does it come from?"

"They pack them with it at the state lab, but also there's a bottle of it in our storage closet."

Ms. Lane noticed how carefully Henry's scalpel cut a surgical line down the dead creature's sternum, flaying the fascia lining its thoracic cavity. He would make a good surgeon someday, she thought.

"Do you think that you'll study biology in college?" she asked.

"Daddy says we can't afford college."

"So what are you going to do after you graduate?"

"My Daddy's lined up a job for me at the lumber yard."

Although his response saddened her, Ms. Lane didn't say anything. She wanted to. But she didn't.

CHAPTER 3

Dorothy and Henry

Dorothy was seventeen. Henry, a little older, and perhaps more aware of time, wasted none and quickly obeyed the Southern tradition of meeting her parents, and asking permission to take their daughter out. Permission given, he came a courting to her house on Saturday evenings. They sat on the bench swing on her porch. Her father had secured the ends of the ropes to the ceiling crossbeam by means of a bolting system sold at the local hardware store. Henry admired it his first time visiting and this pleased Dorothy's father. They swung and laughed into the evening. Henry was so funny, in a corny sort of way.

"What you want to be when you grow up, Henry?"

"I don't know. Happy, I guess."

Dorothy laughed. "You can't make money being happy. What you want to do?"

"I want to be somebody, maybe a teacher."

Henry lowered his feet to the floor, slowing the swing down, and looked deeply into Dorothy's eyes. Faint illumination from a light pole a half a block away passed through maple tree limbs disturbing the darkness of the porch, and allowing Henry to admire Dorothy's smile. Thoroughly captivated, he moved closer.

Dorothy's mother turned the porch light on so quickly she must have been watching, Henry thought. The signal was clear. Dorothy kissed Henry on the cheek. Henry grinned, stood up, and gave her a big hug. She placed her arms around his neck.

"I'm sorry you have to go."

"Me, too."

"See you next week, Henry."

"No you won't."

"What?"

"I'll see you in Church tomorrow. You're supposed to teach Sunday School."

"Thanks for reminding me! I left the Bible text on my bedroom dresser. Guess it's good mamma turned on the porch light."

"I guess."

Dorothy smiled at his sarcasm. "Good night," she said as she walked toward her front door.

After almost three years of courting, Henry did the right thing. It happened after Sunday dinner at Dorothy's house. Dorothy cleared the table and took her place in the den alongside Henry, who was watching a baseball game on television. He excused himself and made his way to the living room where Mary and her husband Alfred were reading the Sunday papers. Mary and Alfred looked up at the same moment as Henry approached.

"Excuse me, Mr. Johnson, I would like to ask you a question in private. No disrespect intended, Mrs. Johnson," Henry said, almost bowing in Mary's direction. Mary's eyes displayed no offense, but widened with a curious expression.

"Is it all right if we step outside?" Henry asked.

"Sure." Alfred replied, pushing himself up out of his chair.

"No need," Mary responded. "Have a seat Henry, I need to check with Dorothy in the other room."

"You sure, Mrs. Johnson?"

"I wouldn't have said so if I wasn't." Mary Johnson always spoke her mind.

Mary stood up, leaving her winged chair empty, and walked to the kitchen. Dorothy's broad smile and nervous disposition confirmed Mary's premonition. Mary threw her arms around her daughter and Dorothy squeezed her hard.

"This is it, Ma! Do you think Dad will give his blessing? Mary's eyes grinned in excitement.

Moments later Henry stuck his head in the kitchen door way and gave a thumbs up.

Their modest wedding was special—a product of a community circle of support for their church-going parents, and a gift from the community for the bride and groom—an acknowledgment that the bride and groom are part of them.

The setting: a small, white, painted Faith Baptist Church decorated at no cost by a florist friend of the bride's mother and father, and with the help of the bride's family and friends. The wedding: presided over without charge by the bride's minister. The reception: in the large hall section of the church where everyone enjoyed a sit-down dinner of baked chicken, yellow squash, sliced potatoes, and caramel carrots prepared by the friends of the bride's parents. The mood: joyous and spirit filled.

Afterwards, there was no thought of a honeymoon for the almost-penniless new bride and groom. Being together under the same roof provided all the joy they then needed—the joy of touch, smell, sound and presence of each other and the joy of the thrilling expectation in discovering how "marriage" works. It was like the trinity, the preacher had said. Dorothy, Henry and their marriage—separate and together at the same time.

Although the job Henry's father thought was available at his lumber yard was phased out, his father found Henry a lumber-yard job through Henry's uncle in Connecticut. It didn't take long for the young couple to face the hard economic fact that they had to move north. They settled in the Elm City.

CHAPTER 4

The Elm City

New Haven is the second largest city in Connecticut and is situated on the north shore of the Long Island Sound. New Haven's population grew after World War II with most of the new inhabitants being African-American from the south and Puerto Rico. New Haven had the first public tree planting program in America producing a canopy of mature elm trees that gave the city the nickname "The Elm City."

New Haven's main thoroughfare is Whalley Avenue, a four-lane, fifteen mile long blacktop road with two lanes in one direction and two lanes in the other, which like an artery moves the life blood of its people on foot, in buses, and in cars from the east to the west side of Elm City. New Haven has many distinct neighborhoods with ethnic groups congregating into those where a semblance of cultural homogeneity prevails. Henry's uncle found the couple a comfortable flat in the predominantly black/Negro neighborhood called The Hill.

Although being surrounded by fellow blacks smoothed some of the transition to northern living, the young couple still were hit by the grim reality that everything was quite different from what they were accustomed. The cost of living was a shock to them—so much so that Henry was soon overwhelmed by the need to keep his financial head above water, and prompted him to take a second job. Dorothy's sense of loneliness of being a stranger in a strange land grew with Henry's long work hours.

To compound the problem, Dorothy became pregnant after their arrival. Some people call them miracles. Where do they come from? Dorothy remembers the preacher during the Christmas sermon exclaiming, "Jesus is born, the Savior is born, the Miracle is here." Then the preacher said something quite startling. He pointed left and right across the entire congregation, saying "look to your left, and look to your right." While Dorothy and the other members of the congregation turned their heads back and forth, he then said "You're looking at a miracle," meaning everyone in the church is a miracle created by God. Remembering being struck by that sermon, and looking at her young ones while they slept, Dorothy smiled at her miracles.

Who created them, she wondered. Is there really a God? Is there one force for all living things: the ant, the tree, the whale . . . things living at the black bottom of the sea? Is there a god for all these?

Yes sir, bringing new life is certainly a miracle, but that is where the miracle ends. As the old cliché goes, having a baby changes everything. Dorothy's first born was a daughter they named Maria. Maria screamed from the time she was born—as though she had a chronic colicky condition—and at eight months often slapped her own legs to keep herself awake at bed time. The effect of lack of sleep certainly had an adverse effect on Dorothy's strength and mental state.

Maria's constant crying not only affected Dorothy but aroused concern from the neighbors. When neighbors knocked on Dorothy's front door and inquired whether everything was alright, Dorothy would reply, "Oh yes, it's just that my daughter is such a poor eater. She's always raising a fuss." This went on for the first two years of Maria's life. Finally a neighbor lady asked to see the child. Dorothy let her in and explained that her daughter just will not eat. When the neighbor took one look at Maria, alarms went off in her mind— the infant was so under nourished. As soon as the neighbor left, she contacted childcare authorities. This marked the beginning of Dorothy's involvement with the State Child Protection Department.

As luck would have it, while Maria was placed in a temporary foster home to regain her normal weight, Dorothy became pregnant again. Another daughter was born and named Katie. Katie was a quieter baby, silent, determined, and less fussy as a child. Soon after Katie's birth, Maria was returned to Dorothy.

Given her problems raising two infants at the same time, Dorothy worried about how long she will have to enjoy them. Investigators from the Child Protection Department called the house yesterday. She wished Henry would spend more time with her.

She enjoyed feeding and playing with them, but the girls could satisfy her just so much. Dorothy was lonely for Henry. Whenever Dorothy pleaded with Henry for more companionship and help raising the girls, his response *"I'm working to provide for my family, like my father did,"* did little to comfort her. She ached for more attention.

Henry worked a full day at the lumberyard starting at 7 in the morning and then hustled to his part-time job in security where he stood guard until ten at night six days a week.

"What time is it?" Dorothy asked, as she rolled over in bed looking for the clock.

"Ten thirty," Henry answered while undressing

"You didn't wake the children when you came in, did you?"

"No, I was quiet."

"The children . . . I . . . miss you."

"I miss you too, but, Honey, you know I have to work this second job just to pay the rent."

Her loneliness tasted bitter green. Being away from her extended family in the South and having little time with Henry left her feeling abandoned. What had begun as discomfort, managing the children by herself, was now pain. She had to plan, she thought: getting the children to day care, arriving at work on time for her part-time job as a teacher's aide at the elementary school, and after retrieving the children, preparing dinner, and then bathing and putting them to bed—all this by herself.

Dorothy bunched the pillow under her right chin. The bed depressed when Henry slid his naked body under the covers. She pushed her hips into the hollow of his stomach, snuggling into him as she drifted into sleep, temporarily less lonely, so much feeling the contrast of this comfort that she willed her tears to stop.

*   *   *

Well, there you have it, the ingredients for the collapse of a family unit. This is Judge Hughes speaking. But before we delve further into the saga of Dorothy, Henry and their daughters, I'd like to tell you a bit more about myself and the Child Protection Department; that is, how it works and why.

CHAPTER 5

Judge Sam Hughes

I am tall, with slightly graying hair, a pleasant face and an easy smile. I adore my wife, my three adult children, and my four toddler grandchildren. I keep a photograph on my desk of the eight of them together. Counting me, there are 9 of us. It's my own little Supreme Court. Glancing at the photograph always brings a smile to my face.

I was in the middle of musing about my family when the letter arrived inviting me to attend a meeting hosted by the Chief Court Administrator at his office in the Connecticut Supreme Court Building in Hartford. Our red-brick Juvenile Court building in New Haven, located near the "hood," where white and black sneakers hang by laces from telephone wires staking out drug sellers' turf lines—pale in sharp contrast to the Italian white marble façade of the Supreme Court.

Thinking about our Juvenile Court brought about thoughts that both impressed and depressed me. I was impressed by the need expressed at a recent Judges State Conference seeking volunteers to serve in juvenile court. And I was equally as depressed to learn that so few judges ever volunteered for the juvenile court assignment. It's a sad place I was told more than once. It was babysitting, others said, and simply below someone who had reached the judgeship. They hadn't signed on to be pastors of the youth and disciplinarians of lazy adults.

But I wasn't convinced that was the case. I had pondered volunteering myself one day. A seasoned judge once told me that "the Juvenile Court Division provides the greatest opportunity for government to intervene and help children and parents in crisis." To say the least, I was also eager to be inspired.

And so I went to the meeting. I parked in a lot reserved for Supreme Court personnel, and walked the short distance to the security checkpoint at the front of the five-story building. After checking my credentials, the security officer directed me through an oval archway leading to the Chief's conference room. My shoes were loud on the marble, and I was conscious of their clipping echo adding a rhythm to the sound of a dozen hurried conversations blended into a swirling ascent of the sound in the atrium. I entered a large, bright room, took the remaining seat at the long mahogany table, and began to count. Twelve trial judges, all seated in tall leather chairs in this room of fourteen-foot ceilings topped with crown molding. Seven tall windows framed the outside view of the gold domed magnificent State Capital Building sitting on the nearby hillside.

The Chief Court Administrator entered and sat at the head of the table. From the date of my appointment as a Superior Court Judge, I wondered how the Chief manages 150 trial judges, many of whom had been fiercely independent trial lawyers and graduates of some of the most prestigious law schools. Before he became the Chief, he had been Legal Counsel to the Governor. At age 60, trim, well-groomed, and sporting a white silk handkerchief and a red silk tie, the Chief looked like a man in charge. After gathering some notes on the table, he stood and began.

"Ladies and Gentlemen, we are embarking on an enhanced initiative to respond to the growing needs of the troubled and troubling youth of our State. As you know, juvenile crime has significantly increased, and the families from whom a lot of these juveniles come are in crisis. The clear evidence of this is the massive increase in the number of delinquency and child protection cases-numbering in the thousands—on our dockets throughout the state, but especially in our urban courts. Teenage muggings, drive-by shootings and drugs are terrorizing our city neighborhoods. They fill our Delinquency Dockets. Child abuse, physical and emotional abuse by parents and adult caregivers fill our Neglect Docket. But this you already know."

He continued. "'Child protection' is not a euphemism. It's what we do in those cases when the state must intervene in a family's private life to protect the children. Whether it is through some form of counseling or other measures, or the ultimate measure: taking children from dangerous situations and placing them in foster care."

I listened to the Chief's voice, and immediately liked him. He was prepared, but not rehearsed. Something in his tone rang of authenticity. The Chief gave a brief history of the juvenile court, most of which I already knew by heart—the movement for the juvenile court started in the United States in the mid-1800s, etc.—and so I took the opportunity to observe the room. A quiet, somber mood prevailed. Sitting at the head of the table, the Chief held up a volume of the *United State's Supreme Court Reporter*, and I was shaken back to full attention.

"Ladies and gentlemen I apologize in advance for reading from the text of the "In re' Gault case," but I believe the language of the Justices of the United States Supreme Court expressed in that case, decided nearly four decades ago, highlights the purposes of the court. In the case, an Arizona juvenile court judge sentenced a young boy to six years in a state industrial school for allegedly making a lewd telephone call."

He began reading in a measured tone.

"The first juvenile court was established by state law in Illinois in 1898, igniting a reform movement. Shortly after that all states and territories of the United States set up their own juvenile courts." The Chief looked up, scanned the faces of judges in the room, and then gestured to a man whose hands rested on a laptop computer at the back of the room.

"Ladies and gentlemen, please cast your eyes to the wall behind me. The remaining parts of the case will be provided to you by a special PowerPoint presentation prepared by the Head of our Technical Support Unit who has been kind enough to join us today."

The Chief nodded. Overhead lights dimmed. From the ceiling, a movie screen unfolded into which black text appeared against a bluish-white backlight. An automated voice vocalized the text.

This is the case of the State of Arizona vs. Gerald Francis Gault

On Monday, June 8, 1964 at about 10 a.m. Gerald Francis Gault and a friend, Ronald Lewis, were taken into custody by the Sheriff of Gila County, Arizona.

The police action on June 8 was taken as a result of a verbal complaint by a neighbor of the boys, Mrs. Cook, about a telephone call made to her in which the caller or callers made lewd or indecent remarks. It will suffice for purposes of this opinion to say that the remarks or questions put to her were of the irritatingly offensive, adolescent, sexual variety.

When his mother arrived home at about six o'clock, Gerald was not there. Gerald's older brother was sent to look for him at the trailer home of the Lewis family. He learned then that Gerald was in custody, charged with "lewd phone call."

The complainant, Mrs. Cook, was not present at the court hearing. Mrs. Gault asked that Mrs. Cook be present "so she could see which boy that done the talking, the dirty talking over the phone." The Juvenile Judge said "she didn't have to be present at that hearing." The judge did not speak to Mrs. Cook or communicate with her at any time. Probation Officer Flagg had talked to her once—over the telephone on June 9.

At the conclusion of the hearing, the judge committed Gerald as a juvenile delinquent to the State Industrial School "for the period of his minority [that is, until 21]"—a period of six years, since he was 15 years old at the time of sentencing.

The automated voice stopped and the screen retracted. Sitting down, the Chief picked up a packet of materials. "On the table in the front of you is an outline of the rights established by the Supreme Court as a result of the Gault case," the Chief said. I collected the packaged outlines along with my colleagues. "As you can see from the outline of additional facts in the case, had Gerald been 18 years of age he would have been entitled to a trial by jury, and had he been convicted of the "lewd" telephone calls, he would have received a fine of $5 to $50 or imprisonment for not more than two months. Instead, he was sentenced to confinement for six years as a juvenile. Please flip over the sheet to the second page."

We turned the page.

"On the second page, my staff has listed the Constitutional Rights which the Supreme Court in this case said that a juvenile has when he is accused of delinquent conduct that could result in being committed to a state institution. They are:

the right to advanced notice of the charges against him or her;
the right to a lawyer;
the right not to be subject to self-incrimination; and
the right to sworn testimony subject to the right of cross-examination.

The Chief continued, "Since none of these rights was given to Gerald Gault or his parents, the Supreme Court ordered the case returned to the Arizona courts for re-trial."

"Therefore, fellow judges, you can see the need for qualified, dignified, intelligent and empathetic individuals to serve as judges in such matters. This topic of juvenile care and justice is why I invited you here to this meeting today. Some of you may be assigned to the Juvenile Division. Those who do will receive updated laptop computers, enabling you to access case law and procedures and resource information helpful in this area. The failure of an adolescent to behave decently is both the fault of his will and of the society that shaped that will. We are here to protect the rights of the innocent and to rehabilitate and where appropriate punish the guilty."

Spicy shrimp on the hors d'oeuvres table were unusually tasty, though my appetite was not what it usually is. I was distracted. After chatting briefly with some of my colleagues, I returned to my car. Driving home, I wondered what my next court assignment might be: Heavy Criminal Court; Family court, Tax Appeal Court; Housing Court, etc. I was willing for any and all. But something inside me felt unusually upsetting. Perhaps it was heartburn. Or a calling. I wasn't sure I'd know the difference.

Two weeks later a letter from the Chief arrived at my house. Sitting at my kitchen table, where I sat to open the first letter from the Chief upon elevation to my judgeship years ago, I grabbed a kitchen knife, held it at an angle, and slit open the left side of the envelope.

Dear Judge Hughes,

This is to inform you that you have been assigned to the Juvenile Court Division for the next two years.

Sincerely

And there it was again, the heartburn, or purpose, or both. I wasn't sure. But I knew this assignment-seeing the children of the nation pitted against the worst of human nature-would challenge my very soul. I reached for the Tums. And I said a prayer.

CHAPTER 6

Judge's Roundtable

The Judge's Roundtable is held in a room set aside from courtrooms. It is sort of an informal judicial faculty room where judges gather to hear each other out on a challenging legal issue in a case, to review any new significant Appellate Court case rulings that might affect their work, and to talk about the new interesting case of the week. And to drink coffee.

At the start of each day, several judges would meet in this room. At times, the feeble attempt at banter would center on our caffeine intake.

"How much coffee would you suppose is ingested by this little group on a daily basis?"

"I don't want to know. Enough to kill a large animal."

"Or a herd."

The men and women in the room gathered in circles, sipping caffeinated beverages and somewhat sharing the burdens of their positions. There was occasional laughter, but very little. The room was not a place for jokes. I remember the day one of the judges asked a question about a child rape case.

"So . . . Should I allow it into evidence?"

"Repeat the information again . . . and from the beginning."

"A pre-teen girl had been sexually abused several years ago in Puerto Rico by her natural grandfather. She presented clear and graphic testimony before the jury yesterday that her grand stepfather, now on trial, is the one who *recently* sexually assaulted her. The girl testified how he closed off the bedroom door when her mother was away; how they played games in the bed; how she said no; how his body smelled and looked; how he gave her candy; swore her to secrecy, and promised not to do it again, but later did."

The judge continued. "Yesterday the State's attorney said allowing evidence of the previous abuse by the natural grandfather in Puerto Rico violates the law protecting the victim, while the attorney for the grand stepfather claims that he has a right to use the information to show who the girl was referring to as grandpa. It's complex."

The consensus was rather unhelpful: it was a tough case. The trial judge did not allow the defense to ask the girl about an earlier possible abuse by another grandfather, because he thought that her graphic description of several acts of sexual abuse by the current defendant clearly showed she knew he raped and abused her. His conviction by the jury was overturned in part because the Appellate Court ruled that he had a right to have the girl's identity of "grandpa" tested by reference to the earlier assault by her natural grandfather. The judicial faculty was right: it was a tough case.

The short morning meeting presented also an opportunity to pass important information about which lawyers to watch out for, those who have a reputation among judges as not filing court papers on time and not preparing well before the trial, as well as the lawyers who file baseless grievances against judges. This was more than glorified water cooler banter.

The judges were unanimous in their view that they would like to look citizens in the face and tell them which lawyers are excellent, and which ones are not; that print and television advertisements are not the litmus test for finding a qualified attorney. The group found a moment of respite in each other's knowing nods.

How many years of law school were represented here? How many degrees, how many hours of service, of training, of reading, of worrying, of working for the common good? Sixty hours a week, sometimes more. Forty-eight weeks a year. Thirty years per career, maybe more. I looked around the table, and in the silence, seized the moment. "What do you all know about Munchausen's by Proxy?"

My question provoked curious stares and a few unhelpful comments. The decision was always mine, always to be made independently, but I had hoped for insight or guidance.

It was cases like this one—parents harming their own little children, for whatever reason, whatever excuse, that I took home.

They lodged in my mind like splinters in skin, cases of little boys sexually abusing other boys and girls, young gangs of boys, with no provocation, breaking the jaw of an innocent man leaving a movie theatre, fathers physically and emotionally abusing the mothers of their young children, while the young eyes watched. These are the seeds of generational violence sown. Though the files remained in the courthouse, the stories remained with me forever.

Can judges suffer from post-traumatic stress just from seeing and hearing these cases? This thought has crossed my mind more than once.

A door into a world of abject neglect and violence against the vulnerable had been opened. I lived in that world now, and I could never fully walk away.

CHAPTER 7

Governor Larry Mulvey

Long before his birth, Larry Mulvey's path to the Capitol Building was paved with gold. Politics and ambition flowed in his Mulvey bloodline. His uncle had been a Senator, his grandfather a State Representative, and his father's cousin a State Treasurer. Various other relatives held offices across the state's history, from dog warden to District Attorney. Political discussions were served alongside mashed potatoes, baked chicken, and green vegetables at most Sunday dinners attended by any Mulvey relation within a ten-mile radius. No invitations were required. His mother, a state commissioner, and his father, an investment banker with the largest financial institution in the state, had only one requirement for admission to the meal: a political connection, a willingness to make that connection a shared commodity, and an ability to discuss politics.

Larry loved campaigning for re-election for a third term, slipping naturally into the role of reformer and inspirer of the masses. His platform had been fiscal responsibility, decent government, and protection of the less fortunate, especially abused and neglected children. He backed up his ethical rhetoric with religious connections as a trustee in the town's Lutheran Church. Well regarded in his community, the tall, handsome, red-haired Larry Mulvey, flanked by his lovely wife and three pre-teen children, appeared as the man whose hands would best safeguard the state's children and taxpayers, at least in the televised advertisements financed by his father.

The pollsters' predictions were right: Mulvey won in a landslide. His victory speech was soaring, and the party a spectacle. It was now important for him to make the right new department head appointments and pick the right new staff. It became clear: he had only to wait for the right time to run for national office. His daddy was very proud. He had just won an unprecedented fourth term. The great Mulvey tradition would continue.

If only he could protect one little secret.

It happened when he was in New Hampshire. His parents were traveling on business abroad and sent him to a special summer session in a prep school—an opportunity, they said, for him to improve his grades and to get ahead.

When they arrived around 10:00 PM, three dozen or so college students were dancing and drinking in a small house. Several guys and girls, half-naked, were laughing in a hot tub. Cups and bottles covered every surface. The music was so loud he could hardly hear Marshal's voice.

"What?" Larry screamed.

"I said I've got something special for you, Sam yelled back.

"What," Larry responded.

"She's hot!"

"What do you mean?"

"The girl."

"What girl?"

"Just come on."

Larry followed Sam and his flashlight on a paved walkway beyond the pool to a shed about fifty yards from the house. Music pounded behind them. As they approached, a teenage boy exited the shed.

"Go on in. She's all yours," he said, grinning.

Larry and Sam looked at each other.

"You go first," Sam directed.

Upon opening the door, Larry saw a young girl—fourteen, fifteen, maybe—lying on a sleeping bag, naked from the waist.

"Come on in," she said. "What's your name?"

"Larry . . . Larry Robert Mulvey," he stammered, nervously. This would be his first time.

She laughed a little. "Well, Larry Robert Mulvey. What are you waiting for?"

Larry unzipped his trousers.

Last month he received the note without a return address. The handwriting had a feminine flourish. Larry Robert Mulvey was

Governor now, and she seemed to remember this one wild night. She didn't want to tell anybody about it—rapes are so humiliating, of course—but she was just a little short of cash, and could really use the money. She really didn't want to tell anybody, but you do what you have to do, the letter read, then concluded with "call soon now and leave a message where I can pick it up. I need the cash, I need the cash, you understand?"

Corruption was only one of the many secrets and problems that Larry's fourth term would face.

CHAPTER 8

Commissioner Mary Strum

Throughout his campaign Larry Mulvey promised that his administration would safeguard the state's children, especially those in foster care. To carry out his commitment he appointed someone without state career baggage-Mary Strum-as the new commissioner of the Child Protection Department.

Mary Strum graduated from the prestigious Eastern School of Social Work with high honor. The heavy medal she wore at graduation is still displayed prominently in its case on her desk at home, next to a miniaturized 'Mulvey for Governor' poster signed by her friends. She had stood next to the soon-to-be Governor on that cold November election night as the precincts filed their vote tallies, one after another. She raised her glass in his honor, and when the party ended at two in the morning, went home and slept for nine hours—the longest night's sleep since she joined his campaign staff eight months earlier. When she awoke just before noon, she smiled.

Mulvey had pulled her aside at the after-party, and asked her to head what would soon be renamed the State Child Protection Department.

"I'm not sure—I mean, I'm not sure I'm the one for this job," she managed. "I'm just five years out of Social Work School."

He had smiled that Mulvey smile. "Your humility is admirable, but sometimes overrated as a virtue. You'll be excellent. You have the maturity, education and sensitivity for this important mission," he assured her. She soaked up the attention, while marveling at the responsibility of her new assignment. The Governor's managers had approved her professional qualifications—and her good looks. Tall, radiant, with "the most perfect cheekbones," her college boyfriend had told her, she had what Mulvey's press secretary called "presence."

Now, nearly four years later, standing at her conference room window, looking out at the State Capitol building, and addressing her five dedicated assistants, thirty-two year old Mary Strum let her mind drift back to those early days. She clenched her teeth, wondering why the hell she had said "yes" to the Governor.

The Commissioner and her department had been under attack on a weekly basis. Today's paper offered the headline: *BABY FOUND DEAD IN DUMPSTER: Is the Foster System Broken?* The editorial page was filled with the ranting of pundits on the department's failure, more particularly, *on her failure.* It was only the latest in a string of similar headlines. Two weeks previous, a young child, severely injured while being put in restraints at the juvenile detention facility maintained by her Department, jumped from regional to national news in less than a day. Mary had stopped watching CNN, and FOX news.

Looking for some kind of affirmation, she spun from the window to the conference table, where she met the eyes of Tom Adams.

"What are your thoughts about these attacks on our department, Tom?"

If only Tom felt free to express what he was really thought, he would have told her that her red dress, slightly clinging to her curvaceous form, excited him. She knew it and could tell that Tom knew that she knew. It was the way Tom quickly looked away from her. Deputy Commissioner Tom Adams, middle-aged, married, and Christian, had never propositioned her, never said anything inappropriate. But she knew that look he gave her, the look he couldn't maintain. It happened more often when she wore red, and she made a mental note of this.

Tom hesitated, opened his mouth, but then closed it again.

Commissioner Strum raised her voice. "What about the successful criminal prosecution of one of our cases in Elm City where the boyfriend tried to cook his girlfriend's two-year-old son in 160 degree boiling hot water while pretending to give him a bath? He said it was a mistake, but the cops saw part of the baby's flesh floating in the bathtub. Why doesn't the press give us a pat on the back for the successful cases we close? No-o-o, they are only out for blood when a case somehow falls through a crack. If it's not the boyfriends of single mothers, it's the mothers themselves at fault."

Commissioner Strum was as they say "on a roll." She continued.

"The way the media is hounding us reminds me of a case the department faced many years ago. I was reading about it recently. It was about a mother who was trying to get attention by suffocating her child. *Suffocating her daughter,* for Pete's sake."

"That was the Munchausen's stuff, yes? Was that for real?" asked Marty, a retired state police officer who was skeptical of psychological terminology.

"Was it for real? Absolutely, Marty." Tom answered emphatically.

"That's so sick. Do people really do that?" Marty asked.

"You've not been here long, but certainly long enough to know that if it's sick, people will do it," Tom was noticeably on edge. "Thousands of children are hurt this way every year. And some of them die."

Mary Strum interrupted. "Well, that was years ago. Let's pray we never have another one of those cases. The department weathered the storm the press kicked up then, and we will weather the storm now. We must do better. We *will* do better. My question for you is *how.*"

Tom cleared his throat, and when he began to speak, his tone was noticeably changed. "Well, Commissioner, I hear that the child protection lawyers are not regularly visiting the children assigned to them. We need to tighten up on that. The lawyers could be instructed to give regular reports to the courts on the status of these children in foster care. At the same time we could have our social workers regularly visit *with* the children, and give their supervisors written reports on their visits—and that gives us another checking point."

"What we need is more retired cops, not social workers," replied Marty who was never shy about giving his opinion. "The federal court order requires that we hire social workers—and see what that's gotten us."

Tom responded quickly. "Those social workers are the only thing keeping this . . ."

Mary slammed her hand on the conference table. "We need a plan to stop this chaos, and this is not it." She looked at the new hire. "Janet, you know the regional manager down in the Southern Section of the state, Region 4. Their number of harmed children after placement in foster care is very low compared with the rest of the state. What is Region 4 doing that the other regions aren't? Or are there just better people in Region 4?"

On another day, the sarcasm would have gotten a chuckle. But the mood was too somber for much joviality.

"Janet, what do you think?" Commissioner Strum demanded.

Janet Mullen was hired by the Commissioner because of her experience in Washington, D.C. and having been an intern for Congresswoman Johnson, Co-chair of the House Subcommittee on Children and Placement, which was never a disadvantage to a resume. Janet had traveled across the country assessing state child protection and foster care placement programs, and made recommendations for federal funding. With state government cutbacks, federal funding was becoming more and more necessary, and it was becoming more and more important for Mary Strum to stay in Congresswoman Johnson's good graces. Giving Janet an opportunity to help improve her agency would also help cement relations with the feds.

Janet knew what she was about to say would prove her worth. She had begun her day at Eileen's BodyWorks at 6:00 AM. After twenty minutes of calisthenics her 5 foot, six inch, 120 pound frame lifted 15 pound weights, pressed the 50 pound bar, and enjoyed a refreshing shower. By the time she arrived at the office, she was full of energy, and ready physically and mentally. Later that day, that energy would be tested.

Adjusting her thin-framed Polo eyeglasses, Janet addressed the Commissioner. "The Supervisor at Region 4 has a triage system, whereby, because of limited resources, they decide who may profit the most from their attention. They log in each call received, whether from the Hot-Line or direct, plus the Supervisor listens to the caseworkers' voice mails each day. You know, in some regional offices the voice mail storage of some caseworkers are so completely filled that if someone were trying to report an emergency situation they couldn't get through. The Region 4 Supervisor requires the caseworkers to voice respond either immediately or within 24 hours so that there is always storage available for additional calls. Each caseworker has a cell phone; and there is a court liaison that has an office in the courthouse and a desk at the regional office."

"Who approved that system?" Tom asked.

"Where did they get the money for cell phones and a liaison?" Mary asked, "And why wasn't I told? Tom, did you know about this?"

"No. This is the first I've heard of it; I just had lunch with Martha Fleming, the supervisor down there, and she didn't mention anything about it to me. Doesn't she need your approval for her system?"

"She certainly does, although I've heard that the Governor is beginning to listen more to the Child Advocate and she may have intervened," Mary responded, pacing back and forth in front of the window. "Janet, maybe you and Tom can attend that State Conference tonight down in Stamford. Martha will be there. You can get some information from her about who is funding that program without my approval. It's something I want to bring to the attention of the Governor's Chief of Staff right away. He's a details man, and I need as much information as I can get before discussing it with him."

Tom scanned his pocket calendar, "I have a meeting with State Senator McCone tonight in preparation for the budget presentation to the Legislature next month. Should I cancel it?"

"No, that's too important. Janet, you will have to go by yourself. You think you can handle that?"

"Yes." Janet replied and then added awkwardly, "Commissioner." She took a deep breath and held back a smile. Sometimes the force of nature delays an opportunity until you are ready, and Janet knew this was her time. Rising from her chair, Janet cleared her throat. "Well, if you will excuse me, Commissioner, I probably should get going. You know traffic on I-95 toward Stamford will be horrendous, and I need to get some materials from my office to take to the meeting."

"Of course, Janet, but do bring back the information we need."

"I certainly will, Commissioner."

After leaving the Commissioner's office, Janet exhaled for the first time, and stepped quickly down the hallway to her office. She could hear her intercom ringing before she even walked in.

"Yes?" she answered, but still a little breathless.

"Sorry to interrupt you, but there is a CPD employee on the phone who says it's urgent."

"Okay, put her through."

It was one of the calls she hated but appreciated. A social worker for the department, calling to report disturbing news, prompted by conscience and duty to make a call to a higher-up. This one was from a social worker in New Haven, Christine Wilkinson, and in a few seconds, she had managed to change Janet's focus from career advancement to the children in the system.

"A lot of children down in Bridgeport—kids in foster care—are being misused by their foster parents."

"What are you talking about?"

"I mean, they are being lent out to clean houses of people and to do all kinds of work."

"How do you know this?"

"I understand that you are the Commissioner's new assistant. Word is you can be trusted. You may be in a very good position to help these kids."

"What do you mean?"

"A friend of mine at the Department, a janitor actually, gave me a copy of a memo he found lying around on the Commissioner's desk after work. He said there were several copies that were covered up with other papers that fell from the desk as he was cleaning it. He took one."

"Have you brought this to the attention of your supervisor?"

"No. And from the memo you'll see why. Also I don't want my janitor friend to get in trouble. Every day this is allowed to go on exposes the children to more abuse. That's why I'm taking a chance in calling you, but you can't say I told you, 'cause they'd fire me for going around the chain of command. But . . . I can't sleep, worrying about these kids."

Janet could hear Christine's voice cracking.

"Why don't you just give the information to your supervisor?" Janet asked again, this time with greater urgency.

"Ma'am, as I said before, this is quite sensitive, and if you saw the memo you would understand. I can't tell you what it says over the telephone, but I can give it to you."

"Where's your office?"

"Regional New Haven," Christine answered.

"I've got to come pass there later this afternoon. You're just off the turnpike. I could pick up the memo in about 45 minutes."

"God bless you. As I said before, my name is Christine, I'll, uh, wait for you by the front door."

"I'll be driving a blue Saab. See you then."

The conversation slowed her down, giving her only time to grab half the material she'd intended to take with her. She rushed out of the building, steered her sky blue Saab through the parking gates, negotiated the traffic circle, and joined the line of cars crawling up the ramp to the Interstate. She dreaded the image of bumper-to-bumper rush- hour traffic to Stamford, but found this a pleasant diversion from the deeper dread of discovering what that Elm City memo might reveal.

CHAPTER 9

Child Abuse

"Will it hurt?"

"What?"

"Will it hurt, you know, the children?"

Twenty-year old Earl had a young face that looked younger when he was worried.

"The boss said it won't, and that's good enough for me," work foreman Vinnie answered.

"The dust is thick, though, you know? And the building is so old—could be asbestos and stuff," Earl continued.

"Would you relax?"

When Vinnie looked at Earl, his older eyes saw only weakness and hesitancy. "You're so stinking paranoid!" Earl yelled.

Dust was everywhere, a kind of film stuck to the walls of the hallways and cabinets and desks through the offices on all ten floors-on the steps of the stair well, on the broken plasterboard strewn throughout the building, on the exposed plumbing. The air itself seemed colored with it, a lingering heavy fog of dust.

"Boss didn't say nothing about asbestos or whatever. Besides, those asbestos codes would add months to this demo job, and we gotta finish in two weeks. Don't have time to be asking these questions."

"But the asbestos?" Earl repeated.

"Dammit Earl, shut up. We're just gonna do this—finish it, turn the building over to the Casino developer, get our money, and move on to the next job. That's what you want right? Money? To live? We're out after this anyway. Kansas City's next."

Standing inside the main oval red brick entry archway, Earl
pulled a white dust mask from the pocket of his faded blue jeans and
handed it toward Vinnie.

"Here."

Vinnie waved it away.

"Don't need it. Been doing demo for a decade; never used one
yet." Vinnie drove a shovel deep into a pile of broken plaster on the
floor and hurled it into a large metal bin by the window.

Earl stood for a moment with his arm outstretched, and then
shoved the mask back in his pocket. He watched Vinnie for a moment,
bent over with shovel in his hands, and thought how he didn't look
half bad for an old guy. Hard work kept his chest and arm muscles
pumped, and his short hairstyle minimized his balding head and
highlighted a few gray hairs. Earl noticed that Vinnie moved with a
military precision—the trash for the dumpsters here, the scrap for
resale there.

"You know, the boss wants to put you in charge of what he calls
our youth brigade," Vinnie called out, without looking up.

Earl held the shovel by the handle against his denim leg. "Why's
that?"

"You're young enough to relate to them. The rest of us are old
enough to be their grandfathers. It's not a problem, is it," he half
asked while tossing a twisted piece of corrugated metal into the
blue bin.

"Oh no," Earl answered quickly. "I just wanted to know why."

"That's your problem. Asking too many whys. Collect your boys
and meet me in the backyard."

"But—"

"But what?"

"I mean, how do we get away with having, you know, underage
workers?" Earl's face looked young again.

"The contractor believes whatever he's told and is too lazy to
follow up. Boss said we were part of some special program for Juvy
Court. Get going."

Earl jumped to attention and headed down the stairs. Vinnie was
a military man, and he'd be pleased to see Earl handle the boys like
troops. So military style it would be. A chain of command—Earl as
the boss of the older boys who would then be the bosses of the others.

Emerging from the side door, he strode quickly up to a kid named Ron, standing with a group of ten boys in a circle.

"Walk with me," Earl said flatly. He could do this power thing.

A light brown-skinned youngster left the group, and walking ahead bowed a few paces behind Earl, raised his eyes and stopped by the side door.

"Yes, sir," he said, cramming his hands in his pockets.

"I'm placing you in charge of the boys for the clean-up project. I'll show you what to do, and then you will show them what to do, okay? Like a chain of command. Since you'll be their boss, you'll get extra money in your paycheck, okay?"

"Sure, Mr. Earl, yes sir."

Earl stared at the boy—about eight years his junior, he figured. The boy made eye contact infrequently, and looked, as Earl did, a little younger than his age. He looked like his little brother—well, not his actual brother, but the brother he'd come to know after he had been adopted. Eleven years old, he was living with his fourteen-year-old cousin in a rooming house when a church lady in the neighborhood for whom he ran errands took him in and raised him. His cousin refused to come along, and is now God knows where, while Earl finished school and now brings home money the government knows about. Looking now at the top of Ron's head, as the young man dug his toe in the dirt, Earl thought for the first time in a long time how lucky he had been.

Earl gave Ron his assignment: he and the boys will work alongside him scavenging usable items from building debris. They will divide the area into quadrants and clear each quadrant of its recyclables. It was a hot day, and by the time the boys had followed Earl through the first floor of the building, they were sweating and coughing. Earl tried to ignore the sound while he pointed out the useful materials— green and gold plated lamps, desk top computers, small printers, chairs in good condition, etc. He walked the group back outside to the yard, where large, metallic, yellow tubes descending from window openings on top level floors and dangling about ten feet from the ground, ended just high enough for the bays of tri-axle dump trucks.

As the bay of a truck filled with demolition debris from one of the huge commercial trash shoots, the grounds crew called up another truck to take its place. The yard buzzed with activity as forty or fifty workers in denim jeans, hard hats and work boots streamed in and out of the building. Several guards stationed at the street entrance to the work site checked each vehicle entering and exiting the yard.

"Hurry up, guys," Earl hollered, "It's almost lunch time!"

Dust masks covering their faces, Earl's rag tag army, ranging in age from ten to fourteen, deposited their collection of recyclables in the southeast corner of the yard. The lunch whistle blew and the boys slipped their masks off and several put their hands on their waists. "The food's paid for. Get whatever you want from the lunch truck," Earl yelled.

Descending on the truck, the boys grabbed hot dogs, hamburgers, sandwiches, sodas, chips, and half-sat, half-fell into a circle, some on the ground, others on upturned empty five-gallon buckets.

"So how'd you get here?" asked thirteen year old Matt looking up from his three hot dogs.

Ron looked at him. "You mean me?"

"Yeah. How'd you end up here?"

The other boys slowed their chewing, listening for an answer. Staring down at the unpaved ground, Ron cleared his throat. "'Bout six months ago, a lady from the Children's office came to my school and asked where my mama was. I told her I didn't know and she made me take her to where I was staying."

Ron paused to bite off the corner of a ketchup package. He spit it out and squeezed red ketchup over the thin hot dog and the bun. He held up his right index finger, signaling them to wait a minute, and took a huge bite, almost half the dog, rolled it around in his mouth, and swallowed.

"God, I could eat ten of these."

"So what happened then?" Matt asked. Several boys, wide eyed, chomped on potato chips from shiny yellow bags, and focused their attention on Ron.

"Well, the principal said it was okay, so the lady put me in her car and drove me to Bob's apartment. She didn't like what she saw though."

"Why's that?" a boy in a short sleeve plaid shirt asked.

"She said the apartment was filthy. There was no electricity. Some animal droppings were in there, and she said it smelled bad. She said the dishes hadn't been washed, and that we didn't have no refrigerator. And there were some critters, you know, roaches and whatever. A hole was in the bathroom floor. I told her I never fell through or anything."

Some of the boys laughed a little.

"And you were living there?" asked the plaid-shirted boy.

Ron nodded, chewing.

"You have a mom?"

"Drug stuff. Rehab now."

"So, who, uh, looked after you?" plaid shirt continued.

"Mom's ex-boyfriend. Bob. He brought food, sandwiches and stuff to me."

"And how'd you get here?" Matt repeated.

"Like I was saying, the Children's lady didn't like where I was staying, so she took me to a foster home. I been in homes before, but this one—God, I hope it's the last. That's how I got here. My new foster mother signed me up for this program. They pay her for me working here Saturdays. I hate it, but she told me it would be good for me—teach me what the real world is about. Whatever that means."

"Why don't you just stay at home, if you hate working here?" Matt asked.

"Cause she said if I quit, she'll send me back to the State. State people say they treat you nice. But there's just too many of us. It's not like they're your real parents. Not like those were any better anyway, right? The state people, we're just their job, you know? They go home and forget about us. Besides, they got a real family at home, and we just come and go. Some state people treat you just like family, I've heard. But I don't know none of those."

Another whistle. The boys tossed sandwich wrappings and soda cans in a trash container.

"Let's do it," Earl signaled, and pulled a mask over his nose.

*   *   *

Lest you think that only boys were being abused, read on.

"I don't want to go!" Eleven-year old Angela stood in protest, her four-foot-six inch body agitated.

"So? We need the money. You're just lazy, expect everything free."

Angela's greenish brown eyes examined Claudia, a fifty-something foster parent with ugly shoes. Two weeks she'd been here with this woman. Not long enough to feel comfortable, but long enough to feel the beginnings of hate. The bowl of oatmeal on the table was runny, and Angela picked at it as she said in a low, almost pleading voice, "But the girls said that you get money from the State for keeping me."

"Not enough! God knows. Now finish your breakfast. Van's outside."

Angela wanted to play with her dolls. This was her third foster home in two years, and she'd never had to do this before. The lady from the State said she needed to be a good girl and obey her foster parents, but . . . something was wrong. Grown-ups were right, though. Supposed to be, anyway.

Angela pushed aside her bowl and headed toward the front door.

"You do what they tell you to do, okay?"

"Yes ma'am." Angela closed the door, and walked toward the big, blue van. She could see the outlines of the others—the ponytails and sunglasses. The door slid open and she made her way to the back and crammed into a small seat next to a black-haired girl who didn't look up.

"Cleaning homes today, girls. Ready to do some good work?" The driver said in a voice that was so stupidly cheerful even Angela reacted to the irony she barely understood. The whispers surrounded her, voices speaking about things she barely understood: illicit services . . . cut rate price . . . percentage to host families . . . sell stolen merchandise. She'd heard some of the girls complain of the "bad touches" in several homes, and the fear made the oatmeal in her stomach swirl. Angela wanted to tell the social worker who visited her home last week, but Claudia had warned her not to.

"You'll go back to the State if you don't watch it," she'd said. "Is that what you want?"

CHAPTER 10

Intrigue

Interstate 91 merged into Interstate 95 in New Haven, and Janet Mullen's Saab nudged into the slow line of traffic. While exiting the Interstate near Downtown, she admired the long stretch of pale blue water of Long Island Sound on her left and the Long Wharf Regional Theatre on her right. Joanne Woodward, Paul Newman and James Earl Jones all graced its marquee at one time. *What was the name of that Newman movie—the one with Redford?* Janet couldn't remember, and it occupied her thoughts until she slowed to a stop in front of a large glass-fronted four-story building.

A woman that Janet imagined to be in her early twenties, wearing a yellow skirt and a green blouse, stood in the parking lot, looking nervous and cold. A relieved and slightly anxious smile appeared on the woman's face as Janet lowered the car window.

"Janet Mullen?" she asked in an upturned voice.

"Yes, and you must be Christine Wilkinson."

Janet noticed Christine's hands were shaking as she offered a manila envelope through the window. "Here's the memo I told you about. It's from Tom Adams."

"And it says that—"

"That the Governor and the Commissioner knew about a child abuse problem all along . . ."

Janet exhaled. "The Governor *and* Commissioner? I don't believe it, for God's sake."

Christine seemed on the verge of tears. "Yes, I'm afraid so. I—I hope this doesn't get me or the janitor in trouble." Janet took the folder with her right hand, and placed it on the passenger seat.

"Don't worry," Janet assured her. "It's not you or the janitor who needs to be nervous right now. Relax. You've done what you should have. I'll call you as soon as I get a chance to read the memo and decide how it should be handled. Right now I've got to get to Stamford for a meeting."

Agony crossed Christine's face.

"Don't worry," Janet counseled.

The Saab slowly pulled away. In her rearview mirror, Janet could see Christine looking around before retreating into the building.

Just enough time to reach Stamford, Janet thought, while a troubled feeling swirled in her stomach. She'd been a follower of orders her entire adult life. Now, *I feel like a double agent,* she thought, and sighed deeply as her cell phone vibrated in the cup holder.

"Hello," she answered.

"I got your message about the Commissioner's office," a man's voice responded. "I can meet you tonight."

"I'm on my way to a meeting with Region 4, and I'll be free around 7 o'clock."

"Good, I'll meet you at the law firm of Jackson, Carmen and Ramsdale. Can you take down the address?"

"I'm driving right now, but it must be in my GPS. I'll be there," Janet said and closed the phone without a farewell. He reminded her that they met at a news conference. *Emanuel . . . Emanuel . . .* that's his name, she recalled.

"God, this is creepy," she said aloud.

When it opened in 1958 the Connecticut Turnpike, a/k/a I-95, was a healthy and vibrant young child, providing a speedy alternative to the slow U.S. Route 1, which, dotted by traffic lights, meandered through shoreline towns one by one. Now I-95 is akin to an overstuffed elderly man, with movement hindered and arteries clogged. Near Stamford, Connecticut, it's a highway to nowhere, over-crowded with rush-hour stop-and-go traffic. Janet looked in her mirrors for signs of troopers, pressed her foot on the accelerator, and, determined to beat the rush hour clog, set the cruise control on 75.

Its small New England green notwithstanding, Stamford's charm has been shrinking by the encroachment of New Yorkers. Tall steel and glass office buildings dot the downtown skyline. Going away from the city center, Janet stopped her Saab in front of a teal-colored two story building, and looked at the GPS: The Regional Office of the Child Protection Department. She glanced once at the manila envelope in the seat beside her, covered it with her coat, and walked inside.

Janet had barely sat down outside the Supervisor's office when a distinguished-looking older man in a three-piece, tweed suit approached her with a smiling face and an outstretched right hand.

"You must be Ms. Mullen. The Commissioner's office told me you were joining us this afternoon. I am Mark Jackson, but please call me Mark."

Janet rose quickly. "Yes, I am pleased to meet you. Call me Janet."

"Please follow me, Janet."

He had an air of efficiency, Janet noticed, and kept a quick pace down the beige, linoleum hallway to a corner office with its walls lined with bookshelves and the ubiquitous gray filing cabinets that filled all the little rooms of state offices.

"Please have a seat," he said, pointing to one of the brown chairs opposite him. She noticed he had unusually bright green eyes.

"The Commissioner asked me to meet with you so that she can find out why your region is so successful while the Northern Region is not."

Subtly, Mark looked for a ring on Janet's left hand. Finding none, he made a dozen assumptions at once: career type, little time for social life, high standards, ambitious, difficulty finding a compassionate male. Janet shifted under his gaze. Catching himself, Mark refocused on the purpose of the meeting.

"Yes, the Commissioner's office called me. I put together a manual that we follow in handling all of our cases. Here is a copy for you."

Janet took the manual from Mark, and opened it to the first page: *Executive Summary—How to Maximize Resources: the Federal Project.*

"As you can see, Janet, we apply a multidisciplinary approach to decision-making."

After an hour of how-to-fix-the-system discussion, Janet felt inspired and equipped to answer Mary Strum's questions. She took the Executive Summary, together with other Southern Region memos on improving the system, thanked Mark, and left without looking back at him watching her.

The hands on her watch pointed to 6:35.

Emanuel Valez' family immigrated to the United States before he was born. His grandfather was a lawyer in Cuba and had a considerable amount of property when Fidel Castro came to power. It was because his grandfather knew Fidel that he and his family were allowed to leave the country—without any significant funds. They caught one of the last planes out. Emanuel had heard the story so often that he sometimes forgot he hadn't been born yet.

A resourceful man, Emanuel's grandfather learned English, worked during the day and attended the Connecticut Law School at night. The American system of law did not accept his foreign legal education, nor acknowledge his having practiced in Cuba. After graduating from the Connecticut Law School, he became a successful lawyer, and fighting for the rights of immigrants, defending members of the marginalized population, he was an inspiration in the community. His stories were a powerful motivator for Emanuel, and the desire of exposing corrupt government drove Emanuel into media studies at the University.

Unimpressed by the lack of aggressiveness from the mainline press, Emanuel, upon graduation, cobbled together a local city sheet, which he edited. With that and a part time job at a book store, he kept the landlord paid and the utilities on. Friends put the paper online, while Emanuel sought that something that would move his paper and web cast to the next level.

It was, miraculously to her, exactly seven o'clock when Janet opened the door of Jackson, Carmen and Ramsdale in downtown Stamford. A receptionist, sitting behind a white U-shaped desk, carved from a single piece of marble, directed her to two massive cherry wood polished doors.

"Mr. Velez is waiting for you."

As she opened the door, a diminutive young man at a conference table stood up. His thick oval shaped eyeglasses magnified his brownish gray eyes.

"Ms. Mullen?"

"Yes."

"Do you have it?"

"Yes." She was nervous when she shook his hand, and the sound of his closing the door startled her more than it should have, causing her to tremble a bit.

He looked different. When she first met him at a conference on media relations and state government she thought he was a total square. He had given his card, and said his start-up was eager for news. She was standoffish, and understandably so, she told herself. He could be a muckraker, grabbing a story at anybody's expense. Still, she'd kept his card.

Now face to face with him, alone in a strange room, she noticed nothing but his intensity. His attention was fully focused, and his eyes were clear and serious. He sat, leaned forward in his chair and placed his elbows on the conference table.

"I need complete verification that the Commissioner knew. That she had personal knowledge of the situation. Otherwise—"

"Don't worry, I have more than that."

"What do you mean?" Emanuel asked.

"This concerns more than the Commissioner," she answered. "It concerns . . . the top."

"What top?"

"The Governor."

"The Governor?" Emanuel straightened, eyes wide, "You can't be serious."

"Yes, I am."

"This kind of claim cannot be made without—"

"This is what I have," Janet replied, pulling a manila envelope from her brief case and sliding it across the conference table. She thought to herself that it must have just been polished. The envelope glided easily. Emanuel snatched it up and opened it. He retrieved the 'memo to file' from Tom Adams, Deputy Commissioner of the Child Protection Department. It took only a moment for Emanuel to understand its implications. In a recent conversation, it said, Adams had told Mary Strum, the Director of CPD, about a large number of foster children in the Bridgeport area being exposed to abuse as child laborers. It also said Mary Strum thanked him for his diligence, honored him for his work, and told him frankly that any investigation would have to take place after the upcoming election.

The memo recorded that Adams protested, citing the urgency of the children's situation and that Commissioner Strum said that the election is only one month away, the Governor knows about this situation, and will take care of it after the election.

Emanuel stopped reading, and then started once more from the top of the page. When his eyes reached the bottom of the page for the second time, he exhaled, and shot those piercing eyes to Janet.

"How did you get this?"

"I have my sources."

"Is this memo accurate?"

"Yes. To the best of my knowledge," Janet answered. Her heart was beating too quickly, and too harshly. She felt she could hear it in the room.

"And why give this to me?"

"Why not you?" Janet replied.

"Because I'm me. And we're small. Why not release this to a mainstream outlet?" he asked. Janet sensed rightly that question was less curiosity than a kind of test of her intentions. She answered quickly.

"Because you know as well as I do—better, I hope—that the Governor has many friends. The media has a history of being kinder to him than his enemies would prefer. Certain things are not allowed to be said. Certain knowledge not allowed to be shared. This—" she pointed to the memo, "—is of that kind. The story would be squashed, and I'd be labeled an irresponsible, disgruntled employee. No, this needs to be made public by other means—means that cannot be traced to me or to my source."

"And if your source is not reliable?"

"She—my source is reliable."

Emanuel stared at her, and she again noticed the intensity behind his lenses. She returned the stare without blinking, as though all her credibility rested on her winning the old playground game.

He broke away first, and glanced at his watch. "I need to talk to my people. Will you leave your number?"

She nodded. It wasn't until she sat down in her Saab and turned the key that she realized what she had set in motion could not be stopped.

CHAPTER 11

Juvenile Court

The Juvenile Court Courthouse sits at the midpoint of what some would call a major thoroughfare in New Haven. The name on the building—Superior Court for Juvenile Matters says it all. One hundred fifty linear feet separate the two story red-brick courthouse from the street. Nine-foot private hedges running the entire one-block distance in front of the Courthouse shield its visitors from passerby's prying eyes. Adults remove their watches, belts, and jewelry as they pass through the metal detectors at the front door. The first floor is a large waiting area with rust colored ceramic floor tiles. Visitors have a choice: walk up the flight of stairs on the left to the second floor or turn right toward the clerk's window to see one of the probation officers whose offices are accessed through the doorway under the clerk's buzzer control.

Once inside one enters the land of confidentiality. In this court, parents, juveniles, and anyone whom juveniles may have offended are heard, juveniles sentenced, children placed in foster care, and some sent away for rehabilitation—all outside the presence of the public, all done in confidentiality, and all for the protection of society and those young bodies and souls.

The juvenile justice system consists of two divisions: neglect and delinquency. The neglect side deals with what the term implies; namely, that the parent is in some way neglecting the child by actual physical or emotional abuse. Subcategories here are families in need of social or medical services; children who are out of control; runaway kids; or children who, acting as young adults, abuse their parents.

As an example of neglect, a tough fourteen-year old boy threatened to slit his mother's throat with a knife, telling her that since his father is out of the house he, the boy is the man of the house. After the boy is locked up, the mother appeals to the court for his release, saying she must have done something to anger him. The court must decide whether it's safe to allow him to return home or whether it is likely her son will carry out his threat. Hearings and trials wherein neglect is found result in the court either providing counseling to keep the family intact or placing the child in foster care or in an institutional facility for the child's safekeeping and well-being. And God forbid if the court makes the wrong decision.

Then there's the delinquency side. It deals with violations of laws, which, if committed by adults, would be called crimes, but when committed by juveniles are called offenses. Violations range from simple physical assaults to robbery, rape and murder. Punishment is proportionate to offenses and ranges from the juvenile being placed on court supervision and ordered to report to a probation officer or locked up in a secure facility for a number of years.

At this point, I'd like to take you through a typical day in my court. Samantha Smith is the Chief Prosecutor for the juvenile delinquent docket. Let's look in on the goings on in Samantha's life in Courtroom B.

CHAPTER 12

Troubled Youth

For seven years, Samantha Smith has been a juvenile prosecutor, long enough to inherit her spacious corner office. Her Phi Beta Kappa mind sorted through the hundreds of cases crossing her desk each month and struggled with whether to recommend incarceration, a rehabilitation program, or, the most serious judgment, a referral to the adult court for prosecution as an adult.

Although no trial was scheduled, Samantha knew the number of cases coming up would keep her office busy. She finished her mint tea in one long gulp, gathered her files, and leaving her office door ajar, walked a short distance to Courtroom B to review the day's docket with Lauren Wilcox, my clerk.

"Got time for me, Lauren?" she asked, upon entering the Courtroom.

Lauren looked up from her station desk, anchored high to the right of the judge's bench in Courtroom B. "For you Samantha, always. Although we have quite a crowded docket today—and would you believe there's media outside for two cases: the rape and the assault near the movie theatre. And we have the neglect docket."

Samantha placed her files on the dark wood desk parallel to the judge's bench as Jack Griffin, long-time public defender hurriedly burst through the courtroom door, rushing toward Lauren. She groaned audibly.

"Lauren, can you put me ahead of the rest of these cases? I need to finish my delinquency docket early this morning because I have a major investigation this afternoon."

"No 'excuse me?'" Samantha asked.

"I'm sorry. You're right. My mother taught me better," Jack replied.

"Maybe I can help you," Lauren said. "But you'd better pull up that tie. You know how the judge is about appearances. Nice suit."

"Thanks. An original J.C. Penny," Jack replied with a smirk, his boyish, ruddy face belying his upcoming 40th birthday. He could lose some weight, and he knew it. A stumpy 5'2", his red and yellow tie did little for his midsection.

Samantha stood a few inches above Jack's height, a fact which always bothered him a little, and was a few years younger, a fact which bothered him a lot. She dressed mostly in blazers and skirts, generally blue-gray or gray-blue, and almost always looked better than he. She was svelte and stunning in her blue blazer, pleated gray skirt and white scarf. This made Jack distinctly aware of himself.

Barely 23, Lauren allowed herself to still be amazed by how much power she held with lawyers, simply by being able to position the cases to be heard. Lauren looked down at Jack through the glasses on the bridge of her nose, feeling that power strongly at the moment.

"Have you met with all of your clients in lockup?" Lauren asked.

"Yes I have, mother, and I finished my breakfast, too. I'm ready. I just hope the state is too."

"The state is always ready," Samantha answered. "My inspector and I have interviewed all the necessary witnesses, and we are ready not only for detention review but also for trial."

"I guess I'm ready to watch you two go at it," said Lauren, shuffling the docket in Jack's favor.

Sheriff Cindy Newman, a tall woman in a blue uniform, white shirt, black tie and gold leaf on her lapels entered the courtroom through the door adjacent to the judge's bench. "I hope you folks are nearly ready," teased Sheriff Newman.

"The state is always ready—"began Samantha.

"Oh, get a better line," joked Jack.

"Are the people from child protection here?" Lauren asked.

"Yes," Sheriff Newman answered. "The front desk called up. Good luck, you two."

Newman turned and walked out of the courtroom. Samantha and Jack, sitting at the long desk, looked at each other for a moment and then opened the files which she would prosecute and he would defend. A knock pounded them to attention.

Newman emerged from the door to the right of the judge's bench, picked up her gavel at her station against the right wall, and struck the brass plate three times.

> *"All Rise . . . O 'yea, O 'yea, O 'yea, this*
> *Honorable Court for the District of*
> *Marlborough is open in this place, all here, give*
> *your attention according to law, the Honorable*
> *Judge Sam Hughes presiding."*

God, she's loud, Samantha thought. Samantha, Jack, and Lauren stood as I entered through the doorway behind the bench. Newman struck the gavel again.

"You may be seated," Newman exclaimed to the audience, and then added, "Good morning, your Honor."

I returned the greeting, and inquired about the delinquency docket. Fidgeting with his files, Jack Griffin stood up. "Your Honor, we have a large number of detention reviews on the docket today."

"Well, before I hear them I must advise everyone here in court for the first time of their legal rights." At this point, I generally took a sip of water from the glass on the bench. I looked at the dozens of juveniles and their parents in the courtroom, and began.

"You have the right to remain silent, the right to a lawyer, and the right to a court hearing where witnesses will be sworn to tell the truth. You have the right to have the Juvenile Prosecutor present her case against you by calling witnesses. You have the right to hear those witnesses and to confront them, meaning, you have the right to have your lawyer ask them questions, and you have the right to testify or not testify at the court hearing."

I have said these words so many, many times before that my mouth would utter them while my eyes scanned the room. My mind wondered what happened in the lives of these young children. I would think about my children who are now parents of my grandchildren. I would think about the past, the tradition of nurturing the young, about the present, and the loss of the past. I would think about the neighborhoods of the children now before me, the places both public and private that have brought them to this Courtroom and to my voice booming over them. I would think of what they are accused of doing.

I remembered the case of the child diagnosed with attention deficit disorder and low intelligence, arrested for disturbing behavior and his remarkable "recovery" to a well-behaved young boy of high academic achievement, no longer needing medication, after being placed in foster care with a loving and supportive family. Looking out at the dozens of young faces looking up at me, I wondered which of the juveniles before me today will get that chance, and which would not.

All these thoughts flooded in a moment, and hung around like a cloud. Upon finishing my advisement, the room was cleared of juveniles and their parents. Each family would be called back into the Courtroom individually, outside the presence of the others to ensure confidentiality.

"Where are the detainees?" I asked.

"The guards are bringing them up in the elevator now," Sheriff Newman replied.

All eyes turned to the right—to the door opening slowly. Two large young men, dressed in state-issue blue uniforms, escorted a small teenage boy to the left end of the table. A women in casual attire entered through the back of the courtroom and came forward to join the teenager. She looked up at me.

"I'm his mother. My name is Cynthia Johnson." A mid-fifties woman in brown corduroy slacks and a green blouse placed her arm around the young man, pulled him toward her, and kissed his cheek. He smiled.

Samantha lifted one of several files stacked in front of her.

"For the record, my name is Samantha Smith, Juvenile Prosecutor, representing the State Department of Child Protection. I am here for the detention review of young Derrick Johnson, who is sitting here at the counsel table."

Jack Griffin stood up and adjusted his tie.

"Jack Griffin, your Honor, for the record. Public Defender. I represent young Derrick. I have explained to him that the purpose of the detention hearing is for you to decide whether he will be held in the juvenile lock-up until his trial or will be allowed to go home until then. His probation officer has a positive report, and I recommend that he be released to his mother."

"Let me hear the report," I demanded.

Samantha removed a copy of the report from her file. "Judge, this is the Probationer's report on Derrick. It read as follows:

Derrick is charged with conspiracy/robbery 2nd and 3rd degree assault. Court ordered conditions are to fully comply with program requirements. He agreed at intake to abide by all of the Program recommendations including random urines and breathalyzers tests. While in attendance he participated in the Reading and Life Skills Project, Employment Readiness Group, Cognitive Self Change, Community Service, along with Case Management. His drug screen was negative. He has completed his substance abuse evaluation, HIV education and treatment plan, and he has been respectful to Staff.

Derrick smiled. A contagious smile crossed his mother's face. Finally, she thought. *He is ready to turn his life around and listen to her and stay away from the bad boys in the neighborhood—not to fit in with them. Maybe being locked up in juvenile hall was a good thing . . .*

Then I stared into the eyes of Derrick, his mother, and Samantha.

"Does the State have a recommendation about Derrick's release?"

"Yes, Your Honor," responded Samantha. "It's the State's position that minor Derrick be returned to the custody of his mother until his trial, provided that he complies with the law, he attend school, and he obeys the rules of his household."

"Neither I, my client, nor his mother object to his release," Griffin responded.

I pointed my index finger at Derrick. "You have some serious charges here. But because of the positive report, I'm releasing you to your mother until trial. However, if you violate any of the conditions of your release, including disobeying the household rules, you will be immediately re-arrested and locked up. Do you understand?"

The smile waned from Derrick's face. He whispered, "Yes Sir. Thank you, Sir."

Cynthia Johnson stood, shook Griffin's hand, and with Derrick in tow, left the Courtroom.

"Who's next?" I asked.

The Guards brought in another teenager who sat near Jack Griffin. "For the record, your Honor, Jack Griffin, I represent Jeff Malloy, who is sitting next to me. His mother, Carmella Malloy, is just entering the Courtroom." Griffin motioned Carmella to sit alongside her child.

"Is there a report for this detention hearing?"

"Yes, your Honor, a copy should be on your bench. I gave it to your clerk this morning."

"Ah, I have it. Would you like to present it, attorney Smith?"

"Yes, your Honor, I will read it into the record."

> *Jeff Malloy is charged with rape, robbery, driving under the influence, drug possession, drug use and the sale of drugs within 1500 feet of a school house. At intake he agreed to abide by the terms of the Program. He is enrolled in Cognitive Self Change, CAALM, Employment readiness, substance abuse evaluation, and weekly case management. He failed to report for scheduled groups on three occasions. He rendered four urine samples. First urine scree on July 10—positive for Cocaine/THC 931ng; second urine: positive cocaine/THC 776ng; third urine: positive for Cocaine/THC 893ng, client defiant.*

> *Seized Property: Rawlins Softball bat, Razor blade box cutter knife, Taurus .357 magnum Steel revolver w/ laser sight Ser Td20346, PBX Federal Pistol; cartridges /357, agmi, 125 gr/Hi-shok box containing 45 cartridges 24 each .357 magnum cartridges, Dexter Usa wood handle knife; partial pkg ½ size zig zag rolling papers; partial box zip loc quart size plastic bags; Ohaus model hh 120D digital scale.*

"These are some heavy duty charges," I remarked, raising my eyebrows.

Samantha Smith chimed in. "They certainly are, Judge, which is why as the state's juvenile prosecutor, I intend to file a motion to have this case transferred to Part A- the adult criminal court, so that he can be tried as an adult."

I looked at the boy and his mother. She squeezed her son's hand, removed a tissue from her pocket book and began wiping her eyes.

Public Defender Griffin had seen this coming. "Your Honor, I have prepared a written Objection to Transfer, which I am now filing with the court."

Griffin approached the bench, holding the sheet of paper. I directed him to my clerk Lauren who took the paper and file stamped it.

Griffin resumed. "The objection points out that at Jeff's age of 14 this court can look at extenuating circumstances."

Samantha interrupted. "Your Honor, there are no extenuating circumstances to raping a 13 year old girl."

"Young Jeff is innocent until proven guilty," Griffin countered. "No one has proved that he raped the girl. Besides, they knew each other."

"How does that give him permission to know her in the biblical sense? That girl's parents call me almost every day to make sure that he is prosecuted for what he did to her," Samantha persisted.

"Counselors, counselors," I interjected. "Lauren will schedule the Objection to Transfer for a hearing next week. Today, I need to decide whether to release Jeff to his mother's custody or return him to the juvenile detention facility until next week."

Samantha held up a sheet of paper. "Judge, this is Jeff's rap sheet. He is not a stranger to the Juvenile Court. It says that he was adjudicated as an offender at age 11 for shoplifting, at age 12 for truancy, at age 13 for assault and for failure to appear in court." She then raised her voice. "The state objects to his release. He is a danger to the community, and he disrespects court orders to appear for trial."

With raised eyebrows, I turned my attention to Griffin.

"Judge, those adjudications are in his past. His mother is here to take him home," Griffin said while placing his left arm on Jeff's right shoulder.

As I opened Jeff's case file, and removed the detention review report, my eyes were drawn to the term, "oppositional defiance," and to a request by detention staff for a psychiatric evaluation. "Has a psychiatric evaluation been performed?" I asked.

"Not to the state's knowledge, your Honor," Samantha answered.

"Well, if one had been done, you'd know about it. I'm ordering a psychiatric evaluation of Jeff immediately, and I'm ordering him held over in detention, at least until that's done."

"But would your Honor reconsider and release him to his mother?" asked Griffin. "She has been here all morning, waiting for her child."

I looked in Carmella Malloy's direction, and took a breath.

"Mrs. Malloy, how obedient is your son? I know that you want to take him home with you today, but I don't know whether that's good for you or the community."

Carmella Malloy knew that her son had been in minor trouble before, but nothing like this.

"Well, Judge, he is alright when he's not hanging out with bad boys in the neighborhood. He is very smart, but he's embarrassed to show it in school. Says his friends don't like it. He's basically a good boy, but I do worry about him. He's taking to not coming home every night."

"Ma'am, I think it's best for the time being for me to order your son held here for his own sake and for the safety of the community. Therefore, I order that he be held on the ground that it is likely that he will offend society again. Guards, take him back to lock-up."

John, the 6 foot 2 inch, 275-pound police guard, grabbed Jeff's left bicep.

"You don't have to be rough with him. He'll cooperate," Carmella said, causing John to release his grip. Jeff reluctantly accompanied John and his assistant to the elevator door en route to the downstairs lockup of four-foot by five-foot cubicles constructed of cinderblock walls, a metal door with a small opening about chest high, and a stainless steel sink and toilet.

Lillian Evans, the other of the two female-team prosecutor staff, opened the door of Courtroom B. A file in her hand read case number 21, 'Donna K.—Runaway.'

"What do you have for the court today, Prosecutor Evans?" I asked.

"Good morning, Judge. This is case of Donna K. She is a bit out of control, as I think even her court-appointed lawyer, Martin Cashman here, will attest.

"Is that true, Attorney Cashman?"

"I'm afraid so, Judge. As you may recall, you appointed me last winter to represent young Donna. Because of her troubled past, you ordered her to be placed by the Child Protection Department at the Grace Home for Girls in Bridgeport where I visited with her as late as last week."

A recent graduate from law school, Cashman recently began accepting fee cases from the Juvenile Court to help pay his office rent. Despite his young-looking face, he had gained a reputation for diligent representation of his clients. Cashman, dressed in a blue pinstriped three-piece suit, exuded confidence without arrogance.

"So what happened?" I asked.

Prosecutor Evans began, "Judge, you ordered 14 year old Donna K. taken into custody because the lady at the shelter asked the Department of Child Protection for help. The report in the file says that she was staying with her mother and her mother's boyfriend at the Westerly Campgrounds, when one morning others at the camp heard her screaming. Donna woke up and her mother and her mother's boyfriend were gone. She was alone in the camp. They left her. A couple at the camp brought Donna to the shelter downtown. We took her on a 96-hour hold. The folks at Grace Homes say she's out of control."

"Where is she now?" I asked.

"The Sheriff is escorting her in. She was meeting with her mother in the conference room down the hall. I just wanted to alert your Honor to her sensitive condition."

"Attorney Evans, what is the State's plan?"

"Therapeutic foster care or placement in a structured residential program, but there's a waiting list for each. Right now she's in a temporary treatment shelter." Prosecutor Evans looked over her shoulder as the door at the rear opened. "Here she is now, your Honor."

A teenage girl, who looked five years older than she was, dressed in faded blue jeans, white sneakers, and a grey pull over, walked slowly to the front. Unkempt dark hair hung like vines on the side of her sallow face. Evans gestured for the girl to take a seat beside her. Following behind, a middle age woman carrying a frown and a large brown pocket book, limped slightly.

"This is Donna and her mother," Evans announced.

"Good morning, ma'am. You may have a seat. Please state your name for the record," I directed.

"Judge, I am Margaret Klemins—that's my girl."

"Attorney Evans?" I asked with a furrowed brow.

Lillian Evans composed her thoughts.

"Judge, the department has tried to help Donna. We located her mother and offered her mother money so that she can take the train to visit with her daughter. The mother always has an excuse for not visiting when given the chance."

Margaret Klemins stared at Lillian Evans with fierceness that four years ago would have made her shiver. Now, she simply glared back. "It's true," Evans said. "The mother doesn't visit and the child blames us because it's easier to blame the department than to admit that her mother is disloyal to her." Young Donna's face twitched, while her head shook back and forth.

"The girl appears pretty distraught," I said. "Sheriff, see if you can get her some water, while the Court takes a brief recess."

A short ten minutes passed before I opened the Courtroom to the pounding of Sheriff Newman's gavel. The Courtroom Clerk informed me that Donna K. and her mother stayed in conference with the Court Services Officer—an attempt at resolution through mediation. If successful, the result would be brought to my attention for my approval. I acknowledge this information as Prosecutor Samantha Smith entered the Courtroom.

"Judge, excuse me, but we have an emergency Neglect Matter. May we be heard?"

"Of course, Prosecutor Smith. Name of the case?"

"It's the matter of Maxine Wright. She and her mother are in the hallway. I am giving Lauren the file."

"Tell the Sheriff to bring them in," I ordered.

Sheriff Cindy Newman returned, leading a woman and a girl into the courtroom. "What's the problem?" I asked.

"I'm Carolyn Wright, the mother of Maxine, my 15 year old pregnant daughter here. She may look grown, but she's only fifteen. We're from Jamaica. My ungrateful daughter here called the police, saying that I was abusing her."

"You were," the young girl replied.

"Is there a probation officer here?" I asked.

"Yes," answered Smith. "Officer Jim Allen. He's sitting in the back of the courtroom." "Officer Allen, please step forward."

"It's a Family with Service Needs case, your Honor," said Officer Allen, a lanky young man in a green blazer, now a veteran probation officer assigned to the Juvenile Court.

"Have you met with the mother and the daughter?"

"Yes, Judge, I followed protocol. I met with them separately, and then together. They are from Jamaica. Been here ten years. The mother is a hard worker. The problem between them started when the mother's boyfriend moved into their apartment. There were frequent arguments between the daughter and the boyfriend—which mother blames on the daughter. Then the problems started between the mother and the boyfriend."

"Judge, he was cursing at my mother and he broke her arm. That's why I argued with him."

"Is that true Mrs. Wright?" I asked.

"Yes, it's true," Maxine interjected. "In fact he's been arrested for it."

"Young lady, I am asking your mother whether it's true."

Carolyn Wright nodded, uttering "Yes, Your Honor."

"Anything else?" I asked Probation Officer Allen.

"Yes, Judge, the daughter is pregnant and says her mother threatens to evict her, but the mother denies it. Child Protection Department wants a court order."

"I need some testimony," I said, and a moment later Carolyn Wright was seated in the witness box.

"Judge, I don't want her to become dependent on the government. When I was a child I had one pair of shoes, and my mother cut a hole in the front of them to accommodate my growing feet. I just don't want the government to provide a home for her in a home for pregnant girls. That's paid for by the government, right? She's pregnant now—I know what that means. The state will provide her with an income. It's welfare, and as a proud Jamaican, I don't accept none of it."

"What about the boyfriend who broke your arm?" I asked.

"He's out of my house. I got a Court Order putting him out."

Reassured by Carolyn Wright's testimony, I suggested that the parties meet with the Court Services Officer and make an agreement, to be approved by me, to live together peaceably.

Within five minutes after leaving the courtroom, Court Services Officer Linda Grady, accompanied by Prosecutor Samantha Smith and Probation Officer Jim Allen, re-entered the Courtroom and sat, waiting for me to finish reviewing the docket with Clerk Lauren Wilcox.

"Yes?" I asked, removing my eyeglasses, and focusing my attention on Linda Grady.

"It's the case of the mother and daughter," Linda Grady replied.

"What happened?"

"Just as they were about to sit down in my office down the hall, the mother started yelling at her daughter, shouting *baby out of wedlock, I warned you,* and then calling her all sorts of names, threw two dollars at her and left."

Prosecutor Samantha Smith interrupted. "Judge, you may want to hear from the girl herself. I spoke briefly with her and Probation Officer Allen in the hallway. The girl tells quite an upsetting story. She's sitting in the back of the courtroom and ready to testify."

I beckoned to Maxine. The weary-looking girl walked to the witness box and swore to tell the truth.

"Judge, if you don't mind, I'll direct the questions," Samantha Smith requested.

"By all means."

Samantha walked toward the frightened girl. "Maxine, just relax and tell the Judge what you told me and Officer Allen a few moments ago."

Maxine lowered her eyes.

"It's alright, just tell the truth. You'll be fine," Samantha pleaded with her.

Maxine began. "Two days ago, Theron, that's my mother's boyfriend, tried to run over me and my mother with his car. We were getting away from him, but then he got out of the car, and started hitting her. They struggled and he broke her arm. Somebody called the police and he was arrested."

"Anything else?" Evans asked.

"Oh, yes, his clothes are still in my mother's closet, and she threatens to return to Jamaica with me to keep me away from my boyfriend. I can't live with her. She starts arguments and then threatens to throw me out into the street. Last week she picked up a butcher knife from the kitchen counter and threatened to cut the baby out of my belly. I don't know what's wrong with her. I don't know what to do—" Maxine continued, her cracking voice trailing off.

"What do you think should be done here?" I asked.

"Judge, unfortunately there are few options. There are no other family members in this country, and she doesn't want to return to Jamaica with her mother. She's essentially homeless. I request that you issue a Take into Custody Order, and we'll place her in a foster home for pregnant girls."

"What do you think of the proposed solution?" I asked, directing my attention to Linda Grady.

"I reviewed the option with her, Judge, and she agreed to accept it, if it is a court order."

"And you?" I said, looking at Jim Allen.

"I agree," Jim Allen responded. "My office will keep in contact with her and her mother, just to make sure everything's alright."

I turned toward Maxine. "Well, young lady, is it okay with you?"

Maxine placed both hands on her belly, and rocked back and forth. Tears rolled down her cheeks. "Yes," she muttered.

"Also I'm going to appoint a Guardian ad Litem, that is, a Legal Guardian, to keep track of you. Okay?"

Although not knowing what a Guardian is, and somewhat assured by the sincerity in my voice, Maxine nodded her head in agreement.

One case followed another until the end of the court day. Parents distraught, kids upset, resources taxed. I reminded myself that I must, as best I can, and mostly I cannot, leave each day's troubles in the courtroom, to be picked up and tended to the next day, folded in with new cases on tomorrow's docket. *Fret not about tomorrow,* I thought, *each day is enough trouble of its own.*

CHAPTER 13

The 96 Hour Hold

Sheriff Carlos Rodriguez looked up from his station at the metal detector and greeted the perky young lady who had just opened the front door to the courthouse. Accustomed to her late Friday afternoon arrivals, Carlos beckoned her through the metal detector.

Hurrying to beat the 5:00 p.m. deadline, Michele asked breathlessly, "Have the judges left yet?"

"Judge Jackson had to go to a meeting, but Judge Simione is here. She may be on the bench doing delinquencies."

"Thanks, Carlos." She ran up the steps, opened the door, and walked twenty feet to the waiting area of the Clerks' Office Window.

Michele was delighted to see Angelina working the clerk's desk today. The sight of her gave Michele an extra breath.

"Hi, Michele! Can I help you?" Michele liked Angelina's ebullient personality. Having worked here only three months, Angelina and her personality had not yet suffered the effects of the position. The crushing emotional weight of cases in this court would change her, though Michele found herself hoping again that it wouldn't.

"Sure am glad you're on duty today, Angie. The Department gave me these last-minute OTC's and I know the clerk's office is not happy about it, but I have to do my job. Is a Judge available?"

"I think so."

Angelina lifted a large red book from the counter and examined several of its pages. "Judge Simione is still in court. She likes to stop at about a quarter of five, so she should adjourn court pretty soon."

At the sound of the buzzer, Michele pulled open the door leading to the conference rooms and courtrooms.

As the door closed behind her, Joyce Cooper, the court liaison, greeted her. Michele looked surprised.

"Oh, Michele, the Regional Office called and told me you were on the way. I haven't seen you in a long time!"

It had been a long time. And Michele noticed that Joyce's hair was grayer than when she saw her last. She still dressed very well. *Is that jacket a Christian Dior? Goes nicely with her dark gray slacks . . . Where does she get her money?*

"What do you have, Michele?"

"It's a horrible OTC request."

"Okay, come with me to my office."

Michele began her explanation while the two women walked down the long hallway past the public defender's office, the prosecutor's office, to Joyce's small corner office.

"Joyce, this is one of the worse cases I have seen—"

"Wait until we're inside."

Michele hesitated, and Joyce opened the door.

"Close the door."

Michele obeyed, and sat facing Joyce who had taken her chair behind the desk. Michele's eyes focused on the large window behind Joyce's chair, through which she noticed people boarding the city bus near a corner store. Life goes on as usual.

"So . . ." Joyce prompted.

Michele refocused to the moment. "We, uh, we haven't had a case like this before. It's strange. Infanticide: a mother suffocating her little baby."

"My God!"

"I know."

"How could that happen?"

Michelle handed Joyce the Petition *for Child Taking*.

"Here, please read this."

Joyce took the paper and her eyes began their journey through the disturbing words of discontent, beginning with the caption.

Petition for Child Taking

History

Mother, Dorothy Simmons, and father, Henry Simmons, have been involved with the child protection agency since August of 2000. Earlier, there was a confirmation of "failure to thrive syndrome" for Maria, then age 2. Maria was placed in foster care for a short time during which she gained her normal weight, and thereafter she was returned to the parents under protective supervision of the child protection agency.

Reason for Petition: Infant Katie Simmons

On January 15, Department of Child Protection investigator, Mary Holden, received a report filed by Julia Smith, social worker at Braintree Hospital stating that young Katie, seven months old, had been admitted to their facility on December 18, after a referral from Southport Hospital. The reason for the referral was repeated, **unexplained episodes of apnea—a temporary cessation or absence of breathing.**

Apnea can cause brain injury or death. Social worker Smith stated that the treating medical providers suspect that the mother is causing the episodes, for they only happen when she is nearby and at no other time. On January 15, investigator Mary Holden reported to Braintree Hospital and met with Sam Sorrento, R.N., and Sheila Mack, R. N. Nurse Sorrento informed investigator Holden that the child was referred to their facility by Newport Hospital and she was told, at the time of the referral, that Newport Hospital suspected Munchausen's by Proxy.

Nurse Sorrento stated that the child had only one Apneic episode in her two-week stay at the hospital, and that once again, only the mother was present at the event.

Dr. Murray suggested a 96-hour hold, pending receipt of some outstanding tests and further consultations. Dr. Murray then provided an affidavit to the Child Protection Department. The affidavit said that she suspected Munchausen's Syndrome by Proxy and that she believed the child's life would be endangered if returned to her mother's care.

Based upon this report the Child Protection Department invoked the 96-hour administrative hold at 4:36PM and placed the child in a foster home under the Department's supervision, pending the department obtaining **an**

Order of Temporary Custody (OTC) *allowing it to keep the child in foster care beyond the 96 hours and until there is a court hearing on custody in the Juvenile Court.*

Joyce looked incredulous.

Michele nodded her head. "If I can't get this OTC signed today, the Department has to release the child back to her family. Our department is under a federal court order that we must either get an OTC before our administrative 96-hour hold expires, or we are in contempt of federal court. I need a judge. Now."

Joyce swiveled her chair to look into the parking lot.

"Judge Simione's car isn't here."

Michele winced. "What can I do, Joyce?"

"I don't know. Let's see if the Chief Clerk is still here. Maybe he has some idea."

The two women moved quickly to the door, and leaving Joyce's office, stepped into a jog. As they turned the corner, Joyce bumped into Mitch Freeman, the Chief Clerk, sending him staggering.

"Oh, excuse me, Joyce, I was just on my way out. You two look—"

"Mitch, I was coming to find you. Michele has brought an urgent OTC and Judge Simione has left—what should I do?"

"No, Joyce, she's still here. I just saw her. She didn't drive in today. She's waiting downstairs for her son to pick her up."

He hadn't finished his sentence before the two women shot off down the hallway and through the doors. He watched them for a minute, before buttoning his coat and walking to the stairs.

CHAPTER 14

The Assistant Attorney General

Jean Mecelli sat at her kitchen table, scribbling notes on a legal pad. Husband Steve ladled what he named "his specialty dish" of spicy hot scrambled eggs, diced Vidalia onions and cilantro onto her plate. Taking a mouthful, she looked up at him and smiled.

"Thanks, hon—"

"Don't talk with your mouth full." He smiled. She swallowed.

"Right. Thanks, though. This dish is as good as our new kitchen is pretty. The stone company did such a nice job with the countertops."

Steve nodded. "I wasn't sure that one guy, his helper, and that spotted dog he kept in his van were going to finish the job this week. But they did. It turned out better than expected." He placed the platter on the table, and studied his wife's face.

"So are you going to tell me?" He asked.

"H-m-m?"

"What's wrong? Are you going to tell me what's wrong? Your face is worried. Which only means I am too."

Jean adjusted her eyeglasses and ran her fingers through her jet-black hair. "You know, when I first took this job, I wasn't an idiot. I didn't think I could save them all. I had no Messiah complex. But I also thought I could just work and work and none of this would get to me."

Steve smiled silently. He knew when not to talk.

Jean raised herself from the table and walked to the kitchen window facing the distant marsh. She checked her watch, smiled slightly at the crimson, blue, and white streaks of sunrise, and turned to look at her husband.

"Every day reading about, hearing about, and dealing in court with the suffering of all these little children . . ." She paused. "There's just so much sadness, darkness . . ."

Steve walked to the window and placed his arms around her from behind. She let her head fall back on his chest. Her voice lowered.

"We were so lucky to have the parents we had. They worried about bringing us up the right way. My mother was a little too protective. And look at all the stuff that we and our neighbors had. A lot of children I deal with in court have nothing, not even hope."

He kissed the top of her head.

"They have you."

"That's not much."

"You're their hope, Jean. An excellent lawyer—everyone says you are. Your exhilaration trying cases keeps you enthused for days. So many children have different and better lives because of you."

"I've been getting pretty teary at work lately."

"It could be that time of the month."

"I don't think that's it. I've been feeling this way most of the time."

Jean turned around and fidgeted with the collar on Steve's yellow shirt, setting it on the neck of the sweater, before turning away in search of her briefcase. Steve gestured toward the living room.

"You say I'm a great lawyer. I'm such a great lawyer that I can't solve my own family problem with my mother and Christina."

"I know your dad would like to end this family feud."

"You know how she is: she's so overbearing. She's still, as she says, 'trying to protect me.' Mom thinks she can boss me around—telling me how much money I should have, what kind of clothes I should wear, what church to attend—and she still wants to instruct me on how to raise Christina. Mom openly complains to Christina that I am not raising her the right way. Enough is enough!"

"When I tucked her in bed last night she said she misses her grandma," Steve said.

"I know. But I told Mom to stop it, and we could talk about letting her see Christina again. It's uncomfortable. We live in the same small town. I avoid her at the supermarket and at the downtown shops. She's always bossing everyone around. I don't know how my dad puts up with it."

"After 40 years, he's not going anywhere."

"I guess my mom meant well—the way she raised me when I grew up—but she did her best to control everything. At least she didn't set out to intentionally harm me."

"You turned out just fine for me."

Almost ignoring Steve's response, Jean continued, "Mom's lawyer has convinced her that visitation with Christina can be forced through the grandparent visitation law. I just think he is milking this case because mom has the ability to pay his legal fees. She lost at the trial court level and now she is appealing to the State Supreme Court. My God, Steve, when will she stop?"

"Her lawyer's fees are your inheritance. And you have to work nights to write motions and briefs for us because we can't even afford to hire an attorney for the situation. By the way, when is our response to her appeal due?" Jean checked her pocket calendar.

"It's due on Monday."

"Is it ready?"

"It will be."

"Look at me." He was serious now. "You have one of the best legal minds in the state. You turned down first round offers from the top law firms to do child protection work in juvenile court. You're capable, and this will work out."

"Yeah, yeah—I'm smart enough, good enough, and doggone-it, people like me! Any more affirmations?" Her sarcasm was warmed by a smile.

"Give me a hug."

She squeezed him hard, paused, then picked up her briefcase.

"Got to go. There's an early-morning meeting in the prosecutor's conference room today; something about a Munchausen."

Steve watched as his wife, thermos of coffee in one hand, briefcase in the other, leaned her shoulder against the door to the attached garage. He thought to himself, *she's the most gorgeous child protector in the state.*

But this affirmation he kept to himself.

Chapter 15

The Munchausen Syndrome

"Hi, Dutch."

"Morning Mecelli," Sheriff Van Deusen muttered. "Go right in. There's some big meeting here today. They told me to stand by the door. Feel like a traffic cop."

"Which room?"

"It's in the conference room right down the hall from your office."

Jean took a deep breath before shoving the door open to her office suite. Robert, her young administrative assistant, handed her a file folder.

"Mrs. Mecelli, this is the file for today's meeting. Just dropped off by Administration this morning." Jean opened it immediately.

"What lousy notice. I'm glad I'm not on the program. What's the meeting about?" she asked, skimming the paper.

"Something about a syndrome. The meeting is in the big conference room down the hall."

Jean placed the folder back on Robert's desk and headed down the hallway. The room was full of regional supervisors of the Child Protection Department—people used to being in charge were now seated quietly. And reluctantly—she could sense it. She noticed Lois Grumman, head of the Children's Institute at the University whom she met at an agency function last month. Lois stood behind a white pine lectern.

"Good morning, I am Dr. Lois Grumman. I am here this morning to talk to you about a mental disorder called Munchausen's Syndrome by Proxy, also known as MSBP. We are seeing more of the symptoms in our clinical review of cases at area hospitals. Presenting with me today is Sam Conley, who as the vast majority of you know, is the Chief Investigator for the State Child Protection Agency."

Sam walked slowly to the podium. "Ladies and gentlemen, Dr. Grumman and I just returned from an international conference on child protection dealing with Munchausen's Syndrome. It is very important that we share some of our findings and some of the things to look out for in making your recommendations to the court. I will now sit down and Dr. Grumman will address you."

"Quite a pair they make," Jean remarked to herself. A woman beside her chuckled.

Lois placed a file on the podium, adjusted her gold wire rimmed eyeglasses and began. This, Jean thought, was going to be a drag.

"The term 'Munchausen's Syndrome' describes a situation in which a person feigns illness in order to get attention from doctors, neighbors and friends. The term 'proxy' in this context means surrogate or substitute. So instead of a person, such as the mother, herself playing sick in order to get the attention, she substitutes her child as the sick person. She still gets the attention as the loyal caretaker. People—friends, neighbors, doctors, nurses—comment on how dutiful she is looking after her sick child. They think the mother must be a saint, or even a victim of a difficult situation. She basks in the attention given her by society's approval of all she is doing to 'help or save' her child."

At some point, Jean started paying attention. After a minute or so, she had a white legal pad in her lap, and her pen was sliding quickly over the paper recording the words by the Gregg shorthand she taught herself while a teenager one summer. As soon as the last word is spoken, she floated to the front of the room, and huddled with Lois Grumman.

Leaving Lois, Jean walked to her office with one thought. She removed a medical report from a manila folder stamped "Confidential." The intercom rang.

"I know you told me not to put her through, but your mother says it's urgent . . . something to do with Christi."

"My daughter is fine. But put her through," Jean said, her shoulders slumping. "Hi, Mom, how can I help you?"

"I'm not in need of help. I'm just calling to see how you and everyone are doing."

"Oh we're fine. How is Dad?"

"He's recovering well from his by-pass surgery. We're preparing to go on a cruise to the Dominican Republic, and were wondering whether we could see Christi before we go."

"What about the lawsuit, Mom?"

"What do you mean?"

"What do I mean? How can I let you see Christi while you are suing us for visitation with her? Is your lawyer going to argue that since we let you see Christi, it's no big deal for the court to grant you visitation rights? Did your lawyer ask you to make this call?"

"Whoa, whoa, one question at a time. No, my lawyer didn't ask me to call. I'm calling because I miss her and you, and we want to see both of you before we leave."

"When are you leaving?"

"In two weeks. The ship sails from Manhattan on Sunday the 18th."

"I'll see you and Dad before you leave, but as long as the lawsuit is pending, you can't see Christi."

"That makes me feel bad."

"Well, I'm sorry, Mom, but if you withdraw the lawsuit with prejudice, then Steve and I will consider visitation, provided you agree to parent counseling."

"Parent counseling . . . why? I *raised* you. You're an important lawyer; I'd say you turned out alright."

She went for humor. Jean sensed it.

"But not before a lot of individual therapy."

"My therapist taught me how to deal with the control messages you have given me since I was a little girl. I had anorexia in college, for God's sake. I've told you what you have to do. Let me know. I've got to go now. Big trial coming up. Bye, Mom." She hit the button and the sadness permeated the room. It has been two Christmases since she'd spoken at length with her parents. Her life had lost some of its texture. Her relationship with her mother had always been strained. But she missed her father.

Jean shook herself back, returning to the medical report from the confidential folder. Prepared by their investigator, it summarized the hospital data on a Dorothy and Henry and their two children, including myriad tests and procedures to which an infant had been subjected to determine the cause of her mysterious illnesses. She read the affidavits from social workers describing their contacts with the children and their parents. She wrote down the names of witnesses with whom she would meet and whose testimony she would review prior to putting them on the witness stand. She made a note labeled 'CRITICAL: To meet with the experts that the department will present at the trial for two reasons: to cover direct examination and cross-examination.'

During direct examination, Jean would explain that the expert would define MSBP in a story-like format. She must tell her expert that there will be questions, such as "Doctor, please explain what MSBP means. Doctor, what is its origin? Doctor, is MSBP present in this case? Doctor, is it harmful?"

Jean must explain cross-examination and the art of doubt-planting. "Doctor, isn't it true that MSBP doesn't explain every apnea incident?" She must explain the hypothetical reasoning. "Doctor, assume a, b, and c facts, don't they lead to d as a result?" Her expert would be prepared, must be prepared. Her expert would pause before giving an answer, and re-phrase the hypothetical question to include relevant facts.

Her expert witness would be thoroughly familiar with her material, and would not be shaken. "Doctor, you're familiar with the Diagnostic and Statistical Manual on the subject of MSBP, do you agree with its conclusion?" The expert witness preparation must go well. A young life depended on it.

She unlatched her large three-ring brown leather backed trial note-book, and flipped to the Law and Evidence Issues. She reached for the calendar and marked Monday as the day she would interview social workers.

Jean Mecelli took a breath and sitting back in her chair, confronted the feeling in her body and the thoughts that raced through her mind: This case mattered. This child mattered. And she must win.

CHAPTER 16

More CPD Troubles

After a half-hour of swimming the breaststroke at the local college Olympic size pool, I made an early arrival in my Courthouse chambers. Awaiting me on my desk is a manila envelope from the Review Committee. I removed a document labeled "Official Complaint," and let out a sigh. Whatever its specific contents, the feeling I anticipate having upon reading it is the same: frustration. I began to read.

Because of poor oversight the Child Protection Department had placed six foster children in a home of a woman whose live-in boyfriend was a known and convicted child molester. The complaint detailed the raping and sexual assault on three of the girls, and one boy.

A simple background check—how hard is that? All of this could have been avoided.

Some of the incidents, it appeared, had been reported but not investigated, and now the children were not receiving therapy. I wondered when the Department would learn to police itself.

Removing a binder from my left desk drawer, I flipped to the law section: *Federal Act: Child Welfare.* Under this law each state must investigate charges of child abuse and neglect, provide necessary treatment, and have a plan of action to avoid further abuse and neglect.

Making a note in the binder, I penciled in the date of the upcoming Review Committee meeting, and turned my attention to the list of cases on the day's docket.

CHAPTER 17

Order of Temporary Custody

When Jesus returned for the Second Coming, 100,000 people would be spared.

The original Puritan colonists believed it, and built a sixteen-acre park designed to hold them all. Jesus hadn't yet come back. They had planted Elm trees all along the border of the large rectangular park-like setting called the New Haven Green.

In the center of downtown—across the street from a corner of the vast New Haven Green— a tall Greco-Roman white marble column Courthouse, reminiscent of the sculptures adorning the palace of the Roman gods, overshadows the buildings nearby.

For decades, this Courthouse has hosted innumerable conflicts. Who murdered whom, whose feet would receive the laying of fault in a divorce, who should be evicted and why, who caused the injuries, who was to blame. The guilt and blame were passed out by men and women every day for a hundred years.

Bobby Seale, the infamous Black Panther was tried here. It was a memorable trial in an unkempt, emotional tide. The demonstrations. The anger. The fear. The New Haven Green filled with placards, while grass turned to mud beneath the feet of protesting thousands. Police sharpshooters, rifles in hand, watched the gathered crowd from their fourth floor roof-top stations on nearby City Hall. And still Jesus had not returned.

Dorothy walked through the massive doors of the Courthouse, having been summoned by Sheriff Esposito to give cause why the judge should not order the Child Protection Department to keep her little child Katie.

"Second Floor, Ma'am; take the elevator or steps," directed the Sheriff guarding the vestibule.

Dorothy decided to use the marble steps. She needed the exercise. Well-dressed young men and women, seated on the dark mahogany benches that lined the marble walls, watched as she ascended the stairwell.

"What can I do for you?" the Sheriff at the Courtroom door on the second floor inquired. Dorothy pulled papers from her pocketbook and handed them to the uniformed man.

"Am I in the right place?"

The Sheriff took the papers from Dorothy's extended hand.

"You sure are," he said after a glance. "Go in, and listen for your name."

Dorothy glanced around the huge Courtroom—a room about half the size of her church. Its aged elegance was reflected in its high vaulted ceiling and mahogany walls. A judge in robes spoke to a man and a woman near his bench. A man and a woman in suits—his blue, hers black—stood at the tables, talking. They looked young. The man turned, and then walked toward her.

"I'm Attorney Christopher Lawrence. Dorothy Simmons?"

"That's . . . that's me."

"Please come with me, Mrs. Simmons. We should take a seat at the counsel table. After court is open, the judge will take a brief recess, and I will review your case with you."

Dorothy followed the young, blue-suited man, while staring at the well-dressed woman she saw earlier, sitting at the table to the right of hers. She had seen magazine pictures of women dressed like that. She liked her scarf. But her hair was too short.

"Hear Ye, Hear Ye! All who have gathered here, rise, and pay attention according to Law! Judge Samuel Hughes presiding!"

Only a few persons were present. Dorothy wondered why the woman holding a raised gavel in hand was yelling. The sound of shuffling feet and scraping chairs erupted as everyone stood up. Dorothy felt that someone was about to lead the Pledge of Allegiance, and she instinctively placed her hand on her chest. From a door in the front wall, I emerged in my black robes, just as Dorothy had seen in the movies. The scene looked so familiar, Dorothy imagined she'd seen me before. It was from television, or from someplace else maybe.

I took my chair and looked up immediately. "Good morning counselors, what case is before the court today?"

"Good morning, Your Honor. For the record, I am Jean Mecelli, the Assistant Attorney General. This is the case of the Commissioner of Child Protection of the State versus Dorothy and Henry Simmons."

Attorney Christopher Lawrence stood alongside attorney Mecelli and jumped on the end of her sentence.

"I represent the Simmons', your Honor, and they are innocent of these charges."

I looked down from my bench at the two attorneys. If I added their ages together, they might reach my age.

Jean Mecelli resembled my daughter, and I recognized the danger in this.

About thirty years of age, I guessed. Mecelli's relaxed upper class accent and immaculate attire—striped black business suit; black pumps; brunette hair in a bun; pearl horn-rimmed eyeglasses—speak of the respect she has for the position and herself, as well as for her well-off parents and the great political connections that landed her the Assistant Attorney General job.

I looked over at Christopher Lawrence. Lawrence is a young man, conservative, with a look of controlled intelligence. Started his own firm last year, so I heard. Known as a meticulous researcher, he also prepared his clients well. He wore interesting ties, which I suspected were strategically purchased to lighten the mood and to start conversation. Today Christopher Lawrence sported a paisley tie of a mixed vermilion and blue hue, and a dolphin tie clasp. He probably got them at a discount store.

Regaining her opening, Mecelli continued, "This is not a criminal case. This is a civil neglect petition which says that these parents, Dorothy and Henry Simmons, have neglected their infant, placing her in grave danger."

Jumping up, Dorothy yelled, "I've done nothing wrong! I want my baby back!"

I banged my gavel. "Sit down, young lady, you will get your turn."

Lawrence placed his hand on Dorothy's shoulder, and motioned her to sit. He then opened his hands in a friendly gesture.

"Your Honor, I apologize, but the clerk's office just assigned the file to me yesterday afternoon, and I must request a continuance to confer with and prepare my client for this OTC hearing. I just met her, and I haven't even had a chance to tell her what an OTC is. With all due respect, Your Honor—"

That said, Lawrence lowered his 5'10" frame into the chair beside his new client. I was known to be a reasonable judge. Lawrence hoped that I would do the right thing and grant him the continuance.

Mecelli rose to her feet. "Your Honor, I object. The state must move this process along. The children are so young. Earlier this year, the CPD took Maria. We need to prove that the parents neglected this child, Katie, so that we can begin the next phase, termination of the parents' rights, and then put her up for adoption."

"What!" Dorothy yelled, rising wild-eyed from her seat.

Lawrence's firm hand on her shoulder restrained her forward movement. Sensing the anxiety in the room, I spoke quickly, and with authority.

"Hold on, Counselor Mecelli. As the judge, I decide when the case will be heard, and Attorney Lawrence needs time to confer with his client in order to prepare for the hearing. Attorney Lawrence, your continuance request is granted. Two weeks." I stood up.

"Thank you, your Honor. And my client-"

The Sheriff banged the gavel, then yelled once more, "All rise! Court's in recess."

Everyone in the courtroom stood again, but Dorothy was late in joining them. As the courtroom emptied, Lawrence turned to Dorothy, "Mrs. Simmons, please follow me to one of the conference rooms outside. I need to discuss your case with you."

I left the courtroom through the door behind the bench.

Christopher Lawrence escorted Dorothy out of the courtroom into the cavernous marble hallway, all the while looking through the glass panel in the door to each conference room on the right side of the corridor. They walked past Conference Rooms 1, 2 and 3—all occupied by lawyers and clients. Dorothy watched their arms moving quickly and their foreheads wrinkling.

They reached Conference Room 4, a dark, small room with a table and mismatched chairs. The heavy door slammed behind them as fluorescent lights flickered. He gestured to Dorothy, "Please come in Mrs. Simmons."

Dorothy entered the room and sat facing the paneled door and her new lawyer. Swallowing hard, she removed the paper from her pocketbook, placed it on the small table, and with watery eyes asked, "What does this mean, Attorney Lawrence?"

He smiled. "Please call me Christopher. And what should I call you?"

"Oh, everybody calls me Dorothy . . . You can call me Dorothy too."

"Well, Dorothy, as I told the judge just now, I just got this file. I looked over it briefly last night. Let's just review it together, okay?"

"Sure," Dorothy replied.

"Here, let me give this back to you, I'll just look at my file copy. The paper is called the petition. I'll read it and you can follow along with your copy."

Taking his reading glasses from the inside left jacket pocket, Christopher started his explanation with a friendly but formal tone.

"This petition begins by listing the names of the people before the court. It has the name of who brought the case, the Commissioner of the Child Protection Department, the CPD, then your name, Dorothy Simmons and the name of your husband, Henry Simmons. Both of you are listed as the parents of Katie. By the way, where is your husband?"

"Henry is still working. He works at the lumber company down on Stiles Street by the Quinnipiac River. He tried to get off but his boss wouldn't let him." She raised her voice with pride. "You know, Henry is an assistant foreman now. He's been on the job for some time. His boss still rides him hard, though. He said he would be here as soon as he finishes loading lumber for a big construction job."

Christopher began reading the petition. "The Child Protection Department seeks an OTC in order to—"

"What's an OTC?" Dorothy interrupted.

"OTC means 'Order of Temporary Custody.' It means that the Child Protection Department has asked the judge for a court order giving them permission to take your child into their physical custody for safekeeping."

Dorothy jumped up from her chair with a look of shock and despair.

"What do you mean 'safekeeping'? Katie has always been safe with me. I bathe her, feed her, and make sure that she gets plenty of rest."

"I understand, Dorothy, these things are upsetting, please sit down."
Dorothy paced back and forth.

"Please sit down, ma'am, it is my duty to read and explain this to you."

Reluctantly, Dorothy sat in the wooden chair. "Please follow along with your copy as I read this."

"Well, I am no good at lawyer language."

"Most people aren't, ma'am, just bear with me."

Christopher took a deep breath. He knew the reaction she would have to the petition, but he had to read on. The gravity must be faced. And her truth must be told.

Christopher was certain that he lost the case two years ago because he did not convince his client of the seriousness of those charges; otherwise his client would have told him the truth and he could have maneuvered in such a way to have defeated that prosecution. He would not make the same mistake in this case. Motioning to Dorothy to focus Christopher resumed reading.

"The Child Protection Department hot line received a call from the hospital saying that young Katie was overly fussy, with almost a terrified look on her face when being held, and that she is okay when laying in her bassinet. Investigation revealed that there were three hospitalizations for apnea episodes, but only one reported by the mother. Investigation also revealed that the family has a history with CPD. The CPD suspects that mother is subjecting the child to suffocation, maybe by Munchausen by Proxy. Wherefore, the Commissioner of CPD seeks a court order to place Katie in foster care under CPD supervision pending further court order."

Dorothy's hands trembled as Christopher finished. She looked up at him. "What does this mean? Munch—"

"Munchausen's."

"—by Proxy? What . . . Where is my baby?"

"Munchausen's means that someone is faking an illness to get attention."

"What does that mean? Where is my baby?"

"The Department has her in temporary foster care under the 96-hour hold."

"96 was on the paper they gave me in the hospital. What does it mean?"

"By law, the CPD, if it believes it has reasonable cause, can remove a child from a home and hold the child for what it believes as safekeeping for 96 hours. CPD must within those 96 hours get a judge's order to allow them to keep the child longer, until a court hearing is scheduled. Today is the initial date for that hearing."

Dorothy's voice quivered. "I don't know what all of this means, everything I did was to help my baby . . . to get her the best treatment."

Christopher looked into Dorothy's teary eyes. *Is she telling the truth?* She looked so befuddled, sitting with the petition in her hands, appearing as a child.

"But I didn't do it."

"You must come to my office so that we can prepare for trial. The burden of proof is on the CPD."

"What does burden of proof mean?"

"Here—take my card, and be in my office at 10:00 Monday morning with your husband, I'll explain it to you then."

"What happens now?"

"Now we get ready for trial."

Dorothy looked at the card in her shaking hands, but could not read it through her tears.

CHAPTER 18

The Pre-Trial Conference

A late afternoon sun shown brightly into the Courthouse conference room where people in suits were engaged in deep discussion.

Sitting around a rectangular table, Linda Grady, the Court Services Officer, asked attorney Susan Bishop whether her client, Henry Simmons, would contest, or stand silent in response to the petition to terminate his parental rights. She looked directly at Susan Bishop, paused and rested her elbows on the table.

"Well, I asked him yesterday what he wants to do, because if he's going to contest, I need to prepare him for the trial. He seemed hesitant."

"Why?" asked Jean Mecelli.

"He said he believes his wife."

Jean sighed.

"His wife told him the girls were ill, and that's why she took them to doctors and hospitals. He works all of the time. Why shouldn't he believe the mother of his children?"

Linda gave a direct response. "You know the court can't keep this case open much longer. Your client has had every opportunity to rehabilitate himself by showing greater interest in these girls. The Child Protection Department scheduled visits, which he did not attend, and counseling sessions, which he missed. His time is up."

"I know," sighed Susan. "He says that he loves his girls and knows how to take care of them, but right now he has to work."

Linda looked in the direction of Christopher Lawrence. "And where is your client?"

"Linda, she definitely will be here. This mother deeply loves these girls."

"Loving them and being a good parent are two different things," interjected Mia Benchley, the court-appointed legal guardian, charged by the court to speak to the children's best interest. Mia, middle aged, but with the kinetic energy of a teenager always held her ground.

"I visited your client the other day. It's a sad day when a mother with Munchausen's Syndrome doesn't realize the harm she places her child in. You can see what my legal guardian recommendation will be."

"Okay," Linda responded, asserting control. "The judge will ask me how long the trial will take, and how much resistance the parents will present. What should I tell him?"

Christopher, sitting at one end of the table, lifted his arms in prayer. "My client has good days and bad days. She says she is a good mother, but says sometimes she should put the children in temporary foster care so she can get a rest. Other times, she says she'll fight this to the end. Sometimes I think she has a thought disorder, but she will be here for the trial next week."

"Why is she prolonging this agony?" implored Mia.

Christopher raised his voice to a shout. "She's their mother! She has a constitutional right to a trial. She wants to plead for her children. Wouldn't you?"

His breathing slowed. He frowned in judgment, and added, "And, you know, you have some problems with one of your social workers who worked on this case. So unless the state is offering an open adoption, the foster parents should not get too comfortable with these girls."

"Counselors," Linda interjected. "The heat in this room is too much. Better save it for the trial. Let's finish going over the exhibits. You know Judge Hughes is a stickler about the exhibits."

CHAPTER 19

The Courthouse

I usually begin my day with toys—red, yellow, and blue blocks in a plastic container—and a tiny football with a Redskins logo. My nine-month-old grandson will visit later today. I filled the cylindrical green meshed birdfeeder hanging from an extension hook above the kitchen window, and stared out at the gray dawn.

Last night I reviewed the file in the case of Child Protection Department against Dorothy and Henry Simmons and that produced today's somber mood. The first day of trial had arrived.

On the drive to work via Interstate 95, I listened to the sound of my automobile, wary that something may be wrong with the transmission. I sensed something was off. Waiting for and dreading a slipping sensation, I slowed my Honda before taking the exit ramp marked "Chapel Street—Downtown." I followed Chapel Street past the Town Green and pulled into the parking space reserved for judges near the back door of the Courthouse.

"Good morning, Your Honor."

"Good morning," I replied to Sheriff Johnson who was in her usual guarding the door position. Normally an elevator man, today, I climbed the four flights by foot. As I settled at my desk, I heard a knock.

"Come in."

Sara Morley, the assistant clerk, entered with two files in her hand.

"Judge, I know you have a trial scheduled to start this morning, and this isn't your week to review OTC's, but Judge Green is covering another court today, and we wondered whether you can review this one."

"Sure, just hand it to me."

"Please ring me on extension 28 when you're done. I'll come and pick it up."

I opened the file, removed the paper entitled "Petition for OTC," and held it with both hands, concentrating on each word.

Petition for OTC

The Department of Child Protection has had an open file on this family since 2001. Two neighbors of the family called the department three days ago and reported that the girl was screaming. They heard her screaming before. A social worker from the Department went to the girl's school and spoke with her. Her name is Mary. She is eleven.

The Social worker noticed some bruising on both of Mary's arms. The social worker and the female principal took Mary to the school nurse. Mary told them that her brother, Ralph, hits her for no reason. When asked what her mother did about it, Mary says that her mother tells him not to do it and she tries to keep Ralph in his room.

Mary also said that it's hard for her mother to stop him because her mother is blind, and Ralph does not always stay in his room. Ralph sometimes enters her room, hits her, and puts his fingers in her privates.

This has been going on for some time. Ralph threatened to hit her if she tells. Ralph is fourteen. Mary says she is scared and doesn't know what to do. According to the school records, Mary's mother's blindness was caused by a tumor that grew on her spine and gradually destroyed her sight.

Because the situation poses a risk of moral and physical injury to Mary, the department took Mary from the school and is keeping her under a 96-hour emergency administrative hold, which will expire today. Wherefore, the department requests that a judge of the court issue an Order of Temporary Custody allowing the department to keep Mary until a court hearing is set for the mother to appear to address this critical situation.

This clearly cried out for a court order of protection. I signed the Petition for Order of Temporary Custody, and left a message for Sara to collect it. I slipped on my black robe, and looked out the window of my Chambers at the vast waters in the distance—that blue that separated New Haven and the Connecticut Shoreline from Long Island. I could be on a boat. I could sail across for a light lunch at a bistro on the other side.

When appointed to the bench as a former civil rights lawyer, some suspected I might be overly protective of the family constellation. But it was the returns that influenced me. Children returned to parents. Then returning to court. Then returning again. The cycle must be broken, and severing rights was sometimes the only means of preserving hope.

If parents were sincere in seeking help handling a troubled child, the judge makes sure that court-ordered resources, such as psychological evaluations and counseling for the child, as well as counseling parents on effective parenting techniques are provided. However, if the parents were not sincere and available to their child, I wasted no tears in deciding they had legally abandoned their child, and then terminating their parental rights. Only then would the child have an opportunity for a fresh start through adoption or foster care.

"Each case must be decided on its merits," I said aloud to no one.

I adjusted my robe, picked up the case file on my desk, and knocked on the adjourning Courtroom Door. As it opened, Sheriff Cindy Newman rose from her desk and banged her gavel.

Chapter 20

Opening Valley

Some judges got used to it. But not me. Every time the gavel pounded and the inordinately loud voice echoed through the Courtroom, I shuddered. All that I knew seemed too little, and all that I didn't seemed too much.

". . . Honorable Sam Hughes presiding."

I wanted so badly to be honorable.

The crowd was standing when I entered. As always. *Here they stand while I sit,* I was the one with authority. "You may be seated," I commanded. "Parties ready?"

Prosecutor Jean Mecelli looked across at defense attorney Christopher Lawrence, whose tie today boasted a long-necked giraffe. Both nodded in agreement.

"Very well, let's get started."

Jean Mecelli stood and circled the open space before the bench.

"Before I call my first witness, your Honor, I would like to describe the nature of the beast."

"Objection, your Honor!" exclaimed Christopher Lawrence, jumping to his feet. "She can't call my client a beast. It's outrageous, and highly unprofessional!"

I struggled hard not to roll my eyes, and overcompensated by bringing my gavel down hard, while staring at Mecelli. "Attorney Mecelli, your language was unfortunate, at best."

"Excuse me, Judge," she responded meekly. "I should have made myself clear. I'm not calling Mrs. Simmons a beast; I'm talking about what the State will prove. It was a figure of speech."

"Yes, and overly metaphorical for this court," I added. "Please continue. Mr. Lawrence, your seat awaits you."

Christopher Lawrence sat down slowly, and Mecelli gathered herself. She removed a thick book from the table in front of her, and held it out for me and Christopher Lawrence to see the large gold letting on a black background: *MSBP—MUNCHAUSEN SYNDROME BY PROXY.*

The book landed on the table with more than necessary force. "Judge, MSBP exposes thousands of young children each year to serious injury and death. And that's just an estimate. No, Judge, it is not Mrs. Simmons, Katie's mother, that the State is calling a beast. The beast is MSBP. The State will prove that it is this beast that caused injury." Mecelli gestured toward the book, and then to Dorothy Simmons, who lowered her head. "Because we intervened, we avoided death to young Katie. But because of this beast, Katie must be removed from her mother.

Lawrence barely paused before launching to his feet. He picked up the black book, and turned its gold lettering face down.

"Judge, not only is my client not a beast, there is no beast. Pure affection for her child controls her."

Mecelli reached for the book, but Lawrence kept his hand resting heavily on its cover.

"Counselors, keep things under control," I commanded. "Call your first witness."

Still on his feet, Lawrence turned back to his table and yellow legal pad. "Your Honor, Attorney Mecelli, on behalf of the State, has agreed that I may call Dr. Steven McMahon as the first witness. He has early important clinical procedures that he must perform at the hospital this morning. I would like to call him as a witness first, so that he can get back to the hospital, with the Court's permission, of course."

I addressed the courtroom. "As we know, because the State has the burden of proving the charges against the parents, they normally put forth witnesses first, but because it's important to the doctor's patients to accommodate him, I'm granting that you may call him out of turn."

"Dr. McMahon?" Lawrence called out. In response a middle-aged man dressed in a blue blazer, dull yellow tie and gray trousers walked from the back of the courtroom toward the judge. I beckoned him into the witness box.

At the Clerk's request, he raised his hand and swore to tell the truth.

"Please be seated, Doctor," I implored. "The respondent's attorney, Christopher Lawrence, has a few questions for you."

Moving from the lawyer's table to within two feet of the witness box, Christopher Lawrence began. "Doctor, are you Board Certified, and, if so, what does that mean?"

"Yes, I am certified in pediatrics and forensic psychiatry. Pediatrics, of course, is the treatment of children, and forensic psychiatry is the application of psychiatry to the law or to legal situations such as this. Board certification means that I passed the required number of national tests in my field."

"Thank you, Doctor. Tell us, what is Munchausen?"

"Munchausen is a cluster of psychological findings. It's a syndrome in which adults feign illness or even create or lie about their medical problems in order to get attention for themselves."

"What's a 'syndrome'?"

"A syndrome is a group of symptoms that characterizes a condition."

"And where does Munchausen come from?"

"The term originates from the antics of a German raconteur by the name of Karl Frederick von Munchausen. He lived in the 1700s and fought with the Russians against the Turks. After returning from the war, Munchausen told exaggerated stories and winning lies, such as defeating scores of Turks with nothing but spoons, riding cannon balls to the moon, and pulling himself out of a bog by his own hair. People thought he was hilarious, telling such tales from tavern to tavern throughout Bavaria."

Christopher interrupted, "Doctor, are you serious?"

"Absolutely. Karl's adventures are widely published in Russia, and the high arched theme of his 'truths' has migrated into medicine, based upon the principle that even in medicine, lies can be the basis for commanding attention, and thus, entertainment for the liar."

"So, Doctor, please tell us the precise definition of Munchausen by Proxy?"

"It's official name, Munchausen Syndrome by Proxy, was given by the Royal College of Pediatricians and Child Health in Leads, England. It means a caregiver, usually the mother, feigns or induces an illness in another person, usually her child, to gain attention and sympathy as the worried parent. She's not lying about her medical condition. She's lying about her child's condition, and therefore lying by means of proxy—her child."

"Doctor, is it a psychological disorder?"

"Yes, it is. It's listed in the Diagnostic and Statistical Manual of Mental Disorders, called DSM under Factitious Disorders."

"Doctor, if the mother in this case has this condition, is her child at serious risk?"

"Yes."

Christopher positioned the yellow legal pad on the podium near the witness box. He walked toward the witness, placed his hands in his pockets, turned, looked directly at the judge, and slowly asked the ultimate question.

"Now, Doctor, in your professional opinion, does Mrs. Dorothy Simmons suffer from this condition known as Munchausen Syndrome by Proxy?"

The doctor leaned into the microphone. "Absolutely not."

Christopher looked over his shoulder at Mecelli.

"Why do you say that, Doctor?"

"Because I administered a battery of psychological tests to the mother and she passed them. Of course, she has anxiety about what's going on, but she is no danger to the child."

"Thank you, Doctor. Attorney Mecelli may have some questions for you."

Mecelli calmly stood. "I don't have any questions of him on cross-examination, Judge; however, I may call him as a hostile witness in my part of the case."

"You're dismissed for now, Doctor," I told the witness.

"Dr. Marsha Kendrick to the stand," Mecelli said loudly.

A mature woman, impeccably dressed in conservative fashion, walked to the witness box.

Jean Mecelli commenced questioning her from her seat at the counsel table.

"I am a pediatric pulmonologist," Dr. Kendrick said in reply to Mecelli's initial question. "And what is a pulmonologist?"

Straightening herself upright, Doctor Kendrick began her explanation. "A pulmonologist is a medical doctor who specializes in the treatment of lungs and breathing disorders."

Mecelli, seated for these opening questions, now rose from her chair and walked toward Dr. Kendrick.

"May I approach the witness, your Honor?"

"You may."

Standing close to Dr. Kendrick, Mecelli inquired in a subdued voice, "Doctor, what is apnea, and how does it work . . . or not work? Please explain that to the court."

Dr. Kendrick straightened again. "Apnea essentially means 'not breathing.' During breathing human beings take oxygen into their lungs and their lungs exchange or expel carbon dioxide. There is a tightly regulated relationship between carbon dioxide, oxygen and the pH level of the blood. It is important that there be a flow of gas between the lungs and the environment."

"So not breathing can produce severe injury to the human body?"

"Objection, your Honor," Christopher interjected. "I think we all know what a human body needs to breathe."

"Overruled. Patience, Counselor!"

"What is the level of breathing sensation that exposes a person to injury?" Mecelli asked.

"The studies that we have done at the Pulmonary Institute show that humans who are not trained cannot maintain voluntary apnea for more than one or two minutes. At that point the brain triggers an involuntary breathing response. However, some well-trained divers, for example, can hold their breath underwater for several minutes. An apneist is defined as someone who can hold his or her breath for quite a while."

With a puzzled look on her face, Mecelli asked, "Doctor, why only one or two minutes for the average person?"

"Because of the way we are built, the human body does not store oxygen for later use. Our bodies, especially our brains, need oxygenated blood, meaning oxygen in our blood from breathing."

"And, again, Doctor, what happens when our bodies don't get oxygenated blood?"

"As I said before, harm results. After a few minutes permanent brain injury may occur, and several minutes after that . . . death."

Lawrence was on his feet again. "Your Honor, this is a very fascinating science lesson, but—"

"Get to where you're going, Counselor Mecelli." I directed.

"Yes, Your Honor. Thank you, Doctor, now I would like to ask you some questions of particular concern in this case. By the way, Doctor, you said that you are a *pediatric* pulmonologist. What does pediatrics mean?"

"Pediatrics means treating persons from birth to 18 years of age."

"Thank you. So what is considered a normal pregnancy, in terms of length?"

"We at the hospital find that 40 weeks is a normal length, and 38 weeks is considered a full term. A baby born before the end of 38 weeks is considered premature."

"Doctor, do you know when the baby in this case was born?"

"Yes, 32 weeks."

"So baby Katie was premature?"

"Yes."

"Doctor, is prematurity a cause of apnea?"

"Yes, because of the underdeveloped lungs of a premature baby."

"And is it your opinion, Doctor, that repeated episodes of apnea in such an infant is dangerous to her health and survival?"

"Definitely so, or I wouldn't be here testifying."

"Thank you, Doctor. Attorney Lawrence may have some questions for you."

Lawrence studied his notes on the table. "I have no questions for the doctor."

"Does the State have any other witnesses?" I asked.

"Yes, your Honor, the State calls Dr. Mary Johnson as its next witness."

A bespectacled woman with a professional air rose from the audience and made her way to the witness stand. In response to the Clerk's request, she raised her hand and swore to tell the truth.

"Dr. Johnson, I have a few questions that will allow you to tell the judge and jury about your qualifications." Mary Johnson turned from observing the faces in the back of the courtroom and focused her attention on the woman lawyer in the double-breasted jacket standing before her. "Doctor Johnson, could you tell us your specific occupation?"

"Yes, I hold a medical doctorate in pediatrics. I am a professor in pediatrics at the University of Manchester, and I am the Clinical Director of the Children's Hospital of Manchester."

"Doctor, are you Board Certified, and are you familiar with Munchausen Syndrome by Proxy?"

"The answer is yes, to both questions. I am board certified, and I have diagnosed hundreds of cases of Munchausen Syndrome by Proxy."

"Doctor, do you do any lecturing?"

"I am a visiting scholar at the University of Stockholm in Sweden, and at the Institute of Medicine in Florence, Italy, where I oversee committee forensic reviews of MSBP cases reported from cases presented internationally."

"Doctor, what is MSBP?"

"Munchausen Syndrome by Proxy is a term which describes a caretaker, generally the mother, creating or feigning an illness in a child so that she gains attention."

"How does that work, Doctor?"

"Well, she gets the attention of doctors in the hospital and her neighbors and friends express their approval of all she is doing to 'help or save' her child. There is also a theory that the mother gets satisfaction from pulling one over on authority figures."

Jean Mecelli raised her voice as she strode from the counsel table toward Dr. Johnson. "Ma'am, I mean, Dr. Johnson, what are the criteria for determining MSBP?"

"There are essentially five criteria: an inordinate amount of time spent at doctor's offices or hospitals; emphasis on what a superb mother she is; giving doctors direction on medical care; a vigorous denial, shifting blame to others; and a negative medical history, meaning no objective findings of anything medically wrong."

"One other preliminary question, Doctor. What are the causes of this syndrome?"

"We don't know for sure. But it's speculated that as a child the mother got attention by feigning illness, and/or that now she is feeling inadequate as a parent or is suffering from some feelings of anxiety."

"Doctor, does this constitute child abuse?"

"Yes. Because it exposes the child to harm from false illness."

"How so, Doctor?"

"Let's take apnea for example. First, there is tampering with the normal breathing of the child to produce the symptom of apnea, and then there is exposure of the child to invasive medical procedures to confirm and/or rule out whether the child is suffering from apnea."

"Doctor, has there been child abuse in this case?"

"Objection, your Honor!" shouted Christopher Lawrence, quickly rising from his chair. "The state Legislature recently passed a law restricting an expert's opinion to information she hears or sees while a case is being presented in the Courtroom."

"Objection sustained. The answer to the question is premature. But you may continue your foundation questions, Attorney Mecelli."

"Doctor have you seen the affidavit accompanying the OTC, the Order of Temporary Custody, the hospital and doctor reports, and the family history?"

"Yes, I have."

Christopher Lawrence stood up.

"Objection, your Honor, to the affidavits, family history, and medical reports. They are all hearsay—they all report what someone else, not present here today in this courtroom, said. I can't put these reports on the witness stand and question them about the truth or accuracy of the information in them, as I would have a right to do if an actual person were here testifying on the witness stand about the same information."

I rubbed the back of my neck, and noticing Mecelli's frustration, asked how she would respond.

"Well, your Honor, the reports do fit the definition of hearsay, meaning a report telling what the writer or someone else said—therefore, 'hear-then- say.' But the state legislature passed a law making these reports admissible for use in a court proceeding or trial, such as this."

"Not true, Your Honor," Lawrence countered. "I have a copy of the statute law right here. It says that the reports are admissible during, and I quote directly, your Honor, '*in the dispositional phase of the trial.*' It's a direct quote from Section 46b-18, your Honor. We're in the early adjudicative phase."

I asked my Clerk for the law book, and speedily read the section.

"You are correct, attorney Lawrence. The statute you quoted from does say that social worker reports can be presented during the dispositional phase of the trial."

Returning the book to this Clerk, I continued, "And it is the adjudicative stage, the part inquiring into whether the parents have abused their children, that the hearing today is focused on. That is, the role of the court in this part of the hearing is to adjudicate whether the children have been abused."

"Precisely, Your Honor," Christopher Lawrence added. "As we all know, only if the court, meaning your Honor, decides that they have been abused, would the court then move to the dispositional stage, the phase of the case when you will hear evidence about what your Honor will do with the children—whether to return them to their parents under court-ordered supervision, place them in foster care, or terminate the parents' rights to the children so as to free them up for adoption."

"Yes, I am aware of my job, thank you."

"Forgive me, your Honor, I was only—"

"Well, attorney Mecelli," I said, ignoring the unnecessary apology, "it looks like the State needs to call live witnesses to the stand for this phase."

"I anticipated the ruling, Judge. May I now ask Doctor Johnson to step down so that I can call a social worker to testify to the underlying facts?"

"Yes, you may," I answered.

As Dr. Johnson left the witness stand, Mecelli called Lorraine Holder, a social worker at Child Protection as her next witness.

Under oath, Lorraine Holder testified to her long involvement with Dorothy and her family, including their other child, Maria, taken earlier by the State for her protection. She continued by giving a detailed history of Katie's medical treatment, as well as the concerns of the Child Protection Department. During her testimony copies of hospital records and tests were introduced. At the end of her testimony the court took a fifteen-minute recess.

Upon the resumption of the court hearing, Mecelli recalled Dr. Mary Johnson to the witness box.

"Now, having heard the testimony of Lorraine Holder and having seen the exhibits introduced into evidence during her testimony, what is your opinion regarding whether MSBP was the agent of injury to the minor child in this case." Dr. Johnson turned toward Judge Hughes.

"I believe to a reasonable degree of medical certainty that MSBP caused injury to this child."

"And Doctor, do you know who caused the child to suffer injury?"

"Yes."

"And who would that be?"

"Her mother, Dorothy."

"Why do you say that?"

"Because of the history of the case. I have examined in detail all of the hospital records for this child."

"Doctor, do you have notes that you would like to use, to refresh your memory during this testimony?"

"Yes, thank you."

"Any objection, Attorney Lawrence?" I asked.

"No, Your Honor. I reviewed the notes during the recess."

I nodded. "You may proceed then, Attorney Mecelli."

"Doctor, using your notes, tell us why you believe Dorothy Simmons injured her child."

Dr. Johnson removed a pair of white pearl rimmed eyeglasses from her purse, placed them on the bridge of her nose, glanced at a small 10" x 5" pad, cleared her throat, and started her report.

"On December 23, the mother brought this child to the emergency unit of the Hillsborough Hospital, complaining that she was turning blue and wasn't eating properly. Hillsborough admitted her and administered several tests, some invasive. Several days later, having no objective findings for the mother's complaints, the hospital discharged her to her mother's care."

"And Doctor, was she admitted to another hospital shortly thereafter?"

"Yes, to the prestigious Steinwake Children's Hospital Center, which is two towns away from the mother's home."

"And Doctor, please tell the Judge what happened to the child at the hospital upon her admission."

"May I answer by reading the hospital record?"

"Yes, you may."

"It's exhibit 5," Mecelli answered, handing it to Hughes.

"Very well, I will read it out loud."

February 15. The child presented with low oxygen blood levels, blue lips. She was at risk for brain damage and near death. The medical history shows that the child was born on May 30, eight weeks premature at 32 weeks, suffering from apnea due to prematurity, and a central nervous system phenomenon. The discharge summary from Hillsborough Hospital concluded 'current cause of apnea and Brachardia seems to be most likely reflux.'

Dr. Palmer, a renowned pulmonologist administered the spirogram examination, testing for undiagnosed chronic obstructive pulmonary disease, the results of which were negative. Dr.

McKinley, the cardiologist, conducted an electrophsysiologic study, using a catheter inserted in her heart, which was also negative, and Dr. Harris did an endoscopy, or upper gastrointestinal scope, again with negative results. The baby was released, in perfect health, into the mother's care.

"Doctor, could you explain how the endoscopy is done?"

"Yes. The endoscopy is quite invasive, requiring the use of a scope inserted into the esophagus and then into the stomach."

Returning exhibit 5 to Hughes and without invitation from another question, Doctor Johnson spoke firmly, and in a raised voice.

"I don't call these 'suffocation episodes'; I call them 'attempted murder' or 'medical child abuse!' The unnecessary medical tests, consisting of magnetic resonance imaging, probing the body, and requiring sedation, constitutes certain abuse in my eyes."

Across the distance from the witness stand to the table, Dorothy stared at Dr. Johnson for a prolonged moment, before dropping her head and saying to no one in particular, "This is torture." Her voice retreated into her mind. *When I was a sickly little girl my mother and the doctors were always looking after me. That's all I've been doing with my girls. All a good mother would do . . .*

Two weeks later, the trial ended, and I remained convinced from the trial evidence that the children would be in grave danger if returned to their natural parents at this time. Clearly the mother was exposing the children to danger through Munchausen, and the father, so busy with his work, was not an effective safeguard. I reviewed the status reports, which describe the natural parents' situations and troubles. I issued another Court Order requiring the natural parents to undergo therapeutic counseling, as a step toward qualifying them to seek the return of their children. I also ordered that the Court Services Officer should bring the case in for periodic status reviews to see how the children and the natural parents are progressing. I had little hope that the biological parents would follow through.

CHAPTER 21

The Mannings

The Child Protection Department frequently sends requests to the public through television, radio, print commercials and ads for potential foster parents. It is not a role for everyone. Some are more suited to foster parenting than others and Beatrice Manning was one of those. John Manning, on the other hand, required the subtle technique of gentle persuasion. Let's see how that played out.

They always said that Beatrice Manning was born with too kind a heart, and kind hearts make complicated lives. She never mastered the concept of "mine." As a little child, when other children asked for her toys, she would give them away, even while her parents protested.

She grew up, but important things remained the same. So it was no surprise that she couldn't resist the pleas from the Child Protection Department. In her late thirties and still fit, Beatrice believed that now it was her time to give back to the community by helping out those her preacher called "less fortunate."

John, Beatrice's husband, was closing in on retirement. He married young Beatrice late in his life, and had paid off the mortgage on their contemporary colonial home. He put in 30 years teaching and administering at the local community college, working his way up to Academic Dean. However, the job was getting, as he would say, long of tooth. Mediating inter-faculty turf skirmishes and fending off takeovers of his department by younger assistant professors was not pleasant. Playing golf full time—hitting the tee shot in the middle of the fairway, blasting the little white ball from the sand trap onto the green—bicycling in the middle of the day, lounging at the beach, being out with nature and watching sunsets without a worry about work—yes, those are the rewards of retirement, John mused.

He remembered the foster-child conversation started at the end of one of his long work days. His trusty silver 1989 Volvo transported his tired bones into the attached garage. Through the door he smelled his favorite meal. A pleasant mid-week surprise he thought, as he entered the kitchen. Kissing the cheek of his "favorite chef," John's eyes smiled at the sumptuous offerings on the dinner table.

Things changed mid-meal.

"John."

He knew that tone.

"We've got to help out," she said. "We must adopt some of these children."

Startled, John looked up from his plate.

"What children? What are you talking about?"

"Look at all that we have, for God's sake! What's it all for? We have hundreds of thousands of dollars and no children to inherit it. We must give back—"

"But we *do* give back. We give thousands of dollars in scholarships to inner-city kids every year, and to other charities. And you and I do a lot of volunteering."

"But there are hundreds of children waiting for pre-adoptive foster homes," Beatrice countered.

"But we're not parents, Beatrice."

Beatrice pushed back from the table. Emerging from the kitchen a moment later, she placed a cake pan in the center of the table. John's favorite—German chocolate cake, layered with a deep, dark chocolate and finely crushed nuts, lightly glazed with mouth-watering caramel icing.

"What did I do to deserve this treat? It's not my birthday."

"Here, let me cut this for you. It's just for being you."

Beatrice slid the cake to him on a papery thin turquoise plate. John ran the pad of his right index finger around its beveled edge. "Where did we get this?" he asked.

"You remember, it was in the shop near the Charles Street Bridge in Prague."

"Oh yes. We had the cups, saucers and plates shipped back to us. I just haven't seen them in a long time."

"Would you like some ice cream?"

"You bet," he answered.

"Are you sure this doesn't have anything to do with asking me to take in some foster children?"

"Well, you look a little tired for this conversation tonight. Besides, I've got some papers to grade after dinner, and we can talk about it another time."

Beatrice would bide her time. She had brought up the subject and she knew John would think about it.

Early the next morning, awake before the 5:30 alarm, John slipped out of bed without disturbing Beatrice and headed for the bathroom. Exiting the shower, he glimpsed his naked image in the mirror on the bathroom door. Not bad for 55 years on this earth—a little gray and some thinning hair; but somewhat youthful; not a terrible declination, thanks to regular gym workouts.

Turning away from the man in the mirror, he walked to the dressing room, put on the attire set out the night before, and opened the door to the hallway. Beatrice called to him from the bedroom.

"I want to finish our talk about the children. I had a dream."

"Can't it wait until the weekend? I have a meeting with senior faculty. I'll call you right after."

John walked downstairs, made coffee, pressed the garage door opener, backed out the Volvo, and headed off for another day in the world of academia.

Beatrice lingered in bed. She realized that as an only child, John was accustomed to having his privacy. But she also knew her own heart and its vulnerability to children.

If she told him that the state paid foster parents to take care of the kids, he'd only reply, "We don't need the money." That was certainly true. But there was that other, lingering thing. Caring for their Golden Labrador and the Siamese cat hardly satisfied her mothering instinct.

She regretted that they'd been unable to conceive—he was simply resistant to having someone else's children. She understood. But she knew that he had never once said a flat out "no" to her. Not for anything.

Beatrice's thoughts lapsed into memories of when she became a stepchild. Her mother died after giving birth to her younger brother.

Her father remarried quickly. The neighborhood stirred. And people whispered. Just interested in the house, people rumored, about her new mother. They had the biggest house in the neighborhood. She could do nothing to please stepmother Catherine, who had little time for her. No hugs and no kisses, just jealousy about the affection that her father showed her. How he loved her! Easy to hug, and quick to embrace. Beatrice remembers sitting on the front steps on summer afternoons, waiting for him to come home from work. As soon as she saw the black Buick turn the corner she ran to open the wooden gate to the driveway. Her father brought the car to a stop near the porch, and stepped out, always with a grin. His arms were strong.

"How's my princess today?" he always asked. Then he would place his hands behind his back, bring them back in a closed fist, and say, "pick the right one and the prize is yours." Most of the time she won the prize—be it a nickel, a dime or a piece of candy. Only later, she'd learn there was something in each fist. With her father, she could never lose.

Until she lost him.

Often sickly after the father's death, hospital medical reports suggested Beatrice was suffering from more than grief. Minute traces of poison were found in her blood. Aunt May and Uncle Joe arrived on the same driveway as their father had so often. This time the gate was open, and her packed bags waited on the front porch.

Aunt May and Uncle Joe told her that it was time to leave Catherine's home and to live with them. Aunt May didn't mention the poison. Beatrice slept in a bedroom formerly occupied by Aunt May's sewing machine. She called the room her own until Jenny, her first cousin, and Aunt May's favorite daughter gave birth.

A month before the arrival, Aunt May and Uncle Joe moved Beatrice into a small rented house, co-signed the lease, and took her shopping for used furniture. Aunt May showed her how to set up a house and arranged for her to get work.

Beatrice's mother had left her early. Her father later joined her mother in heaven. Step-mother, Catherine, had rejected her. Even years later, after marrying John, and becoming a successful teacher, the rejections plagued her. She wondered why.

Beatrice sought help from Pastor Morgan, whom she saw periodically for years. He repeatedly told her to let go of her childhood hurts and not to nurse them. Then one day he said in a stern tone. "Let go of the pity party, and live in the now!"

Those words and his unexpected harsh demeanor shook her away from him and from her Church. These were searing hurts, and she thought that he had simply gotten tired of her complaining. She knew it was taking a long time, but even today she resented his trying to catapult her into the "now." There was nothing in the now to make up for the then.

Until this now.

If John agreed to take in foster children, she could nurture her hurt through nurturing them. She wouldn't reject them the way Catherine had abandoned her.

Chapter 22

CPD Investigation

Sally Chandler thought back to the CPD meetings headed by the Commissioner as she reviewed two proposed foster care placements for Maria and Katie.

"Is the background investigation completed?" Sally asked, sitting behind her desk.

"Not yet," answered Joe Jackson, the foster care placement supervisor. "But it's almost done. I've checked the court records and ours—all clear. No prior history or involvement with this department. I've spoken with the neighbors and no problem there. The Mannings are well liked, friendly, and mind their own business. His employment checks out, but I'm still waiting for the national criminal records report. That's the last piece."

Sally possessed an almost religious eagerness to help the unfortunate; a need to give them a listening ear, to point the direction out of difficult situations, to offer advice and education when needed. She supervised the Child Protection Department parenting class program that taught parents how to better raise their children. She oversaw the substance abuse program, monitoring parents' attendance and encouraging them to break free of additions so that they can be effective parents to their children. She monitored the employment and housing referral programs run by Child Protection for parents. And she supervised the therapeutic and counseling programs offered by Child Protection for parents in need of those services. She did not sleep often, or much.

But it's not just Sally's inscrutable devotion to helping the less fortunate, extending to volunteering long hours at the local food bank, which impressed Joe. He also found her looks irresistible—a striking forty with a bright face, shoulder length black hair, and boundless energy. And there was something besides her sharp mind, feminine disposition, good looks, and determined resolution—Joe thought back to his youth in the South and found it: Sally Chandler was a lady.

After working in social work for seven years, Joe clung to the rare moments of beauty and grace he could find. Sally was one. Now, he hoped the National Crime Information would send back a clear report, so he could count John and Beatrice Manning as another one of those moments.

CHAPTER 23

Foster Parents

I am always amazed with the speed with which the CPD can move when there is an emergency.

You see, John finally agreed with Beatrice's pleas, but with a multitude of *Ifs*; only *If* there were children in a desperate situation, only *If* it were only temporary, only *If* the word adoption were not uttered. Lots of luck with that. At any rate, Beatrice left a message with his secretary that he must be home no later than 4 p.m.

At exactly 3:45 PM, a blue van drove into their driveway with "CPD" in white lettering on the driver's door. Beatrice escorted its occupants into the house.

At exactly 4:00 PM, John arrived, and parked his car in front of the house. Beatrice embraced him before he reached the front step.

"They're here!" she shouted.

"Who's here?"

"We passed the background test."

"What background test?"

"If all goes well with the home inspection and interview, the Department would be ready to bring two children who need emergency shelter today."

"What test?"

"You—you told me if some children were in a crisis, we could help out temporarily, so I called the Child Protection Department and told them to put us on the list. They did a background test. The folks from Child Protection are in the den."

"Why didn't you tell me they were bringing children today?"

"Because I didn't know. An *emergency* situation popped up. It's not planned in advance, John. Now be nice to them."

Walking to his favorite part of the house, John suspected that the moment was one of rubber meeting road. If he accepted the children, his favorite recreational space would be filled with games, his routine of leisure reading and watching sports on TV would be interrupted by children's sounds and games. He had hardly enough time to begin feeling sorry for himself when he spotted the two strangers in casual attire. The taller of the young couple, wearing a pale yellow cardigan, extended his hand.

"You must be Mr. Manning. I'm Alfred McGuire from CPD—Child Protection—and this is Shirley Davis, also from CPD."

He shook Albert's hand and nodded at his companion. A little shorter than Alfred, Shirley looked even younger. She spoke and John was taken aback by the confidence and authority of her voice.

"Mr. and Mrs. Manning, thank you for seeing us today. With these children—it was an emergency."

"What do you mean?" John asked.

"We got a call from the hospital saying that a baby girl was in grave danger from her mother, and she had to be taken by us for safekeeping. The baby has a sister who was taken as well."

"There were no other relatives?" John asked. Beatrice stared at him.

"None that the department can trust," Alfred answered. "So we took the children under a 96-hour emergency hold."

"Please have a seat, both of you. May I get you something—"

"No, thank you ma'am," Alfred answered.

"I'll take a tea," John said. Beatrice did not move to get it, but sat down next to Shirley on the couch.

Lowering himself into John's favorite recliner, Alfred noticed John's tense face. "Oh, I'm sorry, is this—?"

"No, no. Don't be ridiculous." He paused, sitting opposite Alfred on the couch, next to Beatrice and Shirley, and then leaned forward, looking intently at Alfred.

"What's a 96-hour hold?"

"Something like a police power. It allows the Department in an emergency situation to take kids into temporary foster care for their safe-keeping for a period of 96 hours."

"If we accept them, do we have to return them to you after 96 hours?" Beatrice asked.

"Oh no," Shirley responded. "It means that within those 96 hours the Child Protection Department must go to a judge and seek an order of temporary custody—."

"An OTC," offered Alfred. "So that the department can keep the children in its temporary legal custody until the parents have a court hearing at which a judge will decide whether the children should or should not be returned to them. We don't have a place at the department to keep the children. We just have office buildings. We place the children in foster homes. That's where you come in."

"That's where we come in, John," Beatrice said, looking at John, as though he did not understand. And he probably did not since things were moving so fast.

"Also, Mr. and Mrs. Manning," said Alfred, "there's a court hearing going on. The Department is asking the judge to issue an Order allowing us to keep the children with a foster family until the outcome of a trial on whether the parents' rights will be terminated."

"So I guess if we like them, we'd better not get too attached," Beatrice responded in a guarded tone.

"I'm sure you'll like them," Alfred replied. "And they're baby sisters. They're quite special."

"Where are they?" John broke his silence.

"In the day care room of our main office downtown. We personally needed to see your home and interview you before bringing them along," Shirley added. "So . . . are you sure you're willing to take the children on a temporary basis?"

John turned his head toward Beatrice whose face was holding back a smile. The corners of her mouth were twitching, as they did whenever she was nervous.

"Yes," he said, and the smile released. "We'll give it a try."

Alfred stood quickly. "Great, we will bring the girls later tonight. Seven o'clock, if that is all right, Mr. and Mrs. Manning?"

"Sure, we certainly have enough room for them, but what about . . . you know . . . Pampers . . . little girl's clothes?"

"Oh, don't worry about that," Shirley interjected, as they moved toward the door. "We have plenty of baby clothes, toiletries, and toys. When we bring the girls, we will bring everything they will need."

"Baby food?" John was eager now, and it surprised him.

Shirley smiled. "Including baby food."

A short two hours later the doorbell rang, and Shirley, Alfred and two CPD aides entered the Manning's foyer carrying baby clothes, bassinets, high chairs, foodstuffs, multicolored toys and two car seats. John rushed over to relieve them. In the doorway Shirley held a tiny human wrapped in a pink and white cotton blanket. Alfred's right arm supported a toddler's bottom while his left hand cradled her tiny head against his chest. They asked where to put the items.

"Guest room on the second floor, second door to the right," Beatrice responded, pointing to the staircase.

"The bassinets?" the aide asked.

"You can just leave them here."

With arms filled with boxes of baby clothes, the aides began the first of many climbs to the guest room.

Beatrice beckoned Shirley and Alfred through the French doors and into the parlor. Alfred sat in a wing chair by the piano. He lowered the toddler to the floor, and turned her so that she could see the new faces. Shirley, rocking the baby back and forth in her arms, sat in the other wing chair near Alfred.

"Here they are," Shirley said, holding Maria.

Beatrice found no words, but two. "Small and Vulnerable."

She extended her hands and arms to the toddler and walked toward Katie. She leaned down and placed her hands on the child's shoulders. Katie turned away, and looked to Alfred. "What beautiful eyes she has," Beatrice thought.

John appeared in the doorway, having finished transporting the supplies. Shirley met him and filled his tired arms with Maria.

"Hold her head up with your other hand," Shirley instructed. John, smiling, began slowly pacing the floor, rocking Maria back and forth.

Beatrice led the procession to the second-floor, with John holding Maria, Beatrice cradling Katie, Shirley holding a Pac and Play bed, and Alfred carrying a bassinet. John turned to look at the group. It was a sight, alright, a sight indeed.

CHAPTER 24

Court Status Review

"What's next?" I asked, noticing a hint of weariness in my own voice.

"The case of Dorothy and Henry Simmons, scheduled today for a status review. Our last case for the afternoon session," Lauren, his clerk, answered. "It's just a status review," she added.

"Are the parties here?" I inquired, looking out into the courtroom from my bench.

"They're just coming in now, Judge," Jean Mecelli, the Assistant Attorney General replied.

Attorney Christopher Lawrence escorted Dorothy Simmons, her face troubled, into the courtroom.

"What's the status?" I asked, taking the file from Lauren.

Assistant Attorney General Jean Mecelli stood up. "Your Honor, as I explained to Attorney Lawrence before we came in, the policy of the Child Protection Department is family re-unification, if that can be achieved. And at the end of the trial the court imposed several steps which the Simmons' must take to be able to get their children back."

"Yes, I recall, and they're here in the court file," I added.

"Judge," Mecelli resumed, "the Simmons were required to admit to exposing the children to danger, and then undergo extensive counseling. Those were the first major steps required of them."

"How's your client doing, Attorney Lawrence? And where is Mr. Simmons? Have you explained the steps to him as well?" I asked, in a matter-of-fact tone.

"I didn't do nothing to harm my girls! You had no right to take them!" Dorothy Simmons shouted while rising from her seat and pointing a defiant fist toward me. "Sit down, Mrs. Simmons," I commanded, pounding my gavel.

Sheriff Cindy Newman pressed a silent emergency button on her small desk, pulled out her black baton from its holster and moved aggressively to position herself between Dorothy Simmons and the bench.

Attorney Lawrence grabbed Dorothy's arm. "Please sit down!" Lawrence urged her. "This will only make things worse."

"But my baby—"

"May we have a recess, Judge?" he asked.

"Recess granted! Get your client under control!" I responded in a threatening tone. "I could hold her in contempt and send her to lock-up, with that attitude."

"Yes, Judge, I know," Christopher Lawrence replied. "Thank you for your patience.

I considered the status reports, which describe the natural parents' situations and troubles, and signed a Court Order keeping the girls with a family named Manning. The Mannings are providing a good home for the girls, according to the preliminary reports from both the legal guardian and CPD. I issued another Court Order requiring the natural parents to undergo therapeutic counseling, as a step toward qualifying them to seek the return of their children.

It was clear to me that the parents of Maria and Katie could not admit to harming them and that going to intensive counseling was out of the question.

Subsequent periodic case status reports produced no better results, only pleas from Attorney Christopher Lawrence not to terminate the Simmons' parental rights. Court Services Officer Linda Grady reported at subsequent in-court status reviews that the National Crime Information Center produced no negative reports with the Manning's treatment of the girls and that the Child Protection Department is pleased with the Court Order placing the girls in their care as long-term foster parents. The Manning's saw no particular legal advantage to terminating the Simmons' parental rights, since as long-term foster parents they were granted the ability to make the important decisions in the lives of the two girls, now completely bonded to them. I approved long-term foster care placement in lieu of terminating the Simmons' parental rights.

Months moved along. Seasons slipped by.

The girls' middle and high school years were exceptional at Amistad Academy, a public charter school which emphasized REACH values, respect, enthusiasm, achievement, citizenship, and hard work—all very productive years under the vigilant eyes of Beatrice and John whom the girls called Mom and Dad.

CHAPTER 25

The University

The University in the Elm City is an American private Ivy League research institution. Founded in 1701, it is the third oldest institution of higher learning in the United States. Katie felt herself fortunate to be one of its students.

Katie scanned her identification card and walked through the massive wrought-iron gates of Temple Hall—a student complex laid out in a rectangle row of attached four story red brick buildings—spackled with ivy—enclosing a vast area of green grass. The kids called it the quad. When classes finished for the week, after answering difficult questions and taking the notebooks full of scribbled lecture points, Katie always felt a sense of homecoming as she passed through those gates. For three years, it had been home. A Frisbee flew over her head and she vaguely heard a student yell an apology. She waved and smiled, and looked in the direction of "I'm sorry."

Katie had just stacked her books on the olive-colored pine desk in her room when a tall girl with reddish-brown hair entered briskly, wearing nothing but a white cotton bathrobe, and wet hair.

"God, what I wouldn't give for a shower in our room instead of down the hall."

"Going out tonight?" Katie asked.

"How'd you know?"

"The new outfit on your bed."

"Oh, it's nothing," Lisa shrugged.

"Silk skirt and black striped jacket! Your parents love their baby girl. Who's the lucky guy?" Katie concluded with a grin.

"A fellow I met in our Spanish class. His father owns an insurance company in Phoenix."

Lisa tied her hair in a bun, and spun open a container of foundation. Katie passed her a makeup bag and Lisa emptied its contents on the desk—eyeliner, lipstick, and blush. "What are your plans?" Lisa asked.

"I just need to recopy some notes from the last lecture about Keats. Professor Ashford is quite picky at test time. He wants to see his words repeated in our answers."

"Oh, what a bore."

"I know, but you do what you got to do. I need an A in this one."

"Sounds like me in Victorian Literature. The questions on those exams—I have to read them three times."

Finishing her makeup, Lisa lifted a new skirt from the bed, placed it on the hanger hooked on her closet door, and held up two blouses taken from her side drawer.

"Which one, Katie?"

"The pale green one goes better with the beige skirt."

Lisa smiled at her image in the mirror on the back of the closet door. The green worked.

"Katie, I don't know what I would do without you."

"Look silly. And never go to fancy places that require good taste," Katie joked, then said, "Tell me about the mystery man from Spanish class."

"He's a junior. His parents are from Montevideo, Uruguay. He's really nice. This is the second time he's asked me out."

"So where are you going?"

"We're going to see this new play by Michelle Tucker at the Shubert Theatre. I should be home by eleven. I'll call you if there's anything to say about my evening," Lisa smiled shyly.

"Are you going out too?" Lisa asked, as Katie began to change into a pair of khakis.

"Yeah, but not on a date. It's the group that helps out in the Juvenile Court."

"Where's the meeting?"

"In the Warren Building. Far cry from the Shubert."

Lisa slipped on her new Morrise pumps, turned around in front of the mirror, and looked at Katie for approval.

"You look terrific. I'm sure your new date will approve. Don't wake me if you come in too late."

"See you later! Wish me luck."

Five minutes later, Katie lumbered down the red cobblestones sidewalk that ran along the border of a grass covered park-like area called the Upper Green. She noticed the regular homeless people who had taken their stations on several benches adjacent to the walkway that crisscrossed the Upper Green. She pushed her right hand into her jeans pocket and fingered three coins: two quarters and a dime. Out of the corner of her eye, she counted the figures on the benches: five, maybe six. Their heads were turned away. Regretting that she had not picked up some of the change on her desk, she quickened her pace, and avoiding the crisscrossed pathway, headed to the sidewalk that boarded the green.

Upon reaching the other side, Katie glanced back to see if the beggars' eyes were following her. Their hands were outstretched to others. Feeling less guilty, Katie continued walking, and passed several nouveau clothing stores and boutiques, each displaying vibrantly colored mannequins cloaked in green, gold, and turquoise. She stopped in front of a brownstone building. Its dark red exterior was impressive, and elegantly contoured to reflect the Gothic architecture of nearby University buildings. She checked her notes. This is it.

Katie pushed open the heavy paneled front door, and lunged up the steps, sensing her lateness more now that she was inside. The meeting in the "Child Support Center" was already in progress when she entered. A young Asian woman, neatly attired, handed her a booklet and motioned her toward the only empty aluminum chair in the front row.

The large room reminded Katie of her high school auditorium, except for the wide plank hardwood floors rather than the faded linoleum at Manchester High. Thirty or so people were seated in five rows of six chairs all pointed in the direction of the speaker. Katie took the seat in the first row center next to a middle age woman.

A petite, articulate, brown-skinned African American woman, in her mid-thirties by Katie's estimate, pointed to words on the easel board beside her.

She read the words out loud. *"NATIONAL CHILD GUARDIAN PROGRAM (NCGP)."*

The lady continued. "At this moment, there are more than a half million children in foster care in the United States. More than a quarter of a million of these children enter and leave foster care each year. On average, a foster child is placed in six foster homes before she is eighteen years of age. You can imagine the trauma of a child who moves to a new family home six times, uprooted five of those times, and having to adapt to each home situation. It's easy to see why many of these children have emotional attachment problems."

A hand is raised in the back of the room. "Just give me a minute or two more," the speaker said before returning her pointer to the easel. Katie's eyes moved from the pointer to the speaker's white pearl necklace and earrings.

The speaker took a sip of water and resumed. "NCGP is a national organization with local affiliates. Here in this state, we train and provide legal guardians to help kids in foster placement. We are similar to the National Court Appointed Special Advocate (CASA) Program which provides over 200,000 children with a volunteer court—appointed legal guardian each year to speak to what's in the child's best interest, including foster care placement. According to CASA's website 1900 children are victims of abuse or neglect yearly, some resulting in death.

Katie watched the emotion in the speaker's face move down her forehead to her chin. "It's enough to break your heart. But we—you— are here to help them," the speaker said, then added, "I'm going to give you a few minutes to read the booklet handed out when you came in, and afterward we'll take questions."

CHAPTER 26

National Child Guardian Program

Katie opened the booklet. A photo of the speaker appeared on the front page and below it her name: *Martha Hammer, Executive Director, NCGP*. . . Katie glanced at the other people in the room who were turning pages, some using pens to underline passages. Katie began reading.

> *The foster parents receive the children under a court order, which sets the length of the time the children are to be with them before they are returned to their natural parents, or adopted, or become adults themselves.*
>
> *The role of the natural parents while their children are in foster care differs from case to case. Some children have 'no contact' orders on them, meaning that the court has ordered that the parents have no contact with their children until there's a hearing in court, and the court decides when and under what conditions they can see them. This is usual in cases where the children have been physically abused by the parents—so the judge is very cautious, and may not want the parents to be around these children in a foster home setting. Some foster parents may be nervous about having the natural parents, whom they do not know, visiting in their homes. In other cases, some visitation is allowed, often in a neutral environment.*

Katie turned to the second page.

> *First, someone reports a child as having been abused. The child shows up at a hospital with a suspicious injury, such as a*

burn. The doctor prepares an affidavit stating whether he or she believes child abuse has occurred. If the affidavit states that the child has been physically abused, the Child Protection Agency by law has the right to take and keep the child for 96 hours in a safe place. The agency has a list of people who've signed up for foster care placement.

Such heavy stuff, Katie thought. She took her favorite bluish green ballpoint pen from her purse and poised it over the next paragraph.

After ninety-six hours, the child must be returned to the parent, unless a judge issues a different order. However, upon taking the child into custody, a social worker from the Child Protection Agency is immediately dispatched to the courthouse to ask a judge to issue an Order of Temporary Custody, called an OTC.

Katie underlined *OTC*, then *Order of Temporary Custody.*

The social worker takes the doctor's affidavit substantiating likelihood of abuse and prepares her own affidavit based on her investigation after talking to the child's care givers, in most cases the parents, about how the incident happened. The social worker prepares the background information on the family, and puts all this information in a report. This information is typed up on a form, called a Parental Neglect of Abuse Petition and given to the clerk of the court who takes it to one of the judges.

Katie also underlined *Parental Neglect or Abuse Petition*. She paused, stretched her arms, and concentrated on the next paragraph.

A section of the petition, called the OTC, indicates whether the Child Protection Agency is asking the judge to issue an order granting the agency temporary custody of the child for safekeeping until a hearing on the case takes place before the judge.

The man in the back of the room raised his hand again. "When do you go to court?"

Now, Martha Hammer answered, reading from the writing on the easel.

"The court case begins when the social worker gives the Petition to the clerk of the court. That's called the filing of the case-handing the paper Petition to the clerk of the court. The clerk places a 'filed' stamp on the Petition. Then the clerk takes the Petition to the judge. The judge reviews it, and returns it to the clerk who sets a date for a court hearing on the petition, whether or not the judge signs the Order of Temporary Custody section. If the judge signs the Order of Temporary Custody within the 96 hours, the Child Protection Agency then has authority to keep the child in foster care until the hearing date. If the judge does not sign the Order of Temporary Custody section, the Child Protection Agency must return the child to the parents, and wait for the court hearing date."

She turned her eyes directly to the audience. "So, you may be thinking, 'what's my role in this?' And I'm happy to tell you. We're looking for individuals to serve as 'Guardians ad litem,' meaning, 'Guardians at law or Legal Guardian.'"

Martha turned over the paper on the easel, revealing large bold black letters on the next page, and read aloud:

Role of Guardian ad litem:

Meet with the child and the child's parents;
Visit the child in the foster home;
Speak to the child's teacher and principal if the child is
in school;
Make sure the child's medical and dental needs are met;
Speak to the child's lawyer;
Attend all court hearings;
Write a report to the court regarding what in your opinion
is in the child's best interest.

"As you can see," she finished, "it's a large task, and a wholly necessary one."

A young man—seated in the first row, attired in gray pants and a blue short sleeve dress shirt, rose and walked to the front of the room. Martha said, "I would like to introduce you to Mark Clark, my assistant. Mark is the associate director of the NCG program in this state."

The man began to speak in a full, energetic voice. "Thank you, Martha. As she said, I'm Mark Clark. I have been with the NCG program now for about five years. I can tell you this is the most meaningful program for children who find themselves in foster care. What you as a guardian of their interest can do for them is tremendous. You can make a real difference in their lives. There are thousands of cases in Juvenile Court, and therefore thousands of children who are in need of the services of guardians ad litem. We and they urgently need your help." Mark looked toward Martha.

"So, this is the overview of the NCG guardian program," Martha concluded. "Thank you for coming out to listen to our presentation and plea. We will take a short break for coffee and muffins. For those of you who can stay and help, Mark and I will give specific instruction on how to perform your role, for example, interviewing techniques, talking to a child and parents; and how to's and how not to's; what kind of security protection you will need for certain neighborhoods and what to put in the report to the court. Again, thank you."

Katie did not care about the muffins. She made her way to Mark, and expressed to him her keen interest in being a guardian ad litem.

"What motivates you to want to do this?" he asked politely.

It was the easiest question she'd ever been asked.

After impressing upon Katie the importance of the program," Mark added, "*in fact, we were just involved in one case where the baby was placed in scalding water in the bathtub. In that case of a suspicious child injury, the hospital placed a call to the Child Protection Department, which sent a social worker to investigate.*"

Because her senior year final exams were approaching, Katie informed Mark she couldn't volunteer now, but would like to in the future."

"We always need help," he responded.

CHAPTER 27

Gary Maxwell

Katie stepped out of her morning shower, and stood naked before the vanity. She wiped the steam from the mirror, examined the few fine lines above her right eyebrow, and felt for the small grainy nodule in her left breast. Inexplicably her mind drifted to her first meeting with Gary—it was in the ornate University President's Reception Room with its plush deep dark maroon carpet, mahogany walls and pale gold, milky-white, dark red and blue colored stain glass windows overlooking the college courtyard.

She recalled it vividly. It was there that the intrigue was born. A tall, slightly older man approached and asked what she was majoring in.

"Political Science," she answered.

"Interesting, especially in today's times. Need all the science possible to straighten out the political mess the world is in now," he said, extending his hand. "Matt Jordan, I'm a Professor in the History Department."

"Katie Manning," she replied. Not bad looking for a professor, Katie thought. Short beard, thick eyebrows, square-shaped face, steel blue eyes, slight hints of grey in his hair line. She glanced at his left hand. No ring. The corner of her right eye caught a younger man moving through the crowd toward them.

"Professor Jordan," the man called out as he approached.

"Hi Gary. Gary, this is Katie Manning. She's a Political Science major," he said, envious of Gary's single status, then added "Gary Maxwell's one of our new Assistant Professors."

"Pleased to meet you, Miss Manning," Gary responded, almost bowing.

Later Gary would tell her how serendipitous their meeting was, for he rarely attended faculty-student get-togethers, and how a feeling inside compelled his attendance at this one.

She knew from the time she looked into his hazel eyes that first day that she would sleep with him—her inauguration into the intimacy she had heard all the girls talk about. It would be her first time and he was the right one. A few months later, it happened. What a joy she had in the intense *head rush, I can't get enough of you* moments when every touch, smile, and utterance was a discovery as precious as marveling at a new baby's smile.

Months of trips to museums, dinners with candle lights, nights out at the movies, camping in state parks, and enjoying nature and each other drew them even closer. Even a false pregnancy couldn't disconnect them, yet another nemesis did—his aversion to long-term commitment, which he hoped he could shake.

A half of a year later it ended, not with a desire to punish him, but with great sadness. His burning desire for excitement and making a concrete difference catapulted him from intellectual pursuits at the University.

But why did he decide to become a U.S. Marshal—the tough people who chase and capture violent convicted criminals across the country, returning them to jails and prisons—she couldn't imagine. Maybe to safeguard society? Long after their goodbyes, he called and left his special cell phone number just in case—the one that doesn't register on any caller ID.

CHAPTER 28

Professor Jordan

Gary's departure left an aching void in Katie's heart, leaving her vulnerable for romance.

It started so innocently. Professor Matt Jordan, breakfast tray in hand, was searching for an empty table when she waved him over.

"You don't mind?" he asked.

"Oh no, please have a seat. It's pretty crowded in here."

Katie was honored to have a good looking full professor sitting with her. Her classmates would be envious.

"You don't eat in the student cafeteria?" he asked, removing the plate from the tray, and placing it on a side panel.

"No, I get up kind of late sometimes and this place is close to my classes," Katie responded, buttering a burnt piece of rye toast, then raising her eyes to him and glancing around at all of the students in jeans and sweaters gobbling their food while reading text books and scribbling notes.

"Gee, I haven't seen you in months. Gary, my former Assistant, always spoke so highly of you." He paused after swallowing a mouthful of scrambled eggs. "Are you in contact with him?" Hoping her relationship had ended, his tone was controlled but friendly and disguised to conceal his interest in this lovely junior.

Katie wondered whether the gaze from Professor Jordan mirrored a genuine interest in Gary, or something else. He seemed to be closely analyzing her.

"No, we're not seeing each other anymore."

Sitting across from this beautiful girl deeply stirred Matt, giving him an elevated feeling he hadn't felt for his wife or anyone else in a long time—too long, he thought. He didn't know this girl. But her beatific smile, her delicate manners, and her smooth, creamy skin in that yellow sundress captured him. He must be careful. Propositioning a coed could be trouble.

"Don't let your eggs get cold," she said smiling.

"Oh yes, thank you, my mind was wandering," Matt blushed in embarrassment. "You're sure I'm not intruding?"

"Oh no," she replied, looking at her watch. "But, if you'll excuse me," she said, rising from her chair, "gotta rush off, I'll be late for my 9:30 class."

Matt's six foot frame rose in recognition. "Have a good class."

What a nice man. Only this thought wouldn't last.

CHAPTER 29

Jordan's Deception

It was several months later when Professor Matt Jordan made his overture. He sent a couple of drinks to two young ladies sitting at a front table at the Flaming Mushrooms Gig—a pop jazz band that was the hottest new sound on the scene at the University Club, so named because of its proximity to the campus. Surprised by the waiter's appearance at their table, the girls' puzzlement was answered when his finger pointed to a tall man with a short beard, and full eyebrows clapping his hands to the beat, standing and smiling in their direction.

"Who's that?" Lisa asked.

"It looks like Professor Jordan," answered Katie. "You remember, I told you he introduced me to Gary."

Katie raised her glass in Professor Jordan's direction, signaling a thank you, and turned her attention back to the band. Moments later, Matt Jordan stood a couple of feet alongside her table.

"Mind if I join you?" he asked, in a friendly but elevated tone competing with the loud rhythmic beat of the rat-a-tat drumming mixed with electric guitars penetrating the large darkened room.

Pointing to the vacant seat next to Katie he said "It's pretty crowded in here."

"Sure, have a seat. Lisa, this is Professor Matt Jordan. He's in the History Department. Lisa's my roommate."

"Pleased to meet you," Lisa responded, raising her glass.

"You guys come here often?"

"No," Lisa answered, "but we heard so much about this band. We had to hear them . . . they are awesome." Then she asked, "Do you come here often?"

"Oh, no, there are too many teenage busts for underage drinking here. I took a chance just to hear the band."

When the set ended and the applause waned Matt handed his card to Katie.

"I can't stay, meetings, meetings, meetings, but please give me a call. Gary told me how smart and hard-working you are. I have a project you may be interested in. It's been nice to meet you, Lisa."

That said, he left. And she did call.

Later she would explain to Lisa how she ended up in bed with Matt Jordan. He was charming and attentive. It started out so innocently with her meeting and working on the research project in his campus office. Then there were flowers and a hug for her birthday. Although he asked about Gary, she heard it in his voice . . . a personal interest in her. She was so lonely. Gary didn't answer her letters. Matt was so sensitive or at least she thought.

"So how did you find out?" Lisa queried her sobbing roommate.

Katie swallowed, raised herself up in bed and used her blanket to wipe her tears. "We were working in his office one Saturday morning when a woman burst into the room glaring at me."

"Aren't you going to introduce me?" the woman yelled at Matt.

"Then she bounded straight toward me, shouting 'I'm Eleanor Jordan, Matt's wife, and you?'"

"I told her I was working on a research project with Professor Jordan."

"Some research, she yelled and stormed out the door."

"So what happened next?"

"I was shocked. I didn't know he was still married. He told me he was divorced, and we had to use his friend's apartment because he had custody of his young children. He pleaded for me to stay."

"So, what did you do?"

I screamed at him and ran out of his office. I won't return his calls. He's a creep. Four months I spent with him. Oh God, I feel so used."

Sitting on the side of the bed Lisa took a long look at her distraught friend.

"You could report him to the Dean's Office for unethical behavior. The University should fire him. It's so unethical!" Lisa said, slamming her right fist into the bedding.

What would Gary think? Katie wondered. She still carried a torch for him. Was Matt just a rebound? Should she turn him in? If she did, what good would come of it? Graduation is within a few weeks. And she has no idea where she will be after that.

CHAPTER 30

Another Miracle

Feeling down doesn't even come close to describing the depression Dorothy struggled to conceal. "Are you alright?" Henry kept asking his wife who was wrapped in blankets on the living room couch. "It's not your fault, it's the system. All these damn restrictions. Requiring you to admit you done wrong. Well, you didn't do no wrong. All you wanted to do is take care of your babies. Then requiring us to attend all those damn counseling sessions. Who's got time for that? I'm working my damn ass off. I've got no free time. You've got to snap out of it, Dorothy. What's done is done, besides we need to take care of the new baby you're carrying."

Almost fifteen years have passed since I, as judge and jury, ruled that Dorothy and Henry cannot see their daughters and it has been that long since her discharge from the locked psyche ward of Women's Hospital. *Her Diagnosis: suicidal ideation secondary to depression, and the fictitious disorder MSBP.*

Dorothy's constant thoughts centered on the idea that taking them to the doctor was the only way to help the children. She wasn't, what they say Munchausening them, whatever that means. Dorothy wondered when she will feel better. The only hope she knows springs from the new life growing in her belly. Is that a kick? Intent on keeping this one, Dorothy raised the blankets and rubbed her stomach. Her outlook brightened with the thought; *tomorrow I will see the doctor at the hospital.*

CHAPTER 31

The Hospital Visit

Looking up from the charts on the counter of the beige Formica semi-circular Nurses' Station, Estelle Adams is confounded by the face she hasn't seen in years.

"Hi, Estelle, do you remember me. Dorothy . . . Dorothy Simmons, remember?"

"Why yes, I remember you," Estelle responded in hesitation, the woman's voice filling her memory. "It's been a long time." Estelle paused. "It's so good to see you, how can I help you?"

"I'm here for a wellness visit, a maternity checkup," Dorothy softly uttered, gently patting her stomach. "I don't have a regular doctor; that's why I use the hospital."

Resisting a frown, Estelle walked around to the front of the nurses' station, pulled Dorothy aside, then whispered, "Have you recovered?"

"Recovered from what?"

"You know. Why don't you come with me to somewhere private," said Estelle, gently touching Dorothy's left arm, and pointing with her other hand toward a doorway a few feet down the hall.

Walking slowly beside Dorothy, Estelle commented, "It's been a long time . . . let's see—at least 10 or more years since I last saw you. You haven't aged at all."

"You must be kidding . . . with all my troubles," Dorothy replied.

"Come on, take a seat in my office," Estelle directed, opening the door.

Once inside, Dorothy lowered herself in the chair in front of Estelle's desk, and studied Estelle's face. She must be at least 50, Dorothy thinks, no gray in her dark brown hair, but the color could be from a bottle. A few wrinkles. A restrained smile. Someone said the black upside down V on the nurse's hat means she's important.

"So, you're pregnant?" Estelle asked, breaking Dorothy's concentration, and scrutinizing her face for any hint of personality disorder.

"Yes, I think it's been a few months now, judging from the morning sickness and all," Dorothy replied, sitting back in the chair.

Estelle moved a few papers around on her desk, and then changed her voice. "Have you seen your children?" The question was posed in a more formal tone—a tone heard on a lawyer TV show, like being talked down to.

Crossing her arms across her chest and resting them on her slightly rounded belly, Dorothy summoned an answer. And summoned it was, because for some reason, she hadn't expected to see Estelle here today, and she hadn't been thinking about the children.

The words "No, no, I haven't," slowly emerged from Dorothy's throat.

"Just give me a moment," responded Estelle, turning her head toward the grey desktop computer on her desk. She articulated her long fingers on its key board, and read the file list that opened on the pale blue screen. Pressing a black down arrow key, she accessed the archived file list, then scrolled to *Dorothy Simmons*. A quick click revealed its contents. Estelle scanned the *Background History* section and focused on another section entitled *Expectations*. She then turned her eyes to the woman, dressed in a faded blue dress, sitting across from her desk. Dorothy's caramel skin was still attractive, she observed, her face a bit more mature, but her eyes, though clear and milky white with brown pupils, revealed abundant anxiety.

Anticipating some embarrassing questions, Dorothy lowered her head and studied the run in her stocking, starting just along the left side of her right knee.

"Why?" Estelle asked in a measured tone.

"Why what?"

"Why haven't you seen your children?"

A tear formed in the corner of Dorothy's left eye. She blinked, and tried to clear her voice. "The foster parents don't let me."

A frowning Estelle continued. "Reading from the file given us by Child Protection, you were expected to admit to the abuse, get counseling and then visit with the girls. Did you do that?"

An indignation-stirred defiance ignited a heated response. "No I didn't because I didn't do it! How can I admit to hurting my babies when I didn't do it," she shouted, raising her hands.

"Well, according to our records the judge . . ."

"I don't care what the judge said, I didn't . . ."

Clearly this isn't getting them anywhere, Estelle discovered. "Okay, Dorothy, Okay, please calm down." Motioning with her arms the way pedestrians signal cars to decelerate, she added "I just had to ask you, because it's hospital protocol, that's all, because you're here pregnant, that's all. Nothing personal."

Estelle couldn't believe her eyes and ears. This woman is pregnant again after all these years and coming to this hospital for pregnancy visits—the very hospital from which her last child was taken. She must be out of her mind, Estelle thought, if she thinks this hospital will give her another Munchausen moment.

CHAPTER 32

The New House

Dorothy and Henry Simmons' new house—a red brick bungalow with the master bedroom in an enlarged second story attic—is just the house that Henry could afford with his recent hard-earned raise. He wasn't crazy about the lumberyard, but it provided steady wages, a goodbye to the landlady and a hello to his new home. Plus the clincher—the arrival of their new baby boy—was the perfect housewarming gift.

Almost a month passed before Henry finished painting the interior. An antique white—as the woman in the hardware store called it—covered the walls of the master bedroom, which was also Terrence's room. The new parents couldn't bear having this baby sleeping away from them.

Primary night duty was Henry's. He got up and attended to the whimpers and cries of his new brown baby boy. His large hands picked him up, cradled him on his chest, rocked him back and forth, and gently rubbed his back until his cries slowed and stopped. Dorothy was grateful for this help and for the raise that allowed Henry to quit his second job and spend nights with her and the baby. She felt better with his being more around the house. With Henry's encouragement, she thought about volunteering for weekend duty at the local soup kitchen.

CHAPTER 33

The Soup Kitchen and Dorothy's Mental Breakthrough

The Soup Kitchen was the place where Dorothy met the other important adult in her life—Dr. Alice Patton, a petite five foot four woman with streaky gray and brown hair cut to just above her shoulders.

The Soup Kitchen was in the massive basement of the Evangelical Church. Men, women and children entering the front side door were given tiny square pieces of green paper with numbers, and called to the front of the cafeteria serving area by those numbers. Dr. Alice Patton worked the baked beans station alongside Dorothy who ladled out mashed potatoes on the plates for the needy who moved in an orderly line along a long serving table, starting at the beginning of the line—from picking up trays with paper plates—to the mixed salads and greens, then to the golden baked chicken, the white and buttery mashed potatoes, Alice's dark brown baked beans, and finally to squares of carrot cake and apple juice at the other end.

"How long have you been doing this?" Dorothy asked.

"Oh, for about a year," Alice answered.

"You're welcome," Alice said, smiling to the pregnant girl on the other side of the table whose plate displayed mixed vegetables and mashed potatoes.

Working together at the Soup Kitchen over several months allowed Dorothy and Dr. Alice, as she affectionately called her, to become close—close enough to confide in the doctor how sad she felt about having lost her daughters. And close enough for her new psychiatrist friend to enable her to begin thinking about whether she had done bad things to her girls.

Still, it came grudgingly, creeping bit by bit out of her subconscious during deep sleep. Over the years she had fought the thought, often able to will herself back to sleep and feel her depression smothering it. But after talking to Dr. Alice, bit by bit it kept coming and coming, and finally burst into her consciousness—the thought that she had in fact exposed Katie and Maria to harm at her own doing, and she somehow must make amends.

CHAPTER 34

Katie & Maria to Washington, D.C.

As a Judge, I was invited to speak at numerous social functions. Through my civic involvements I met Margaret Ashmore, a devoted supporter of many worthwhile organizations, including the District of Columbia Museum. By serendipity at one of our civic functions Margaret asked me whether I would give some advice to a bright young lady who may be interested in the law. Of course I said yes. Incredibly that person turned out to be the same Katie Manning that Margaret calls her niece, as well as the infant whom years ago I placed in foster care with a John and Beatrice Manning. Some six degrees of separation, I'd say.

I learned that Katie had graduated with honors from the prestigious college in the Elm City. I heard that not only had she grown into a beautiful woman but she possessed a determined sense of wanting to make a difference.

Through surrogates I reached out to the Mannings and through them to Katie and suggested a possible apprenticeship position in a prestigious firm in Washington, D.C. to give her some exposure to the legal world to help her decide whether law might be a good career choice. Beatrice Manning and Katie liked the idea, as did Beatrice's sister, Margaret Ashmore. So I got in touch with Robert Atmore, a top-notch attorney who once worked for me as a law clerk, to see if he would accept Katie as an intern. He agreed.

Katie's Washington, D.C. story begins with the Mannings' drive from Connecticut to Grand Central Station.

It was near the distant colored lights of Times Square in an early dawn intermittent rain that a dark figure, meandering in the street, ambled toward their car, with hands palm up.

"John!" Beatrice shouted.

Immediately John jerked the car away from the center line.

"I didn't see him," John exclaimed, looking over his left shoulder at the dark figure, now flailing his arms and punching the air.

Beatrice placed her hand on John's shoulder. "Be careful. We have enough time.

John was nervous. He didn't want to admit it, but he was. As he pulled the Volvo onto the Grand Central apron and stopped behind a small line of cars idling near the massive doorway, white mist rising from their tail pipes, he could feel the sadness in his chest. He activated the yellow parking flashers, and the family disembarked. He reached into the trunk to remove Katie's bags.

"Be careful with the cloth bag, Dad," said Maria. "The sidewalk is wet."

Stepping toward him, Katie picked up the canvas bag. "Here, Dad, I'll take it. It's not that heavy."

He released it to her with an unnecessary "You got it?" and remembered the day he unloaded their few bags into that small room at the top of the stairs. Now look at them. Both pretty and young, both somewhat sophisticated but still a little giddy—Katie ready to leave for the Capitol City, and Maria traveling with her to set her up in her new apartment. Then she'll return and Katie will be in D.C. by herself. He felt sadness in his chest again.

"Come girls, give me a big hug," Beatrice beckoned, her arms stretched wide.

Katie placed her bag on the hood of the car, and squeezed Beatrice tightly. John's hugs were briefer but no less intense.

"Be careful now. Protect yourselves," he said, aware of the high tone to his voice. "Be wary of strangers, and keep to safe well-lighted sections of streets."

"Okay, Dad," Katie answered.

"And we won't take any candy from strangers," Maria mocked, with a funny grin on her face.

"Mom, we'll call you on the cell phone," Katie shouted.

Beatrice rubbed the back of John's neck as the girls disappeared into the building. "Honey, they will be fine," she said. "We taught them well."

John nodded. The Volvo responded to the call of its ignition. And they eased out into the half-deserted streets of early morning.

Fifty foot statues of Hercules, Minerva and Mercury guard Grand Central Station at the 42nd Street entrance set adjacent to a 13 foot circular clock. The high arching ceilings and Italian white marble walls frame a cavernous space. Katie and Maria stood, awestruck.

In animated fashion, they carried their suitcases down two long flights of white marble stairs to the white marble floor of the massive station hall. An oddly perky young security guard responded to their question and pointed them to Gate 19. Tickets in hand and suitcases bumping on their legs, they hurried past a large four-sided clock atop a mahogany and brass information booth in the center of the vast hall and joined the line of passengers streaming through the Gate's archway.

The girls stepped into a spacious blue steel train cabin with large rectangular windows, faux leather seats and a retractable shelf extending from the sidewall. Internet connections, and power ports for personal computers and other electronic devices enhanced the fine quarters of their transport machine. Maria, sitting opposite her sister, leaned on the retractable shelf and stared directly into Katie's face.

"Your life is totally changing," Maria said, with barely contained excitement.

"I know," Katie responded with a slight grin.

"So tell me about this lawyer you'll be working for in D.C."

"Robert Atmore. He clerked for Judge Hughes."

"So why's he interested in letting you work for him?" Maria asks.

"Nice talk."

"I don't mean it like that!"

"I know," Katie said, reaching across and slapping her sister's leg. "I may be interested in law or social work. Mom said something about a mentoring program that he runs for the law firm. Aunt Margaret knows more about it. And this is my chance to figure it out."

The adrenaline of catching the train now wearied them, and the steady hum of the train lulled them to sleep. Maria's book slipped out of her hands. In a few hours, they would see the Potomac River.

CHAPTER 35

Katie's Apartment

Beatrice's trust in her sister Margaret Ashmore had been earned through thousands of conversations, dozens of years, and more than a handful of family disputes. They had protected each other during internecine and outside power struggles. It was Margaret whom Beatrice trusted to secure an apartment in a safe neighborhood for her children.

Margaret Ashmore and her husband James greeted the wide-eyed girls at Union Station and ushered them around town for a short day of orientation to the City that Runs America. They drove up Pennsylvania Avenue, passed the World Bank and George Washington University, and finally to a tree-lined street, complete with esplanade and brownstone buildings. In her hands, Katie held the keys to her own place.

"We don't know how to thank you—" Katie began.

"No need. No need for that," Margaret hushed her.

"Well, then, I'm now extending an invitation to you and Uncle James to come to dinner here next Sunday."

"Invitation accepted, my dear Katie," Margaret answered, smiling. "And don't forget to call Judge Hughes to thank him for arranging your internship with lawyer Atmore."

"Won't forget," Katie assured her.

Katie settled into the larger side bedroom with windows facing the courtyard. Maria took the bedroom facing the back yard. A quaint galley kitchen, featuring older appliances and windows with a slight courtyard view, was visible from the living room. Sugar maple hardwood floors creaked beneath their feet.

Something about the space, the separation from the adults that had shepherded them through their youth, something about the coffee made in their own coffeemaker, the living room that was theirs alone, turned their conversation to matters long left unuttered.

"Do you still wonder why?" Katie asked.

"What do you mean?"

"Why they gave us up? Why they've never—why they've not tried—"

"We may never know."

"But don't you wonder . . ."

"Yes."

Katie's cell phone rang. She lifted it to her ear while placing the coffee cup on the table.

"Hello?" She paused and raised her left eyebrow, an unconscious talent Maria used to envy.

"Who's that?"

"Some man from The Child Protection Department in Connecticut. Said a lady who says she's our mother is looking for us. He said he'll call back when he gets more information."

Maria was silent. So was Katie.

"Do you . . ."

"Yes."

Katie took both cups to the kitchen and refilled them.

"Should we do anything, or . . ."

"We'll just wait, I guess. Like we've been waiting all this time. Then we'll see. You know, cross that bridge—"

"When we get there, right. You sound like Mom."

"I know. I've noticed that myself." Katie smiled. "Do you ever think that maybe Mom and Dad would think we were . . . I don't know . . . disloyal or something? For wanting to know."

"They always said they'd help us find them if we wanted. I don't even know what kind of feelings I could have for my birth mother and father. It's like they abandoned us. I love my mom and dad. They're the ones who raised us. But still . . . I don't know what I'd do, if a woman knocked on the door, stepped in the house and called herself my Mom. What do you do? Shake hands?"

They both laughed, and then stopped suddenly. Neither knew the answer.

CHAPTER 36

Katie, Volunteering

The cab slowed to a stop at 14th and U streets around noon. Katie exited and asked a passerby if he knew where she could find the National Child Guardian Office. A studious-looking young man with a book in one hand, and a portable phone in the other, pointed to a nearby building.

"It's right there, ma'am," he said.

"Thank you," Katie replied. *Ma'am?* Katie thought to herself, *when did I become a ma'am? Maybe I need more makeup.*

Katie looked at herself in every passing window, then ascended the steps of the red brick townhouse and rang the vestibule door bell. A buzzer sounded and she pulled the door open.

"May I help you?" asked the young man sitting behind the desk.

"Yes, I'm here to inquire about volunteering. I went to one of your meetings in New Haven, Connecticut and I was told to look you up when I came to D.C."

"Your name?"

"Katie Manning."

"Please have a seat and I'll see if Michele is in."

Sitting in one of the wooden chairs, Katie viewed the large posters lining the wall. Nelson Mandela, the Dalai Lama, Martin Luther King, Jr., Mahatma Gandhi, and Mother Teresa were all neatly framed and displayed above inspirational messages. Scenes of children playing appeared in a neat row of enlarged black and white framed photographs on an adjoining wall.

As Katie reached over to retrieve a magazine from the table in front of her, a tall lady wearing a blue business suit said her name.

"I'm Michele Winter. Come with me—glad you found us!"

Diplomas and citations lined the walls of Michele's office, and if Katie hadn't spent so much time lately with lawyers, she may have been intimidated. The lady's high cheek bones denote a Cherokee lineage, something Katie only noticed because of how well her father had trained her to notice details and pick up on physiognomy.

"Did you go through orientation in New Haven?"

"No, I just went to one of the introductory meetings. I wanted to volunteer, but I couldn't because it was near the time of my final college exams."

Michele Winters pulled open a drawer on the right side of her desk, removed a thick manila envelope, and handed it to Katie.

"Here, I want you to take and study these materials, and then we'll put you through an official orientation after which the court will swear you in as an official NCG guardian ad litem. How much volunteer time do you have?"

"Well, I'm working full-time at the law firm of Swarthmore Jones and Smithtone, but they encourage us to do some pro bono work, so I would say about 15 hours a week during the day and several hours on the weekend."

Michele Winters' eyebrows shot up in surprise, "You look so young to be a lawyer."

"Oh, I'm not!" Katie laughed. "I'm working as a paralegal to see whether or not I like law well enough to go to law school. I'm working directly for one of my relative's friends who is a partner at the law firm."

"You're fortunate."

"Yes, I am." Katie answered.

"Well Ms. Manning . . ."

"Please call me Katie."

"Well Katie, leave your personal contact information with William at the front desk and we'll arrange your orientation so that you get sworn in right away. Also, we'll need to do a police background check. Would you have trouble with that?"

"Oh no, I've never been arrested."

"By the way, Katie, why do you wish to volunteer for the NCG program?"

Katie smiled. "I was a foster child, and I've always wanted to help children who find themselves in unfortunate situations. I was fortunate to have great foster parents."

Ms. Winters nodded knowingly. As she walked Katie back to the reception room, she assured her that if the background check and orientation go well, she had an important case to give her.

"Anything to help," Katie said kindly. Before she was out of the front door, her orientation packet was opened, and Katie started pouring over its contents.

Several days later William called Katie at the law firm and outlined the orientation she would receive: meetings with current Guardians Ad Litem, that is Legal Guardians; some instructional meetings at the center; several visits to the juvenile court; and then finally the oath before the Judge. Only those directly involved in a case are allowed inside a courtroom when the case is being heard. She'd be made privy to sensitive information, and it would be necessary for her to keep secrets and honor confidentiality.

"I hope that won't be a problem," William uttered in an inquiring tone, then added, "If it all works out, your first client is a juvenile named Cheryl Williams. She's just 14 but looks like a well-developed 17, and that's part of the problem."

CHAPTER 37

Robert Atmore, Back-story

His family referred to him as Robert the Successful -- just like a Medieval Knight ---now on track to become partner in the successful law firm of Swarthmore Jones & Smithtone, "which has offices in several countries," his mother would say because she could not remember the list. Assigned to the Washington, D.C. office situated 10 blocks from the White House, Robert paid a high price for his penthouse condo.

More than one ex-wife receiving thousands of alimony dollars each month and distant relationships with his children provided ample testimony to the problems that single devotion to occupational success can bring. Even after all these years, Robert struggled to keep his secret suppressed, a secret seared into his psyche, too frequently bringing his thoughts to the edge of self-destruction. The thoughts were like some devil inviting him into a trance, and beckoning him to take a detour from high status into debauchery.

He was thirteen, visiting his favorite Uncle Milo in Puerto Rico. In the hill-top village, burro rickshaws took tourists around the village, past the center church and back to the little park overlooking turquoise-blue ocean waters. White stucco houses were omnipresent. The village was a safe place—far away from some of the dark streets of D.C. He climbed trees, as many as he could, in the grove sloping down the hillside.

He sat high in a mango tree, his hands sticky from the fruit, his lips sweet, when he saw it. His uncle pulled a young girl into a makeshift in the nearby tall weeds. The girl he did not know. She was no older than he. Robert climbed down the tree, pushed through the tall grass and stood silently. He heard faint sounds. Through gaps in the faded wooden slats he saw the girl remove her clothes while Milo sat on the ground before her. When she finished, Milo stood up and ran his hands over the front of her body. She made a sound as she turned her body away from him. His hands moved up and down the back of her body. Another sound. She turned her body toward him. Again his hands. Again the sound.

The girl stooped down. What was she doing? He couldn't see. He could feel the dust in his nose. The slats blocked his view. She was dressing. He backed away slowly, slowly, to the weeds. Then he ran.

Robert returned to the mango trees often in the late afternoon. A favorable perch. He would see Mino with different girls. He could not look away. He thought about it at night. The sweet young girls—some early teens.

He thought about it always. Maybe someday he could taste sweet youth, or is it just a fantasy?

CHAPTER 38

Robert Atmore, Mentor

The mentoring board of the local school district welcomed Robert, as they did any upstanding member of the community. The manager of the program explained over the phone that the program's purpose is to provide guidance to at-risk youth. A young teen named Frank was chosen as Robert Atmore's mentee. Frank's mother had several children and his father abandoned the family years ago. His brothers and sisters were all in school, all receiving free lunch because of the family's limited income. The family struggled with Frank's mother working full-time in a laundry mat, and having difficulty keeping several of her boys, especially Frank, out of trouble.

On this day Robert met his mentee and his mother at the George Washington Carver Middle School. The moment Robert arrived at the two story red brick schoolhouse, his mind flashed back to the time his middle school principal administered the paddle to him for acting out in class. Once had been enough.

A young man, barely of college age, approached Robert.

"I'm Timothy O'Brien, the school mentoring coordinator," he said pleasantly, extending his hand. "I want to introduce you to Mrs. Gracie Williams and her son, Frank."

A woman stood at the door of a conference room and extended her hand as well. "I'm Gracie, and this is my son." She glanced down at Robert's shoes as she shook her hand.

Robert stuck out his hand to the boy—no more than thirteen, Robert thought—and smiled as the foursome entered the conference room.

"So, Frank, tell me a little something about yourself," Robert said. "What do you want to be when you grow up?"

"I dunno."

"Yes, you do," Gracie interjected. "You told me you like those law shows on TV and you want to be a lawyer."

"Is that right?" Robert asked the boy.

"Yes, sir."

"Well, I know a little bit about that, and it's a pretty good job."

Timothy explained how the mentoring program would work: Robert would meet with Frank in this conference room once a week; discuss school achievement and career planning issues; and answer any questions that Frank may have about life in general. However, most importantly, he must counsel Frank about how to stay out of trouble. Concluding his remarks, Timothy asked whether all agree to these roles. They all nodded.

During their initial mentoring session a week later, Robert stressed the importance of Frank keeping his grades up.

"Do you know the five P's?"

"What are they?" Frank asked.

"My mentor shared them with me when I started clerking at a law firm."

"You had a mentor?"

"Sure, everybody should. So the five P's are: Prior Preparation Prevents Poor Performance. You should study well in advance and prepare for your examinations. By doing so you will be an excellent student, and as you prepare thoroughly to meet life's challenges, you will have more control of things so life will not be so difficult."

Frank nodded—whether thoughtfully or politely, Robert could not tell.

As Frank headed to his first period class, Robert found his way to the principal's office.

"He's a natural leader," Principal Samantha Johnson explained to Robert. "Captain of the basketball team, a smart kid. But . . ."

"In these times, there's always a but, isn't there?"

Samantha Johnson looked at him, and he could read the appreciation in her eyes—that he understood the challenge of being in education in the middle school years.

"At this point, he could go either way. He's easily influenced. He wants to please people—that's how he can lead, but also how he can fall. The next year is critical," she concluded.

"I'll be an active mentor, Mrs. Johnson. Without a mentor, I'd still be lost."

"I'm glad. The last thing he needs is someone who enters his life and doesn't follow through."

"I understand," Robert said, as he stood to leave. "I always follow through."

It was on his third visit while sitting in the conference room near the Principal's office that young Frank explained being approached by local gang members.

"And what did they want?" Robert asked.

"You know."

"To sell?"

"Yeah. I mean, not yet. But . . ."

Robert looked across the table at young Frank. Dope. This young.

"And what did you say?"

"I said no thanks."

"And how did they respond?"

"They said I should think about it because they could take care of me. And the money was good."

"You have to be careful hanging around near them. You could be doing nothing, and be picked up by being in the wrong place."

Frank nodded. Robert sensed it was enough for now, and changed the subject.

"Why do you want to be a lawyer?"

"I dunno. I like the lawyer shows on TV. It looks like they can help people in trouble."

"They do. That's exactly right."

Robert let the silence hang for a moment, hoping to lead Frank into his own thoughts.

"What's it like being a lawyer, Mr. Atmore? You had to go to school for a long time?"

"Don't let the schooling part bother you. It's only seven years after high school."

"Seven years!" Franks brown eyes widened. "That's way too long."

"No..no . . . no," Robert responded. "The time goes by so quickly, you hardly notice."

"Why so long?"

"Well, you have to graduate from a four year college and then law school is three years."

"Boy, I'll be old when I graduate."

"You won't be old, and besides law school is fun."

"How's it fun?"

"It's fun because you meet interesting people in law school. People from all over the country and the world are in your classes. And you get to figure out how our legal system works. Believe me, you will enjoy law school."

"Are you sure?"

"I sure am. I had a ball in law school, and you will too. It tunes up your mind and you meet some terrific people. Besides, I'll be around to advise you with your studies."

"Yeah."

"You know what? I have an idea."

Robert's idea was to have Frank visit him at his law office to see what a fascinating working environment a law office could be. Several days later, Frank visited Robert.

Frank was wearing a loose fitting suit, probably from a Goodwill store. He looked uncomfortable, but proud of it still.

A secretary escorted Frank and a young girl into Robert's office for a day of shadowing.

"Oh, I hope you don't mind," Frank said. "This is my sister, Cheryl."

Robert, startled by the striking beauty of the girl, stood up and offered his hand.

"Pleased to meet you, Cheryl."

"It's just that I told Sis that I was coming to your office today, and she has an interest in the law too. Mom said it was okay to bring her along so I hope it's okay with you."

"Sure, it's okay, please have a seat, both of you."

Cheryl sat in the seat to the left of Frank, facing the front of Robert's mahogany desk. Robert couldn't help but notice Cheryl's perfectly shaped long legs, thin waist, beatific face and discrete cleavage. She is almost as tall as her brother, Frank, but moved more gracefully.

Robert looked at his secretary while she slowly closed the office door. He moved his thoughts elsewhere, careful to resist disclosing any temptation that may mar his reputation. This is a young girl, he reminded himself, probably 16 or 17 at the most, and the sister of his mentee. But she is so innocently alluring, much more so than the mature and powerful women of D.C., and, ironically therefore, more dangerous. He cleared his throat and touched his tie.

CHAPTER 39

Robert Atmore—Swarthmore, Jones & Smithtone

Robert had been a law clerk for Judge Sam Hughes for two years. He was certain that it was the Judge's letter and a personal telephone call that secured his hire at the law firm. An annual Christmas card was the least Robert could do. Because of the Judge's recommendation and Robert's hard work, he is now close to becoming a partner and co-owner of Swarthmore, Jones and Smithtone, "a major firm with 2000 lawyers in offices in D.C., Atlanta, Los Angeles, New York, Miami, London, Madrid, Paris, Amsterdam, Berlin and Tokyo," as he had to repeat at least several times a day to prospective clients.

Robert specialized in family matters of the wealthy, and had made a career of it. Except for the senior partner in charge of their family law division at the firm, Robert had the most experience. Also, he was a regular lecturer at seminars on family law, and head of the Family Law Section of the State Bar Association. Several members of his law firm burned out in this contentious specialty, having succumbed to the pressure of too many night and weekend telephone calls from their divorce clients, some of whom, being in so much emotional pain, cried uncontrollably.

Robert often remarked that most divorce clients are in crisis. The central person in a married person's social, psychological, emotional, and financial support system is his or her spouse. Add children with the accompanying emotional attachment and a divorce is assured to become a crisis. The couple's identity, and each person's psyche, is formed by these connections, and a divorce can cause identity disintegration and flame out. Ergo, the upset at any perceived violation of a divorce court order and, thus the late night telephone calls to his or her lawyer. Nowadays with technological connections, one's lawyer is never more than a button away. Robert understood why so few of the lawyers in his firm chose his specialty.

For some reason, Robert had the right temperament. He saw his role as a mediator of the closing of a marriage partnership that had produced the financial support system for the couple, and perhaps children. Robert saw his function as helping the parties divide the assets of the partnership equitably, and negotiating a custody and visitation arrangement that would benefit the children. There was something in Robert's personality that clients liked—a kind and courtly demeanor, an unassuming assurance. Client year-end reviews ranked him among the best in the country.

If negotiation with the other spouse's lawyer did not work, Robert was ready for the legal war in Court. The opposition knew they were in for a fight with Atmore on the other side. Pre-trial judges told opposing lawyers their clients had to pay a premium of 15% more just because Atmore was on the other side, and they were in for a long, arduous legal brawl that may end with an appeal to the Appellate Court.

Robert was seated, looking over a file on his new intern. Her resume proved she was intelligent and the picture that she was attractive.

His intercom rang. "Sir, there's a young lady by the name of Katie Manning here to see you."

"Send her right in."

A demure, well-dressed Katie walked into his office. Robert extended his hand.

"Finally, the woman whose praises are the stuff of Margaret's songs."

Katie shook his hand. She could hardly contain her wonder at how handsome he is. She can't wait to tell Maria . . .

"Thank you for giving me the opportunity to work for you," she said perfectly.

"It's my pleasure." Robert policed his thoughts—attractive she is, yes, but she still is Margaret's niece.

"Please have a seat. I hear that you are interested in the law, and some time here would be an opportunity for you to get some exposure to it before deciding whether or not to go to law school."

Sitting in the chair opposite Robert's desk she asked, "That's exactly right. What will I be doing?"

"First of all, I'd like to take you around to meet the staff, and I'm working on an interesting divorce case that needs some assistance. I could have one of our paralegals do it, but it would be a good case for you. I'll closely supervise your work."

After making introductions to various staff members, Robert shepherded Katie to her new office. Though somewhat small, especially compared to his, the office afforded an expansive view of the Washington skyline and a bit of the Potomac River. It's here, and in the firm's library, that she would spend numerous hours, he told her, learning about how the law actually works.

"Please make yourself comfortable. I'll have the divorce file sent to you right away," he said, closing the door behind him.

Katie stood by the window in her new office and looked out toward the River. She heard a knock on her door.

"Come in," Gail, Robert's secretary, entered.

"This is the file that Mr. Atmore wishes you to have. He's prepared a transfer memorandum explaining the case and the problem. If you have any questions after reading the memorandum, he requests that you see him."

"Thank you. I'll go to work on it right away." Katie opened the accordion file, and removed a file labeled "case memorandum."

The firm represents Elizabeth Kent, who is divorcing her husband, Wendell, the chief executive officer of a large multinational corporation. She believes that he has been having an affair with Florence, a young woman in Boston. Marriage counseling has not worked. There are ample signs that he is seeing other women. He is willing to give her a divorce. She has some kind of compulsive disorder.

Although he is willing to give her a divorce after 45 years of marriage, her husband feels that she is not entitled to one-half of his financial assets. He argues that with proper therapeutic counseling, she should be able to join the workforce. They started out without either having much money. Her husband's climb up the corporate ladder has rewarded them handsomely. She believes that she's entitled to more than one-half because she is somewhat disabled, and he is an able-bodied executive. She also wishes to use some of the money to help out with the educational expenses of her favorite maid's son.

The memorandum posed the questions of how to put a financial value on Elizabeth's financial contribution to their marital estate since she didn't work outside the home, and what needs to be done to obtain a large alimony and property award for her. The firm needs this information for her upcoming divorce trial, scheduled ninety days from now.

To gain insight to the thinking of his clients, Robert routinely asked them to write out their thoughts about their case. Katie found Elizabeth's Autobiographical Case Statement, removed it from the folder, leaned back in her chair, and while reading it imagined the voice of her 60 year-old client.

I am trapped in my own world and afraid of touching anything, including my husband. How can I touch him when he has been touched by naked women? I know he is unfaithful, especially with a young woman named Florence in Boston. In my heart I know he is still seeing her whenever he's in Boston on business trips. I've heard the gossip. But he denies it.

I wear gloves when I use the doorknobs to our house. Once inside, I take off my street clothes, place them in the laundry basket, and put on what I call a sterilized jumpsuit. I then go into the den overlooking part of the Long Island Sound, and sit in a plastic-covered recliner that my personal maid has washed with a disinfectant cleaner.

I was not always this way. Earlier in the marriage I hosted many company galas at our house. That in part is how Wendell became the chief executive officer. But he didn't appreciate all the work required to put these things together. He would say that the caterers took care of everything. That bothered me the most. I arranged the catering, and I had to make sure that the house was in perfect order. Perfect order couldn't be left up to the maids. It was a lot of pressure always being "on" while entertaining Wendell's office mates. Rumor had it he was sleeping with one or two of them. The corporate wives and young corporate women executives could be quite judgmental. Everything in the house had to be just so. Plus I had to oversee the children before they left for boarding school because the au pairs were too young to do everything.

Anyway, one day something snapped, and I have never been the same.

The outside world saw a brightly lighted masterful house, butlers, caterers, and dilatants arriving in designer clothes for these dinner parties. To me it was so boring. Even the sparkling champagne dulled my spirits. If I can get a proper settlement, I can move on with my life. Please help.

Katie felt Elizabeth Kent's raw emotions, and was struck by the position she was in—looking into this woman's personal world. Certainly this was not information that Elizabeth Kent told her neighbors. "*Please help.*" This plea stayed in Katie's consciousness for some time.

Katie placed the case memorandum on the right side of her desk, opened the accordion folder, and removed a file labeled "Legal." A copy of the alimony and marital assets statute was penned to the left side. She read silently.

In considering whether to grant alimony, the judge must consider
  how long the couple has been married;
  the money and property that each one brought to the marriage;
  the money and property acquired during the marriage;
  the age, health, occupation, and education of the parties; and
  the cause of the breakdown of the marriage.

Katie compared the factors with the circumstances of her new client. Forty-five years qualified as a long marriage. He has extensive wealth and better health. The cause of Elizabeth's breakdown will be the money-maker for Elizabeth.

Katie would tell Robert Atmore that they needed to gather information about Wendell Kent's affair with Florence in Boston, but she had no ideas on how to gather such private data so quickly. She looked at the court date. Time was running out.

CHAPTER 40

Atmore's Estate Case & Sweet Youth

Katie parked the maroon Mini Cooper in the underground garage and handed her key to the attendant. The firm provided a car for each intern to use.

"Working on a Sunday?" he asked, examining the key ring.

"Got to do some work on a case for next week," Katie replied. "Have a good afternoon!" she added as the elevator shut on her shout. She pressed the PH button by the brass plate labeled *Swarthmore, Jones, & Smithtone*. The elevator ascended to the first of the two top floors of the eighteen-story building.

Stepping into a spacious waiting area, Katie passed the large semi-circular black marble receptionist desk, then walked down a long hallway toward her corner office. The entire floor was quiet and dim. Entering her office she looked out the window at the traffic crossing the 14th Street Bridge. She adjusted the blinds on this bright morning, locked her door, then sat at her desk and removed an accordion file marked "Confidential" from her side drawer.

She had taken it from the closed case file room on Friday. Aunt Margaret mentioned that the firm was handling Marie Merchant's estate, and she wondered what was holding up the will.

Katie squinted as she read the small type on the label. *File 1; File 2.* She lifted the manila envelope labeled "Estate of Marie Merchant— File no. 2" from /the accordion file. She placed its contents, including the Certificate of Death, on her desk.

Marie Merchant. Death from Natural Causes. Aged 82.

On the inventory sheet, the asset column showed the late Marie Merchant to be quite wealthy: nearly five and a half million in total assets. The liabilities column, including moderate funeral expenses, large mortgages, pledges against securities, and taxes, totaled a mere two million five hundred thousand dollars. A copy of the obituary revealed the decedent to have been an active community leader until her later years, and childless. Two letters from a lawyer were addressed to Robert Atmore, dated some time ago.

The first letter opened by stating that before she died Marie Merchant had intended to leave a large amount of money to the D.C. Museum which it had not received. The letter questioned Robert's handling of certain transactions in the estate, and inquired whether he was using estate funds as investments, rather than reconciling the decedent's account. His reply letter assured the addressee that all was well. A second letter from the same lawyer detailed the writer's investigation of the case in the Probate Court and again questioned Robert's handling of the decedent's portfolio of assets. The writer said his client had Power of Attorney authorizing access to the assets. It ended in a threatening tone demanding a clearer explanation, lest the matter be referred to the Probate Judge or to the Lawyer Grievance Committee.

Katie's fingers turned the pages slowly, bypassing numerous Probate Court forms, in search of another response. There it was: a short memo from Robert to the writer proposing a meeting to resolve all misunderstandings. Her fingers hunted for more, without success. She searched the file, but did not find a will.

Marie Merchant had told Margaret that money was coming to her. Just days before her death, she had mentioned how much she valued their friendship—they had sat together on the boards of many civic organizations—and that she wanted to tell her so in this way. The money never came, and Margaret assumed Marie had never gotten around to including her. Now, by chance, Katie had found an opportunity.

Katie had used the firm's identification badge number to retrieve the file from the closed file vault. She made a copy, careful to keep all documents in order, and returned the original. Certainly Robert wouldn't check with the vault clerk about such an unimportant file. Why should he?

It was just after six o'clock in the evening when Katie's curiosity drove her into Robert's office, the only other possible location she had access to that might contain the missing file. Inside the small wooden filing cabinet behind his desk she found the folder: *"Estate of Marie Merchant—Executive File- File #1"* Inside, she found the will.

Voices echoed in the hallway. Katie's eyelids fluttered and she lost her breath.

"Working on the weekend again, Mr. Atmore?"

"No, I just forgot to bring a file home to work on tonight. I won't be in your way."

"Take all the time you need, sir. I finished cleaning your office about an hour ago. You'll find it all in order."

"Thank you, Jim. Have a good evening."

Robert opened the door, and ran his index finger along the wall plate, turning on the overhead light, brightening the room. At his desk, he reviewed some client notes on a yellow pad, and then swiveled to remove a file from his wooden cabinet. He picked up the telephone receiver and read from a piece of paper taken from his shirt pocket, slowly dialing a number.

"Hello. This is Robert."

"Yes, it's a secure line . . ."

"I see."

"There is a lot of money involved here, you know."

"We had agreed on a lower percentage, but that is acceptable."

"A special account in Virginia."

"Then, you'll forget this happened?"

"Good." *Laugh.* "She's dead." "She doesn't need it."

Laugh.

"I'll meet you at Clare's in Arlington. Friday at 5:00. You know where it is?"

"I'll bring everything."

"Fine—November 5 at 5, see you then"

The words sounded like murmurs, but carrying through the door, slightly ajar, of Robert's adjourning small restroom, Katie could make them out. She was sitting on top of the toilet seat with her arms wrapped around her knees, head arched downward, and her ears straining for sound.

She heard desk drawers opening and closing several times, then, footsteps and a door opening and closing. Katie stealthily moved out of the toilet stall while listening for any sign of movement in Atmore's office. Peeking out of the restroom, Katie realized Atmore had left his office. Continuing her surveillance, Katie made a copy of the file, then quickly returned to her office.

Katie breathed a heavy sigh of relief and started reviewing the incriminating documents she had recovered when she heard the footsteps and voices of more than one person coming from the elevators. She turned the light switch off and ducked behind her desk. The footsteps continued past her office. She heard a door open and close. Walking on tiptoes through the hallway outside her office, she passed closed office doors, and followed the faint sounds of human voices emanating from the direction of the conference room. A partially ajar large cherry wood and brass door slowed her pace. The executive conference room was occupied.

Even in its now low and whispered tone, she recognized Robert's distinctive voice. She leaned the bridge of her nose against the edge of the doorframe, exposing only one eye to the inside of the dimly lit room. There was Robert, a young girl on her knees in front of him. She heard the young girl's voice. His right hand stroked her face, and slipped down her neck and inside her blouse.

A door closed in some office down the hallway, and Katie pulled away from the doorway and rushed on her toes toward her office.

He had planned it, though he'd never admit it, even to himself. He'd invited her to his office. Mentor to the brother; mentor to the sister. They'd discussed adolescent troubles, and ideas about future schooling. He had been patient. He had been kind. Robert knew that on this particular Sunday the offices would be empty.

An office retreat occupied the partners and junior associates. His attendance at the retreat had not been required due to a judge's insistence that he start the trial in a high profile divorce case Monday morning. He'd chosen the conference room because of the view, and because of its climate of authority and power. He had his excuse if he was asked: needed to finish preparations for the trial. The girl? A mentee with whom he was discussing her interest in the law.

It had been too easy. He was charming, and he knew it. He took small steps—touching her hand, then pulling back, touching her leg for just a moment, and letting his eyes linger on her body, letting her notice. Letting the hand linger a moment longer on her hand. A slight caress. A touch on the shoulder. Then the face. A comment on beauty. A promise of taking care of her later: the right job.

He heard a door shut down the hall. He stood awkwardly, moved to the door, locked it from the inside and turned off the lights.

He touched her, caressed her, and drew her close. He moved between her legs and she trembled. His movements were slow and soft. Feelings inside her escalated. She trembled long and deep, and then held him tight.

It was their secret, she later agreed, looking at his face and feeling safer than she'd ever known. If they were seen together outside the office, she would call him uncle.

CHAPTER 41

Katie's Plan Revealed

Katie was acting differently. Robert could tell. It would have been imperceptible to anyone else, but Robert watched her closely—too closely, he knew, and he tried not to—but now he was certain that something in her demeanor had shifted. Until recently she had been nearly deferential, and had a calming ease in his presence. He thought that even from time to time she had looked admiringly at him. Now, she hardly looked at him at all. Eye contact was rare. Laughter rarer still. Perhaps she was stressed, he thought. Overburdened. Maybe the job was taking its toll on a young idealist. Still, she seemed . . . what was it? *Suspicious.* He had not done or said anything out of the realm of proper etiquette. Though he had often thought—No, she couldn't know that.

It made Robert uncomfortable, and this was not something to which he was accustomed.

He should check her files. Perhaps she made a mistake and feels guilty. Yes, she had done something wrong and was worried about telling him. Such a good girl, such a hard worker. A perfectionist. Of course.

He entered her office on a Friday evening at eight o'clock and turned the master key to open a cabinet behind her desk. He leafed through six files before he found a file labeled "*Merchant.*" Why did she have a copy of this file, he wondered. Opening it, he read Katie's scribbled notes, in the handwriting he had grown to recognize.

Grievance Committee. Attorney Matthew Wilkinson. Office address, 2400 Garrison Highway, Telephone 202 640 2167. Nov. 5, 11:30 a.m. Bring copy of file.

Sweat formed on Robert's face and he swallowed dryly. Feeling unsteady, he sat at Katie's desk and reread the notes.

My God, he thought. My dear God. She could ruin me.

CHAPTER 42

Governor in Trouble

It has been a while since reporting the goings on related to Janet Mullins, Commissioner Strum's assistant, related to uncovering abuse of foster care children: a revelation that could reverberate to the upper regions of government. Let's take a look.

*　　*　　*

The Governor's Assistant walked up to him and whispered "Russ Maynard on the phone, Sir. Urgent, he said."

Governor Larry Mulvey excused himself from the meeting of commissioners in the executive conference room, entered his office and picked up the telephone on his desk. "Hi, Russ! It's been a long time. How are things?"

"Not bad in my world. But we need to meet."

"Why's that?"

"Can't say on the telephone. We need to meet."

"How soon?"

"Right away. Yesterday. Two weeks ago. I don't have long, and I may not be able to protect you."

Larry exhaled audibly. The Nominating Convention is in less than two weeks. What the hell? A picture of his challenger flew into his mind: the wealthy state senator from the shoreline, a down state woman who had garnered enough support to make Larry's re-election campaign more difficult than it should have been.

"Fine. I can meet you at the Hayward Club."

"Too many players at the Hayward Club. Better we meet in private."

"God, Russ, you're scaring me to death," Larry Mulvey said with a forced chuckle. Russ did not respond.

"Okay . . . can you come to the Capitol?"

"Yes," Russ answered quickly.

"What are you driving?"

"A black Towne Car."

"Use the private entrance. I'll alert security."

"What time?"

"3 o'clock this afternoon."

"See you then."

Larry Mulvey lowered the receiver and felt his blood pressure rising. He fished out a 20 milligram blue pill from his shirt pocket, and poured himself a glass of water from the decanter on the desk. He placed the pill on his tongue, moved it around in his mouth, added water and swallowed.

At 2:55, Russ was sitting impatiently in his car at the entrance to the driveway, peering through the vertical wrought iron black bars separating the public from their elected leader. He stared at the small speaker adjacent to two rotating cameras enclosed in small red metal cubicles on a grey concrete stanchion, willing it to speak.

"You may enter, Mr. Maynard. The Governor is waiting. Take the second parking space near the rear entrance."

"Thank you," Russ answered to the disembodied voice. A metal gate raised smoothly, and the black Towne Car cleared the opening.

The sun was bright, and Maynard wished he were elsewhere. The shore would be nice.

A police officer beckoned the Towne Car to the guest parking space at the rear of the Capitol Building. Capitol security escorted Russ Maynard to an eagerly awaiting Governor. Upon the officer opening the door to the executive office, Larry Mulvey extended a warm hand.

"Russ, I haven't seen you in a while. You look good," Larry said, intently eyeing his old friend.

"You don't look too bad yourself, Larry," Russ replied. "How's the family?"

"Everyone's fine, and unless your news is really bad—well, let's sit at the table over there. I've instructed the staff to bring a pot of your favorite tea." The two men stepped lively toward wing-backed chairs near the corner fireplace. Russ grimaced as he adjusted his seating position and started his report.

"It's the good and the bad of hiring exuberant talent."

"What do you mean?" Larry asked.

"People complain that news is about who was shot, who was robbed, who was sexually assaulted, which building caught fire, or how big the earthquake or storm. And then the war, the war, the war. Over and over again. You can substitute one name for another and the news repeats itself like a damn laundry machine."

"So what?" Larry asked.

"So at the last board meeting, I was instructed to hire three investigative reporters. One of them, a young man from McIntyre School of Journalism in New York, placed a story on my desk. The headline was six words. Would you like to hear them?"

"No."

"*State abandons children: Governor to blame.*"

Larry's eyes widened. His jaw tightened.

"Who is this sonovabitch wannabe who put this story on your desk?" Just then a waiter entered carrying a tray with tea and crackers. Nervously, he asked where to place it.

"Wherever you please!" Larry answered impatiently. He paused and spoke more calmly. "On the coffee table by the couch."

The waiter bowed, turned and exited. He made almost no sound on the hardwood floor, and Russ imagined he was tip-toeing out.

Russ took a long look at his worried friend. They had known each other since high school—thirty years, at least. Larry had all of his hair then. He was the center on the basketball team. Larry Mulvey's reddish-brown hair is thin now, and although he could lose a few pounds, he still had that charismatic "vote for me in November" look that had served him so well. Russ' newspapers had always been a "friend of the Governor." This time would be no exception.

Russ cleared his throat.

"Just say it—all of it—from the beginning," Larry demanded.

"Well, Mark James, the reporter, told me that he was answering the metro phone at the newspaper one day last month when an anonymous woman called and said she had a story. It was about the Child Protection Department and some children in trouble."

"So?" Larry asked.

"She said someone in the department was neglecting children and putting them at risk." Larry folded his arms across his chest.

"I've got the Child Protection Department to look after them. I can't watch over every child. I'm the damn governor. What does this have to do—Sorry. Go on. So what happened to them, to the kids?"

"The woman told James that the children were living in squalor and in horribly dangerous situations."

"Where?"

"In tenement houses on the lower west side, down by Extension Street in the old section of Bridgeport."

"What was the dangerous situation?"

"Not only were the children not being properly clothed and fed, their foster parents were lending them out to perform clean-up jobs for others in the neighborhood, exposing them to environmental hazards, and to child predators."

"Well, that's terrible, of course. But the reporter's story is based upon one telephone call? The caller could be an angry employee, hoping to get a boss in trouble. Did he check that out? Do reporters these days know how to do their—"

"Yes," Russ Maynard interrupted. "He confirmed the story through field interviews in the neighborhood. He actually followed several of the children. He took pictures of them working on construction sites."

"On construction sites? How old?"

"Twelve, thirteen, as long as they are big enough. He said according to sources some of the children were lent out to do work at customers' homes, and foster parents didn't care what happened to them as long as they got the cash."

"How many children?" Larry asked.

"Over a period of a year, at least a hundred."

"What?"

"Maybe more."

"Are you sure?" Larry asked, knowing the answer.

"Unfortunately, yes. I had James verify the sources, and we had an investigator check it out."

"I need to do my own investigation," Larry retorted. "How long can you hold the story?"

"Only a week."

"Why only a week?"

"Because James will wonder why I haven't published it already! He's getting suspicious of my sending him back for more verification. We've already done more than is needed. We're bordering on negligent reporting, and he knows it. He's young, so I've managed to intimidate him, told him he's new in the real world and he must do it the paper's way. But he's suspicious, and he's smart. If something doesn't happen soon, he may leak it."

"Why doesn't he just call the Department of Child Protection?"

"He did. Called the Commissioner's office two weeks ago and someone said it would be taken care of, but . . ."

"Damn it, Russ, I've got an entire state to run!" His typically collected countenance now contorted, Larry shouted, "It's done through my commissioners and department heads! The public works department is responsible for public buildings. The motor vehicle department for registering cars and trucks. The State Police for highway safety, and the State's District Attorney goes after the bad guys who commit crimes." Running out of breath, he lowered his head and concluded. "I can't investigate every damn situation."

"I know that," Russ answered.

"So, why is this James blaming me and not the Child Protection Department?"

"I've read the story he's written—and he quotes from your acceptance speech, the one you gave the night of your election, when you said the future of our state is in the hands of the most vulnerable, our children, whom you pledged to protect. In the view of previous scandals involving foster children, you made child protection one of the corner-stones of your campaign. Exit polls showed that pledge got you a lot of votes. I guess he feels in light of your pledge, you should have assigned someone from your office specifically to oversee the Child Protection Department."

"Damn, if you can't hold this story off—the election is weeks away. What can I do? This is ridiculous." Governor Larry Mulvey knew it was anything but.

"Although I shouldn't advise you—and this must never be said to have been my idea—but you can preempt the story. Before I print James' piece, you call your own press conference and say that reliable sources have given you information about a wide-spread foster care abuse situation in Bridgeport, and that you have prepared an investigation panel, which includes representatives of the legislature, the Child Protection Department, the Concerned Citizens for Child Welfare, and your Chief of Staff, and that the investigation will begin right away. Get ahead of it."

Larry looked up quickly at Russ. This was the path through the valley. His friend had come through for him again. Larry stood slowly.

"That's it. Yes, you're right. God, if you hadn't called—"

"We go back a long way, Larry, and I know you mean to do well. Listen, I'm glad if I can help."

"Should I call the conference now?" Larry asked.

CHAPTER 43

Governor's Strategy

"Is the Committee in place?" Governor Mulvey asked.

Governor Larry Mulvey loved the gothic architecture of the State Capitol Building, his handsome austere office, and awesome views overlooking the Capitol City. He loved this job. But the grandeur of it all did little to calm him. Looking at the magnificence of the office—the hardwood floors, the Persian red and blue carpeting, the portraits of esteemed predecessors—only magnified what Governor Mulvey knew he risked losing.

Larry Mulvey had entrusted Joe Graham, his former campaign manager, now his Chief of Staff, to oversee all of the state deparments, from State Police to Tax Revenue to Child Protection. Five feet two inches tall and only thirty years of age, Joe was known for his toughness with department heads. Larry wondered why Joe hadn't foreseen and stopped the mess at Child Protection.

Sitting on the opposite side of the Governor's desk, Joe removed a document from his brief case, and reviewed it.

"Yes, everything's set," he answered. "The Speaker of the House and the President of the Senate were very disturbed by what I told them surfaced at Child Protection, and each designated a representative to the Committee. They are on board. The leader of the Concerned Citizens for Child Welfare herself agreed to be a member of the Committee, and Mary Strum, Head of CPD will be Chair of the Committee.

"Have they met?"

"No sir, but their first meeting is set for Monday of next week in the Executive Conference Room. The notice of the meeting has been posted, and the media notified."

"Good," Mulvey exhaled. "That should nip this in the bud. We'll get it out before the election. Three weeks to clear it up. On to the numbers?"

Anticipating the question, Joe had already removed another document from his brief case and handed it to Mulvey.

"As you can see here, the breakdown by towns and precincts shows you with a narrow lead. However, Clara Shannon, the junior Senator from down state is gaining. I believe that we can hold her off until the election is over, as she's topped out now. Without a major misstep on our part—which won't happen—our polling people predict you will win with at least 54 percent of the vote."

"Sorry to interrupt, Governor," Beverly, his Administrative Assistant, said, sticking her head into the office. "Commissioner Strum has just arrived."

"Give me a minute," he responded, and turned his attention back to Joe. "How did this one get away from us?" he demanded in a stern voice.

Shaking his head Joe answered, "I don't know. I reviewed my meeting notes with the Commissioner's assistants. They assured me their department was okay and there were no serious issues."

Joe rose, scratched his head as though trying to unearth something meaningful, paused, and then began. "Governor, I think this situation demonstrates that we need a system of better intelligence. Maybe we have to plant our own people in sensitive positions."

"You mean someone in addition to the Department Heads and their Assistants that I specifically appointed? Should we be that paranoid?"

"Afraid so, Governor."

"Well, if we survive this one, and I'm re-elected Governor, I'll certainly consider it."

Joe pressed. "These new people would do field investigations in addition to their surface jobs in the departments. They will look for the dirt, and they too could report to me directly."

"Like I said, if I survive, it's something I will consider . . . Tell Beverly to send in our Commissioner of Child Protection."

"You want me to stay for this?"

"No, I should speak to her privately."

Joe picked up his briefcase, gestured a farewell, and exited the office of a solemn Chief Executive.

Mary Strum, sitting in a winged chair in the outer room, studied Joe's face as he walked to greet her.

"Your turn," he said.

"How is he?" Mary asked, rising to shake his hand.

"Upset, to say the least. Worried about how this serious issue escaped early detection, and how it may undo him and all of us. And he's waiting for you."

Discomfited, Mary entered the Executive Office cautiously. Mulvey did not walk toward her, but faced the window, looking downtrodden.

With his back to her, he asked, "Have you found out how this happened?"

"No," she answered sheepishly.

Turning to face her, Mulvey struggled to restrain his anger. His face reddened, a nervous twitch pulsated near his left cheek, as he resisted the temptation to administer a verbal lashing for the unleashing of this horror. He was angry that this embarrassment is out in the open. He had known about it for at least six months. Word had filtered his way before Mary told him about it, but it was too messy. If the worst happens, he will blame her. If this breaks bad, he will act surprised in public.

"We could lose it all, you know—my job, your job, all of our goals and aspirations for this administration." He pounded the desk, and Mary cringed. "I am so sorry."

Her face looked worn, and was nearly as gray as her dress. She slumped down into one of the leather chairs facing the Governor's desk, and clasped her hands in her lap, looking plaintively at Mulvey.

"I always ask all Regional Supervisors at our weekly Friday morning meetings whether there are any situations in any region that I should know about so that they can be addressed. As I told you last month, I became aware of the problem by accident because the Bridgeport region did not report the problem." Then she added, "At our meeting here last month, you said we should hold off doing anything about it until after the election." Mulvey was silent for a moment.

"I remember," Mulvey replied, sitting in the chair centered at his desk. "I remember, but I hear Senator Shannon is looking for some dirt to close the voter gap, and now I can't risk this leaking out before the election."

"So what's going to happen?" Mary asked, a strain appearing across her face.

"Well, that's why I formed the committee that you are chairing."

Mulvey picked up the report left by Joe on his desk, and scanned the Executive Summary outlining the upcoming investigation. "I've got you, the representatives appointed by the Speaker of the House and by the President of the Senate, and I have the state's favorite child advocate, Matthew Robosky, the President of the Concerned Citizens for Child Welfare advocacy group. If any tragedy befalls a child in state custody, Robosky is there commenting on it before TV cameras and on the front page of newspapers. I decided to bring him inside, and make him part of the solution. As Chair of the Committee you should be able to handle him."

The sense of dread felt by Mary almost lifted. She nodded.

"But still . . . you know the easiest way to solve this, don't you?"

Mary dropped her head.

"But I won't do that. You won't take the fall for this. Not yet anyway. There are still other roads. And this committee is the best."

"I should leave to prepare for next Monday's meeting."

"Of course, but watch out for Robosky. When there's blood in the water sharks can't be trusted."

CHAPTER 44

The Scandal Widens

"Damn it, Russ! You said—"

"It wasn't me, Larry. You know that. This story has tentacles, and I can't be expected to handle each arm."

Larry slapped the leather seat of the Executive Limo, prompting Russ to slide away from him and toward the passenger door.

"Damn it!" He paused. "So what happened?"

"The backer of the political blog is a friend of mine. He told me about their lead story scheduled to be posted on November 1st, four days before the election, lambasting the Child Protection Department and, more directly, you for not fulfilling your pledge to safeguard children."

"How did they get their hands on it? Did your guy—"

"No. It's from a leak inside the department. A woman, Janet, handed over a report tied to you."

"What? How is that possible?"

"It quotes Mary Strum telling you about the foster care problem, and that you told her to wait until after the election."

"My God!"

"Don't worry, my friend. I told him to hold up on the story. That it wasn't complete, and the complete version could backfire on his press. So, even though the young editor is not pleased, they are holding off for the time being. That should at least get you through the election."

Mulvey sighed, and patted Russ's knee, thinking vaguely about how many favors he would owe his friend, and when he might be called on to answer them.

Meanwhile, back at Janet's apartment, she waited until 9 o'clock to call Emanuel.

"Have you seen the story?" he said excitedly.

"What?"

"It's the talk of the town!"

"Uh, no, I just got up, and I was checking in to see how things are going."

"Well, they are exploding!" Emanuel exclaimed loudly, causing Janet to hold the phone away from her ear.

"What happened?"

"My bosses took a chance, said they had heard rumors, and checked with our lawyers who reviewed the memo you gave me from Tom Adams and they said it was enough since the Governor is a public figure—and you know if somebody's a public figure slander doesn't apply if you have a reasonable basis for the story—so we published it on our Internet site, and the regional *Gazette* picked it up and printed it on the front page and now—"

"Take a breath, Emanuel."

"Well, now the Governor must be shaking in his boots," he says.

"Wow . . ."

"It's the talk of the town!" he shouted once again.

CHAPTER 45

The Scandal Erupts

Russ Maynard picked up his intercom before it had finished its first full ring. "Sorry to interrupt, sir."

"What is it?" Russ bellowed.

"Uh . . . Mitch Jackson is on the phone . . . says it's urgent?"

"Is that a question? If it isn't, don't say it like one. You may put him through." *Mitch Jackson*, thought Russ. *Why the Governor ever came up with that as a code name, I'll never know. Sounds like a bad cop name from a bad cop novel.*

"Did you see the front page of the *Gazette* this morning?" Larry Mulvey asked frantically.

"Good morning to you too—"

"It's not a good morning! The article says I was aware of rampart child abuse of some foster children and directed Child Protection to hold off until after the election. The election is in three days and my poll numbers are shaky as it is. They're bound to fall after this disclosure!"

"Well . . ."

"Well nothing, what are we going to do?" The Governor's voice was raised in volume and pitch, and Russ thought that he must certainly have had several coffees already. He could hear the paper rustling in the background. *He's probably sitting there reading it over and over again. Compulsive*, Russ thought.

Russ leaned back in his chair, turned off the speakerphone, and brought the receiver to his ear.

"My sources alerted me to this last night—Stop! Don't interrupt. Obviously, it's also on the Internet—a blogger named Emanuel somebody broke it, we think. Anyway, we've prepared an editorial to run in all of our mainline papers and on our National and International Internet sites. Our paper's editorial, opposing the *Gazette* story, and poking holes in their arguments, will appear in tomorrow's Sunday edition, a circulation far wider than the *Gazette*. With some luck, it should hold your poll numbers enough to get pass the election on the 5th."

Russ could hear silence on the other end. No paper rustling. The Governor's breathing had slowed.

"So . . . we're okay."

"Looks like it."

"Thanks, Russ." And then the click.

"You're welcome, Governor," Russ sarcastically said to the air. "My pleasure."

Russ had been doing this for a long time, and he knew the power of the paper. He knew that overnight polling after Friday's release of the *Gazette* story had revealed Senator Shannon closing the gap—48 percent for the Senator, and 52 percent for the Governor. With a 4 percent margin of error, it was getting uncomfortable.

But Russ knew other things, too. He knew that the Governor would have a restless night and that he'd be up before dawn to retrieve the paper when it landed on his lawn. He knew that the Governor would open the paper to the Editorial page. And just like tens of thousands of other readers, he'd find the bold ink reading:

GOVERNOR TO BE GIVEN BENEFIT OF THE DOUBT

The city would read of the unblemished record of the Governor, and the shoddy journalism used by the *Gazette*. They'd all read—in highlights and bold bullets—all that Governor Mulvey had done for the state. They'd read the call the paper put forth—a call to voters to give the Governor the benefit of the doubt until the Investigation Committee, appointed by him to uncover and correct abuse, is complete.

Russ knew that Larry would feel relieved. And he would convince himself that the editorial was right. Larry Mulvey had done great things for his state. He was meant for this position. He should be trusted.

And then, Russ knew Larry would harness a smile, reflecting on the 800 words in front of him that saved his political career, and then get ready for the last non-political photo opportunity before the election: the stately Governor attending his lovely church on a lovely Sunday with his lovely wife and their three very lovely children.

Newspaper man Russ Maynard stared out the window and looked into the distance wondering if rain were coming.

CHAPTER 46

The Polls

Another restless night. Larry Mulvey slept little, if any, and arrived at the State Capitol at 7:00 on Monday morning carrying a thermos of coffee. Opening the door to the Governor's Suite, he noticed his Chief of Staff Joe Graham sitting in the outer room adjoining the Executive Office.

"You're early," Mulvey announced curiously.

"I just wanted to review some numbers and catch you before the phones start ringing. We've been working all night. The election's tomorrow."

"Don't I know it," Mulvey replied in a dry tone. "Come on in."

Joe followed Mulvey into the Executive office. "Have a seat," Mulvey directed, dropping his briefcase by the desk and taking a sip of his coffee.

Joe removed a sheath of papers from his briefcase.

"I swear you carry around more paper—"

"Yes sir." Joe was in no mood for small talk. "Based upon our checking last night with precinct captains, town leaders and our pollsters, Governor, I'm pleased to report that you are projected to win by a clear 8 percent of the vote."

Larry, Joe had assumed, should have looked like a child rescued from a storm at sea, but his face registered no emotion.

"Thank you," he uttered flatly. "Eight percent is close, but it's good enough."

"Yes sir. The poll data says that without the Editorial yesterday—"

"I know," Mulvey interrupted. "Without it . . . well. We won't have to know that result."

"No sir."

"Well now we will be given another chance. And I'll be sure to incorporate your inter-intelligence model in my next administration, to make sure we don't have another major scandal."

"It's an important safeguard," Joe responded, standing up. "I wanted to give you the vote projection in person, but if you'll excuse me, the campaign committee is expecting me at headquarters this morning."

"Of course," Larry said, rising from his chair. "More paper to produce, I'm sure." He offered an unconvincing line of gratitude. "I'll see you at the polls tomorrow at noon."

CHAPTER 47

Eugene Robinson

While the Governor was fretting about his re-election chances now that the child labor scandal was laid at his doorstep, another of the Governor's appointees was delving into more of the Governor's laundry.

The question made him feel vulnerable, but Eugene Robinson, the new Chief State Prosecutor, asked it anyway.

"Are we doing the right thing?"

His deputy looked back, and answered unconvincingly. "I think so."

The first Black American Chief State Prosecutor, Eugene was known to be cautious. Rumors of wrongdoing in the Governor's office had drifted to him prior to his being appointed Chief, but now he must be careful. One blunder at this level meant an end to further advancement, death of his dream of a judgeship, and certainly no chance at a run for Governor. Worst case, it would signal the end of his career, financial ruin, and political pariah-hood. Mortgage, private school for teenagers, the car—there was too much to think of in this moment, and had his pride not being a governing characteristic, he would have asked the same vulnerable question again.

He was an affable man, slightly rotund, with smooth brown skin and quicksilver focus. Having risen from the ranks of Assistant District Attorneys in short order, he had been widely praised in the media for the way he handled a high profile murder case. His courteous but efficient manner of dealing with colleagues and reducing the back log of criminal cases in his district caught the attention of the Governor's office. With community organizations pressing for the appointment of a minority candidate, and with precious few persons of color in Governor Mulvey's administration, Robinson's name surfaced early. In addition to his exemplary work record, he had been editor of the Law Review at Howard University. Good politics and good personnel—the decision was obvious.

Robinson owed his professional elevation to Governor Mulvey, and Robinson was subtly reminded of it. So was his deputy, Lakisha.

"Are we sure we're looking in the right direction?" It was not the same question. But it was the same question all the same.

Lakisha placed a manila folder on his desk. Eugene picked it up, and leaned back in his chair. Reading aloud from her copy, Lakisha directed him to lines 20-23 on the second page of the affidavit.

> *Confidential sources report lucrative government contracts steered to political contributors by those in Governor's office. Must seek audio/video surveillance by court order immediately.*

"'Confidential sources?' The Lieutenant wants me to apply for an audio/video warrant on 'confidential sources?'" Robinson asked with a frown.

"I'm sure I can have him brief us with greater detail," Lakisha replied.

"The devil's in those details. Without them, and without their showing probable cause that the state's criminal laws are being broken . . ." he trailed off. Chief Robinson would not submit a *confidential sources* warrant application to Judge Hughes. He couldn't. Hughes would not only refuse to sign, he would question motives and process.

"Hand me the conspiracy section of the criminal code," Eugene directed while remaining seated. Lakisha walked to the bookshelf, retrieved Volume 13, and handed it to him. Leafing to Section 53a-48, he read aloud:

> **Conspiracy:** *A person is guilty of conspiracy when, with intent that conduct constituting a crime be performed, he agrees with one or more persons to engage in or cause the performance of such conduct, and any one of them commits an overt act in pursuance of such conspiracy.*

Lakisha listened intently, studying her copy of the affidavit and comparing it with the words of the statute. She focused on the phrases "agrees with one or more persons" and "conduct constituting a crime."

"The crime here is bribery, yes?" Lakisha asked. She removed a second copy of Volume 13 from the bookcase, and turned to Part XI: *Bribery, Offenses Against The Administration of Justice and Other Related Offenses.*

"Take a look at Section 53a-147," Eugene exclaimed. Lakisha turned several pages until she reached Section 53a-147. They both read it in silence.

> **Bribery**: *Class C felony. A person is guilty of bribery if he promises, offers, confers or agrees to confer upon a public servant . . . any benefit as consideration for the recipient's decision, opinion, recommendation or vote as a public servant . . . Section 53a-148:* **Bribe receiving**: *Class C felony. A public servant is guilty of bribe receiving if he solicits, accepts, or agrees to accept from another person any benefit for, because of or as consideration for his decision, opinion, recommendation or vote.*

"Class C felony. 10 years, yes?" Lakisha's voice upturned in more a statement than a question. She had a habit of asking facts, to avoid, Eugene supposed, the appearance of precociousness.

"But why does the Lieutenant want a warrant for the Governor's office?" Eugene wondered aloud. "Could a chief administrative aid or a commissioner be involved? But then why not a warrant specifically for their offices?"

Lakisha was silent, wisely. Speculation would be unhelpful at this point, Eugene knew. Hope was unhelpful too, though he could not help but hope deeply that there was no bribery. A scandal in the Governor's administration would threaten public confidence and stall the ability of their office, among many others, to function effectively. What a tragedy. But a tragedy it would be too for a state official to fail to prosecute those involved.

"We need the details right away," Eugene demanded, leaning forward.

"I'll call the Lieutenant," Lakisha responded, and walked out briskly.

Sitting down at her own desk, she looked at the two office decorations given by her mother: a floral oil painting on the wall and a Turkish rug in front of her desk, both complimented by a large brass urn courtesy of the local antique store. This was a call she would remember. She needed her bearings before dialing. Slowly she exhaled three deep breaths, then picked up the phone.

"Is the Lieutenant in?"

"Who's calling?"

"Deputy Chief Prosecutor Lakisha Jones."

"Regarding?"

"He's expecting my call."

A few moments passed.

"Hello, Prosecutor Jones, Lieutenant Ramsey here. How's the warrant coming?"

"Chief Robinson won't sign it. He needs the details, and rightly so. We need to know the confidential sources. And we need to know what they know. This must be spelled out concretely, and documented in the warrant—"

"Lakisha, this isn't an exercise in power playing. The information is from one of our confidential informants, one of *ours*. We placed him, we monitored, and last weekend we 'arrested' him, together with the guys he was placed with—drug possession with intent to sell—at a motel in Clinton. We put him in the police lock up with the others until they go before the Judge in Court on Mon—"

"Sorry to interrupt, but—" Lakisha needed the point.

"Stay with me. The informant said when the guys were discussing possible heavy sentences in the lock up—it was a big drug bust, you'll read about it I'm sure—one fellow boasted he wouldn't be doing any time because he has a big surprise for the prosecutors: he'll rat out somebody in public office. Next thing we know, our informant said he sees this guy just walking around town."

"So the District Attorney turned this braggart into an informant."

"You got it."

"Okay, so, how does that help me with the details?" Lakisha pressed.

"Keep listening. So we checked it out. It was true. The DA took the guy's story, turned him into a confidential informant. Not only did we get his statements, we videotaped him at the police station.

Also we picked up one of the guys, named Lucius, who then ratted out one of the big money givers."

"That was lucky."

"Tell me about it. Turns out we had some dirt on this guy and we threatened to bust him if he didn't cooperate."

"Did he?"

"Oh, yes he did, and he named the group that gave him the dollars for those in high places and the money he delivered."

"And you have all that documented?"

"Of course. Hell, we sleep with that Investigative Manual. Some of the guys get it as a tattoo."

Lakisha picked up her favorite black fountain pen, leaned forward on her desk, and drew a line left to right at the top of a yellow double lined legal pad. Atop the line she wrote *documented*. "So, let's see, Lieutenant—I'm just making a list. We have your *guy, Informant 1*. Care to name him?"

"Might as well—you'll get a chance to interview him. Name's Fred"

Lakeisha wrote *Fred* to the right of *Informant 1*. "Now we have your newly made Confidential Informant. Name?"

"Mike."

"And then we have your courier, the guy who delivers the money. What's his name?"

"For the time being, let's call him Ratner."

"And what documents do we have for Ratner?"

"Affidavits. Ratner is cooperating, and we're setting him up with a wire. Also we have videotapes."

"When can I get a copy of the affidavits and videotapes?"

"I'll have the Sergeant drop everything off first thing in the morning."

"Good," Lakisha said, and paused. "Is this for real?"

"It is. Though I can't say it makes me happy."

"That makes two of us. I'll call you."

She hung up, looked once more at the floral painting, and began to transfer her notes to the computer. Eugene stood at her doorway with downcast eyes. Lakisha looked at him and nodded.

*   *   *

Meanwhile, the police were taking no chances that their informant's testimony might not be deemed sufficient for an arrest warrant.

The computer repairmen were there to install a special series of cables for the purposes of safeguarding communications among executive offices. One couldn't be too careful, they had said, and everyone had nodded. They looked impeccably official, having arrived in a paneled white truck with black company lettering: *Computers International.* The driver said from the beginning that the name was rather unimpressive, but was shouted down by his comrades, who said they were in police work, not advertising. They presented official looking documents to the guards at the front door of the State Capitol, and explained that they were working the night shift so that the system would be in place for the conference scheduled to start the next afternoon.

In the glove compartment of the van were two copies of the surveillance warrant. At the bottom of both documents were the signatures of Prosecutor Eugene Robinson and Judge Samuel Hughes.

CHAPTER 48

Evidence

"Gene, take a look at this," Lakisha shouted, staring at the video monitor on the corner desk in the office library.

Startled, Eugene Robinson dropped his law book on the long oak table, quickly rose from his chair, and walked toward Lakisha. The whites of his eyes widened as he bent down and studied the familiar figure on the screen.

"Where did you get this?"

"Our Confidential Informant surveillance team."

Eugene crossed his arms and leaned back on his haunches. "Can you turn up the volume?" he asked.

"*And that's why it has to wait. Don't you understand? That's why . . .*" Governor Mulvey's words rose in crescendo as he sat forward in his seat, extended his hand, and took a white envelope from the man seated on the other side of the desk.

Eugene didn't recognize the other man. He was much younger and much thinner than Mulvey.

"*But Governor, the children are in danger, and somebody must do something,*" the young man's voice pleaded—"*a scandal would be bad for business.*"

Lakisha and Eugene watched as Governor Mulvey stood up, turned his back and looked out his office window.

Eugene wondered where the camera was placed. The images and sounds captured on the video in the Executive Chamber of the Governor's Office were so clear: the deep blue carpeting with the white and gold state seal at its center, the massive mahogany desk, flanked by the blue and white state flag, the Queen Anne Couch—all paid for by the citizens of the state. And the white envelope. Yes the white envelope now lays in the center of the Governor's desk.

Mulvey removed his hands from his pockets, stroked his chin, and turned toward his visitor. He paused, then lowered himself into his seat, and began speaking.

"Please turn it up just a little more, I think I'm getting hard of hearing sometimes," Eugene said.

"Yes, sir," Lakisha replied.

Governor the boys just want you to know how much we appreciate the state contracts. Our guys have children—you know, families to feed. We also pay taxes, you know," said a large man in a black suit and tie, standing near the Governor's desk. *"Also our money helps you and the misses out. I hear one of your children is about to go off to college, it's a help, right?"*

Mulvey's face flushed with embarrassment. It all began so innocently, it seemed. Just a small contract favor for a "connected" friend—then down on his luck. One favor led to another, and it was so easy. Now, he's dependent, easy money is like drugs, and they could blow the whistle."

Eugene examined the worried look on Mulvey's face. Mulvey's face brightened as he picked up the envelope from his desk and opened it.

"Is it all here?"

"Yes, Governor, it took some doing, but the boys scrapped the cash together. They want to know when the contract bids will be approved."

"Next week. Tell them it's all set."

CHAPTER 49

Atmore's Crisis

Let's return to see how Attorney Robert Atmore is fairing.

*   *   *

Unable to concentrate, Robert Atmore closed a client's file on his desk and felt a corner of the file pierce his index finger. He looked at the bit of blood on his hand and wondered how long it had been since he'd gotten a paper cut.

He interlocked the fingers of his hands behind his head and leaned back in his chair. She wouldn't do it. Would she? Turn him in to the authorities for stealing the dead client's money—would she?

He would speak with her. She had simply misunderstood. She was young and inexperienced, and had stumbled upon something she did not fully comprehend. He would patronize her.

If that didn't work, he would intimidate her. He was powerful. He could ruin or build her career. She was at his mercy.

He had ten strategies moving at once, much as he did in the courtroom. But at this moment, with the air burning the small bit of sliced skin, he knew none of them would work. Damn her young integrity. She would not fold.

He must get rid of her.

It was absurd, he knew. But he must entertain all options. How? It must be done by someone in the criminal world. He could not get too close. Direct contact and they would own him, and use him for their purposes. Tit for tat they would say, and he would soon be representing gangsters from New York to Chicago. God! What was he thinking? He knew he hadn't the stomach for it. Stealing a couple of million from a dead woman was hard enough, now killing—He'd crumble. Or get caught.

In his mind, Robert ran over a list of his clients. Charles. Charles what's his name. *Charles Murphy.* Charles Murphy had connections. It's coming back to him now. He was growing excited.

A decade ago Charles Murphy, then in his fifties, sat in Robert's office looking out of place. He was a referral from the local bar association's pro bono program. Dressed in a faded black and red plaid shirt and blue jeans, Charles looked like a farmer in the city—a blue collar man in a white collar world. Robert felt the class struggle across his desk. Robert, a high-ranking, hard-charging lawyer, was tasked to represent this man, and to treat him as professionally as those who paid the full, exorbitant fees.

But something in Charles' pained eyes drew Robert's empathy. He looked beneath the pale dry skin of Charles' square jaw and wrinkled face. Charles was hurting—not physically, but at a deep emotional level.

He came to Robert not just to defend him in a divorce, but to avenge his honor, and he was almost penniless. He complained that after putting all of his few precious dollars into the marriage, his wife, Carol, left him for another man and took his daughter, Victoria, with her, allowing him no visitation rights. Charles said Carol bragged that she named the baby Victoria because another man's sperm created her, making her, the mother, victorious over him. After saying it, he could not speak for several minutes.

Carol wanted alimony while at the same time sleeping with yet another man. Robert advanced funds from the firm's account to hire a private detective to confirm Charles' story of a cheating wife and to identify the man complicit in her deceit. Within a few days the detective confirmed his story, and provided Robert and Charles with the man's name: Travis.

Weeks later Charles confided to Robert that he had met a man at his rooming house who had a "contact." The meeting had been arranged and a fee discussed. A few days later the "contact" initiated the plan. Two men parked their van on a city street in broad daylight, and called out "Travis!" A man in his 40s, walking on the sidewalk, turned and answered, "Yes."

Before he could scream, his arms were pinned behind him and his face pressed against the cold aluminum of the van. One man whispered the name Victoria in his ear while the other swung a baseball bat with the force of a professional.

Minutes later, as the van sped away, Travis lay unconscious on the bloodstained pavement. He would forever walk with a cane, unless he raised money for knee replacements. Travis vanished from town.

Robert told Charles to tell no one, and to stop smiling about it.

Charles was pleased with how Robert handled his divorce. Robert called him to the witness stand during the trial, and Charles testified that his wife named the baby "Victoria" because she was sired by another man, making her, the wife, victorious over him, and it broke his heart. After Charles stepped down from the witness stand and joined Robert at the lawyer's table Judge Healy, the judge presiding over the divorce case, asked Dan Nichols, the wife's lawyer whether he had any witnesses. He responded by asking Judge Healy for a recess.

During the recess Robert allowed the wife's lawyer to speak with Bruce Doyle, his private investigator, about his report. They talked in the hallway outside the courtroom, and outside of Robert's presence. Doyle was retired FBI and knew the ropes. Robert knew that after attorney Dan Nichols sized up Doyle, and discussed the report, the opposition and the alimony claim would fold. Adultery was, after all, a criminal offense in those days.

Robert reviewed his copy of the report with Charles while Dan Nichols talked to investigator Doyle. Sitting on one of the hallway benches, Robert, using his right index finger, directed Charles' attention to lines 18 through 25 of the last page.

> It's 9:00 p.m. the lights in the bedroom window of apartment B-12 go out. 10:30 p.m. lights back on. 10:45 p.m. Carol and Travis walked hand-in-hand to her car parked about 20 feet from the entrance of the apartment building. He opened the door for her. She sat in the driver's seat. He bent down and kissed her through driver's side window. Travis stood there, watching as she drove off. He waved and blew a kiss.

They won the case. No alimony and ample visitation rights.

If only Robert could locate Charles.

Robert stood up behind his desk, stretched, and walked to the closed files room. He pulled open the cabinet labeled M-Z, and retrieved the file captioned "Murphy, Charles." Most of the contents, such as court pleadings, and legal research memos, had been discarded to save file space; but the intake sheet showed his address: *40 Mount Pleasant Street.* Phone: *None.* Robert jotted down the address, and returned the file to the cabinet. He needed to talk to Charles right away.

Robert left his office and headed for the elevator. As he waited, June, the receptionist, reminded him of his two o'clock appointment.

"Yes, I know, I'm taking an early lunch. I'll be back in time."

He was sweating.

The elevator descended to the basement where Robert's black Jaguar waited. As he emerged, bright sunlight struck his eyes, and he pulled his sunglasses from the visor. He had not visited the Mount Pleasant area since law school. He lived in the neighborhood because of the cheap rent. He recalled walking home from the law library one night and discovering a dead body on the sidewalk next to his apartment building.

Approaching the next intersection off the 14th Street artery, Robert activated the left turn signal and slowed the Jaguar to a crawl, narrowing his eyes and focusing on the even numbers on the right side of the street: 10 . . . 22 . . . Number 38 was a tall multifamily. The next building, pea green, long and low, was 40. He pulled the car to the curb and killed the engine.

Long baggy pants and shirts hanging low on passersby made Robert sense that his black leather briefcase on the back seat was in jeopardy. He pressed the automatic release latch, grabbed the briefcase, secured it in the trunk and turned on the security alarm. Feeling the gaze of several young men hanging out across the street, Robert cast a look over his shoulder as he walked up the steps of 40 Mount Pleasant. He was about to ring the bell at the faded light brown colored front door when a young man in blue jeans and a white t-shirt interrupted.

"Don't bother with the bell, it don't work . . . been busted for a year. Super never fixed it. Excuse me," the young man said as he walked past Robert.

Robert called out. "Maybe you can help me. I'm looking for a man named Charles Murphy. He lived here a long time ago. You know him?"

The man slowly moved his right hand across his forehead as though Braille reading the tiny bumps on his face.

"No, can't say I ever heard of him. Haven't been here too long. Ask the man in the room at the left end of the hall. He's an old timer; he may know."

Squinting to adjust to the dim interior, Robert walked to room 11. He knocked on the door. No sound. He knocked again.

"Coming," someone called. Robert fidgeted. The door opened a crack. A balding, gray-haired occupant stuck his head through the doorway. Robert thought he must be at least seventy.

"Yes?"

"I'm looking for an old friend. His name is Charles Murphy. A long time ago I gave him a ride home to this building. Do you know him?"

The man eyed Robert suspiciously. Robert protested.

"No, I'm really a friend who hasn't seen Charlie in years. Just want to see him for old time's sakes. That's why I came today."

The man stroked his chin, glanced down the hallway then fixed his stare on Robert.

"Charles Murphy, you say? What does he look like?"

"Broad shoulders, about five foot ten, square type face with a mole on his left forehead."

The description matched the man's friend who lived on the second floor, room 22. He and Charlie ate lunch, swapped stories and played cards almost every day. Charlie suffered a minor stroke last year, and he wasn't about to send him any more trouble. Robert didn't look the type to have been an old friend of Charlie's. Charlie dressed in country, not business casual.

"He moved out West last year to be near his family."

"Where out West?"

"Washington State . . . Seattle . . . somewhere near a lake there."

"Do you have his address?"

"No, I had it. He sent me a card with a picture of the lake, but I lost it. Waiting for him to send me another. Seattle . . . the lake . . . that's all I remember . . . sorry."

Robert thanked him and returned to his car. He certainly didn't have time to go looking around Seattle. Several jury trials are on his calendar. In fact, a deposition in one of them is scheduled for the next week. There are long hours from now until his vacation—still several months away. He just doesn't have the time to go searching.

He sat down in the sun-warmed car. What can he do?

Maybe Bruce Doyle could locate Charles. If Bruce didn't have Charles' photo, he'd know how to get one. Robert turned on the ignition and guided the Jaguar away from Mount Pleasant. Driving a little too fast to his two o'clock appointment, Robert worried that Bruce—retired FBI and now private detective—would not be able to find Charles in time.

November 5th is six days away.

CHAPTER 50

To Seattle

Bruce Doyle convinced Robert that the term "expenses" included business class, especially for such a long cross-country trip. At 36,000 feet, and moving at 550 miles per hour, the Boeing 737 jetliner would set down on the Seattle runway by 4 p.m., enabling Bruce to settle into his hotel suite by dinner time.

Bruce pushed a button on the right console. His plush leather seat reclined. He smiled, gave himself a good stretch, crossed his legs, and having the advantage of the window seat, the complimentary glass of chardonnay, and no passenger next to him to disrupt his concentration, looked out into the cloudless sky miles above Mother Earth. Upon pushing another button, tiny rollers embedded in the seat massaged his back. The quiet, powerful, soothing surge of the plane reminded him of the force of the bullet train gliding on magnetic energy above the rails he rode in Tokyo last year. Aerospace, he thought, is grand.

Bruce retrieved a photo of Charles Murphy from his briefcase. Robert Atmore's law firm had a custom of keeping a photo of its clients in a secure cabinet. Concentrating, he burned Charles' image into his mind, although the mole on Charles' forehead made it somewhat easier. Also the photo refreshed Bruce's memory of Charles from the divorce. Bruce closed his eyes. His thoughts drifted to his wife.

"Don't honey-bunny me," he remembers her saying in protest to his taking the Seattle assignment. She had told him well in advance about the special event their son was starring in at the school and how important it was for him to be there. The middle teen years can be so hard on a boy, she had reminded him. As though he needed reminding, he had blocked out entirely his own fourteenth year. He really must spend more time with his son. Though how. . . . he did not know.

Bruce was comforted by his plan to take another job that would allow him to spend more time in their town. He'd bring Eric something special from Seattle: maybe that and a good apology would do for this time.

The plane landed smoothly. At the Ground Transportation Counter at Seattle-Tacoma International Airport, Bruce collected the keys for the dark, late model Ford waiting in the uncovered parking lot, and walked to the car in Seattle's intermittent rain, which the locals called liquid sunshine. Heidi, his secretary, had made his hotel arrangement. Tomorrow he would find Charles Murphy.

Bruce prided himself on being punctual. He left the hotel at eight a.m. sharp, and was determined to find Charles before noon. Nothing's special about noon, only a benchmark to set the pace. He turned the ignition switch of his non-descript Ford and directed it onto the boulevard alongside the Hondas, Camrys, Chevrolets, and other bland mobiles. He'd been to Seattle before, and had never seen a car with any personality.

Multi-colored pontoons, yellow, green, blue and orange, floating in a lake parallel to the roadway added visual spice to a partly cloudy forecast. Although a picturesque site on this partly sunny morning, the water views were distracting. He was here on business, not pleasure. Noticing the up-tick of early morning work hour traffic, Bruce adjusted his rear view mirror, and pressed harder on the accelerator.

His first stop: Department of Motor Vehicles.

After explaining his ex-FBI status to the DMV manager, an employee handed Bruce a note with Charles' new address, and a complimentary copy of his motor vehicle record.

A half-hour later Bruce rang the doorbell at 235 Shore Drive, a magnificent three-story white Victorian perched on a hill overlooking Lake Washington, a long way from the rooming house on Mount Pleasant, in physical and economic distance. A young man—twelve, perhaps, a bit younger than Bruce's own son—answered the door.

"Yes, may I help you?" he said.

"I am looking for Charles Murphy. I was told he lives here."

"Oh, you're looking for my granddad—your name?"

"Bruce Doyle."

"Have a seat on the porch, Mr. Doyle. I'll get him."

Bruce sat in one of the white wicker chairs and admired the sunlight refracting off the lake.

Lucky guy, this Charles, Bruce thought.

A moment later the front door opened and out stepped a middle age man with a mole on the left of his forehead.

"I'm Charles Murphy . . . heard you were looking for me."

"Yes, Mr. Murphy, I'm Bruce Doyle, remember me? Private Investigator, I do work for attorney Robert Atmore. He hired me for your divorce case. That was a while back."

Charles grimaced at the mention of the divorce, but cleared his voice.

"Oh, yes, I remember. You caught my wife with that guy. Brought the report to court showing them together, while she said she wanted alimony from me ... all the while bragging she was victorious because he was the father of our child, ... naming the child Victorious," Charles responded, looking down."

Bruce retrieved an item from his wallet. "Here's his card. He's with the firm of Swarthmore, Jones & Smithstone in Washington, D.C."

Charles took the card. Come on in, Mr. Doyle." Charles escorted Bruce into a large living room and directed him to an armchair near a miniature baby grand piano.

"Nice house."

"Thank you. It belongs to my daughter and her husband. They are good enough to let me live here for the time being. May I get you something? Coffee . . . a glass of water?"

"No, thank you."

"What may I do for you?" Charles asked as he sat opposite Bruce.

"This is a little delicate, Mr. Murphy."

"You may call me Charlie."

"Well, Charlie, Robert Atmore may be in a little trouble so he sent me here to see whether you can help him."

"Me, help him? How can I help him?"

"No, no . . . not you personally."

"Then . . . how?"

"Mr. Atmore said that something happened to the man who was seeing your wife."

A frown crawled across Charles' face.

Bruce backtracked. "No, I'm not concerned about that man. It's just that Mr. Atmore . . . needs the services of the people who took care of that situation for you."

Charles pressed back into his chair and crossed his arms. A few moments of silence passed as he studied the face of his new acquaintance, searching for any hint of trouble.

"Why didn't lawyer Atmore call me directly?"

"Because it's a delicate matter. He can't trust using the telephone. Too much government surveillance these days. That's why he sent me personally. And by the way, the man in Room 11 in Mount Pleasant is waiting for a letter from you."

"Rod? How do you know about Rod?"

"Mr. Atmore found him while he was looking for you."

A small smile formed on Charles' face.

"Come back tomorrow. I'll make the call this afternoon."

Charles didn't invite Bruce in a second time. When he returned the next day, Charles met him with an envelope at the door.

"I've made the contact. Instructions are in the envelope. They're expecting your call."

"Thank you. Here's my card. If there's anything Mr. Atmore or I can do for you, just let me know."

"Thank you, Bruce. I'm sorry to hear that lawyer Atmore needs help. But he deserves this favor. He went out of his way, for free, and incurred all that expense, getting a private investigator and all to take care of my divorce. Give him my best."

On the plane ride back home Bruce considered the situation, and wondered whether he should take the lead for Atmore. He knew the general location of the D.C. address on the paper that Charlie gave him. Pretty troubled neighborhood, but he could handle that. He still had a permit to carry his Glock 36 laser sight automatic with hollow point bullets. Nobody messes with these. And if the undercover police in that neighborhood saw him, he could always say he was working a special assignment.

It's still too risky, Bruce thought. He has a private detective license to protect. Better to use one of his deep contacts to make the arrangement. He'd give them Katie's photograph and office address. That simple. After all, he told himself while he sipped the Chardonnay and peered out at the feathery clouds, there are millions of people in this world. One fewer won't destabilize the planet.

CHAPTER 51

Tony and Ralph

In the darkness of the evening, Tony and Ralph sat on a low dingy concrete wall on 16th Street across from the neighborhood bar. Surprised by Tony's appearance, Ralph asked where he got his homeless clothes.

"Salvation Army and a little rolling around in the dirt. It's D.C., man. Nobody notices the homeless."

"How much did you have to pay the regulars?"

"Less than you'd think."

Ralph had joined Tony's group looking for a "career path," but his faded blue jeans and brown pullover sweater bought from a surplus military store provide little evidence of this being a successful vocation. Ralph's wide shoulders riding above his muscular frame belied a semi- submissive personality—all qualifications that Tony required. So far there had been only small jobs— limited loan-sharking, and boosting stolen cars. Then this. The first chance to make some real money before the holidays. $25,000 for each of them. They needed only to scare her off. They must find her home, her haunts, her habits, and then exploit them. Fear was the goal, and the tool.

"Been two weeks now," Ralph said. "Where are we?"

Tony pulled out a small spiral note pad. "We know where she lives, works, shops, her favorite restaurants and take out places. Her schedule's packed and predictable."

"Good."

"So what happens next?" Ralph asked.

"They'll tell me next week. I've got a hunch."

Ralph nodded.

"Don't ask me that."

"What?" Ralph asked, surprised.

"You want to know why."

His thoughts had been read. "It's a good question. Why this girl?" Ralph inquired, "She seems innocent enough. She volunteers for God's sake."

"You know, sometimes its better we don't know," Tony answered. "She's a woman at a law firm. I'm guessing she's a whistle blower who needs the wind knocked out of her. Come on, let's get a beer."

Ralph looked at Tony again.

The yellow light inside O'Sullivan's bar flattered no one, but most had blurred vision anyway. Dim lights, dark wood floors, and tall bar stools complimented lonely bodies. Three women sat at the bar, smiled at each other and looked too often into a long mirror behind the bottles of whiskey, gin, vermouth, and scotch standing at attention like gentry soldiers. In a well between the mirror and the patrons a bartender chatted up his customers.

The bartender tossed down two napkins.

"Whiskey for me; draft beer for my clean friend," Ralph directed.

The smiling ladies stood with their drinks and retreated to a table diagonal to the two men. Ralph's eyes followed them, and Tony's followed his.

"Don't stare," Tony hissed.

"Damn."

"Like that over there?" Tony asked.

"Huh?"

"The redhead you're scoping out. I thought you had a girlfriend."

Ralph settled onto the bar stool and turned his face toward Tony. "I do, but I ain't dead. Anyway, let's talk about what we've got to do."

"You nervous?"

"So what kind of job is it?" Ralph asked. "To scare her off, knock her around a bit, or what?" Tony paused, looking into his beer glass searching for answers in the amber, and glanced up at Ralph.

"Nobody lives forever."

"What the fuck you mean? Aren't we just supposed to scare her?"

"It will scare her."

Ralph put his drink down and removed a pack of cigarettes from his shirt pocket. "No smoking in here," the bartender warned. "Sign says—"

"Fine—but I need another drink."

"Same?"

"Yes."

Another whiskey arrived. Ralph is quiet, and has forgotten to look back over at the redhead.

"Worried?" Tony asked.

"Always. *Damn.* Why didn't you tell me?"

"This is your first. Gotta get prepared for it. But you'll be fine."

"How do you know?"

"Because the payment is really $50,000 each."

Ralph looked at him sharply.

"For the trouble."

Ralph felt like he couldn't breathe. Fifty thousand dollars! That's way more than just scare them money.

Tony fidgeted on the bar stool while Ralph looked again at the three women. The redhead's eyes caught his, and she turned quickly away. He could barely see only one of her legs, but it was enough. He wondered why beautiful legs and a pretty face turned him on. It must be a hard-wired thing, a genetic response. Dark red hair, a sculptured face, bright eyes, and a radiant complexion. A low-cut dress slithered down her body and stopped just above the knee. Sensing his gaze, she wiggled her ankle back and forth, and then slowly up and down. Tony nudged Ralph with his elbow, shaking him out of his daze.

"Look at that." Ralph said.

"Huh?"

"Her."

"Man, I can't think about that right now; I gotta think about this—"

"Do you know the young lady in the red dress?" Ralph asked the bartender.

"Sure, she's kind of new. Comes here with the other ladies most Thursdays after work."

"I'm offering to buy them the next round of drinks," Ralph said, handing the bartender a fifty. "Keep the change and tell them they are from Tony and Ralph."

A smile on the bartender's face revealed two missing teeth south of the left front low incisors.

"It's been taken care of," he said, pocketing the note.

"And tell them we'll see them next Thursday, when we'll be buying the rounds," Ralph exclaimed in a full-throated grin.

"Come on," Tony directed. "Let's go and get the details."

The redhead's eyes followed the two men out the door; one man thinking of money, the other of death.

CHAPTER 52

Suspicious

Katie considered the phenomenon—having witnessed the misdeeds of others, she was behaving like the guilty one. Not meeting Robert's eyes. Not sleeping well. Reliving scenarios. Looking over her shoulder.

A man near the subway entrance looked at her, and then looked away. Did she know him? He did not look at her again.

She rode the gleaming aluminum and steel escalator down seven stories into Kennedy Station, passed through the turnstile, and stood on the platform watching the lights pulsate through the circular glass panes on the station floor—announcing the arrival of the subway car. In the car, she took the last empty seat across from two students—one wearing a Howard University jersey and the other a Georgetown baseball cap.

She removed a file from her briefcase.

"Howard's gonna win," one student said as the subway train surged forward.

"That's ridiculous!" the other student shouted.

Katie smiled to herself. Her father would be watching that game. She glanced up and down the aisle. No one was looking back.

"Next Stop Columbus Circle."

Scores of people exited at Columbus and joined her on the steep escalator climbing eighty feet to daylight. In the sun, she was greeted by a homeless man shuffling with a plastic cup extended.

"Quarter, Ma'am?"

Katie slowed her pace, retrieved a few coins from her right jacket pocket and dropped them in the cup.

"God bless you, Ma'am."

Katie briefly caught his gaze.

His teeth were white.

She looked away and regained her gate, wondering how a new transient had gotten permission from the regulars to beg at the corner. She retrieved her keys from her jacket and held them in her hand as she neared the steps of the brownstone apartment.

Upon opening the apartment door, Katie was greeted by a smiling Maria. "How's it going?"

"Good," she replied, aware of how unconvincing she sounded. She grabbed a yogurt from the fridge and tossed herself into a chair facing the window. Children were playing in the backyard of the adjacent brownstone house.

"How was the first day?" Katie asked.

"Pretty good. I have a little badge that says 'Apprentice.' Isn't that hilarious? Like I'm living in the Renaissance. I watched the workers arrange all types of flowers. It was crazy—much more complicated than I thought. What about you?"

Katie scraped the bottom of the blueberry yogurt container, brought the spoon to her lips, and turned it upside down in her mouth.

"Oh, I don't know," Katie answered.

"Say, something's bothering you. What is it?"

"It's the case they gave me. I've just gotten involved trying to help this young girl who's having a hard time listening to her parents."

"What about her?"

"She's in Juvenile Court as a run-away. Disobedient to her parents . . . 'oppositional defiance' they call it," she said, looking away. "I'm trying to get through to her, but she won't confide in me." Katie looked out the window. The kids had gone inside.

"Individuation," Maria said, partly to herself. "Gotta push against authority, right?"

"Like a bird pushing against the shell."

"We did it too."

"Not like this," Katie insisted. "We never talked back to our parents the way she yells at hers—right there in court. And we never stayed out all night."

"Well, that's true. We knew Mom and Dad wouldn't put up with it."

"But there's something else."

"What?"

"She's acting too much like a woman. I'm sure she's sleeping with her boyfriend."

"Are you sure?"

"No, but I have my suspicions."

They sat together in silence. The empty container of yogurt lay on its side.

"I think someone is following me."

"What?" said Maria as a strained look appeared on her face. "You're kidding."

Katie looked at Maria.

"You're not kidding?"

"It's a feeling I have. There's this man, homeless-looking guy. And—well, it's hard to explain.

"Is someone bothering you?"

"No, there's not anyone . . . it's just . . . I can't put my finger on it."

CHAPTER 53

Gary Maxwell, U.S. Marshal

The United States Marshal Service is a federal law enforcement agency within the Department of Justice. The Marshals Service is part of the executive branch of government and is the enforcement arm of United States federal courts. The US Marshals are responsible for the protection of court officers and buildings. They also serve warrants and capture fugitive.

The hiring for the US Marshal Service is fiercely competitive and its training program is one of the toughest in the United States. Gary Maxwell passed with flying colors. When U.S. Marshals are not making arrests, they can be found protecting government officials, processing seized assets of major crime rings, relocating and providing new identities for federal witnesses in the Federal Witness Protection Program, and transporting hardened felons to supermax prisons in distant parts of the country.

Four massive propellers of the grey C-130 cargo plane produced an almost deafening sound amplified by the rattling of chains restraining some of the most dangerous felons America has known—now in this large wide steel and aluminum flying tube headed skyward to a secure undisclosed destination. After delivering this group of criminals, Gary and the nine other U.S. Marshals look forward to well-deserved R & R.

Gary had an eerie feeling. He released his seat buckle and walked down the aisle carefully watching the men in orange prison suits shackled to metal armrests in each seat—some looking at the sky through tiny meshed windows, others frowning with hate filled eyes as he passed by. Upon reaching the door of the rear cabin—the

214

space housing government-issued bulletproof vests, ammunition and sawed-off shotguns—he inserted his key and took one step inside.

"What the hell!" Gary shouted, startling fellow Marshal Leo York whose nightstick hovered for another blow. "Stop!" Gary yelled then grabbed Leo's hand forcing him to drop the black weapon. An older man, blood tricking from his right ear, looked up in horror. A thick brown leather strap wrapped around his waist and anchored to iron eye bolts on the floor restrained his movement, with only his arms raised for protection.

"Let me go!" Leo yelled. "This son of a bitch killed my nephew. I'm gonna bust him up."

"No I didn't!" the man sobbed, "I don't know what you're talking about."

"Shut up, you piece of shit! My brother said it was your goons that beat his son to death."

"What?" the man muttered.

"In the Bronx, that's where!" Leo yelled.

Gary quickly studied the situation: the man in orange prison garb shaking on the floor in fear, fresh bruises around his eye sockets, blood trickling down his sallow face; Leo shouting and straining to deliver more blows; the smell of death and sweat in this barely lit cabin three thousand feet in the air.

Accessing the revenge stored in his 180 pound body, Leo pushed Gary back, grabbed the man's throat encircling it with both hands, and pressed down hard, both thumbs on his Adam's apple. The man's eyes bulged, his legs fluttered. "You mobster sonavabitch," Leo screamed . . .

Using a jujitsu maneuver, Gary lunched at Leo, twisted him to the floor, and handcuffed his hands behind his back.

"Not on my watch, Sergeant!"

"But he killed . . ."

"If he did, he'll be punished. You can't kill him!"

"But . . ."

"Settle down, and I won't report this."

Rubbing his throat, and taking all of this in, the mobster realized his life has been spared.

Months later, the mobster got word that Gary needed mob style help. He sent word that he issued a couple of chits that Gary can cash in at any time.

CHAPTER 54

Scare Tactics

A twenty minute walk. She did it every afternoon. The glistening brightness of this day created a translucent canvas showcasing pink and white cherry blossoms floating and falling on red brick sidewalks and scenting the spring air.

A late model black Chevy van cruised up slowly beside her. They were whistling. "Wow—look at that ass. We'll be back for you," one of them yelled, sticking out his tongue. "It'll be good for both of us!"

Katie quickened her pace, and reluctant to go directly home lest they followed her, scurried into a quaint French boutique restaurant on the corner.

The few people in the restaurant, too early for the dinner crowd, turned as she walked in and hurried to an empty table near the swinging kitchen door.

"Just a cup of tea and a plain croissant, please," she said to the male waiter in the tight black cotton pants and collared white shirt.

Katie removed her cell phone from her handbag, and keeping an eye on the wide front window, scrolled down the phone list to the G's. She pressed the green call button and placed the phone to her ear. A few moments passed, until a male voice answered.

"Gary? Gary, I'm so glad to hear your voice."

"Katie?"

"Yes!"

"God, I haven't heard your voice in a long time. How are you? You sound a little nervous. Are you alright?"

"Actually, no, which is why I'm calling. I hope you don't mind."

Katie told him about the guys in the black Chevy. Gary instructed her to stay inside the restaurant until he arrives.

She'd never been in favor of Gary becoming a U.S. Marshal until today.

Thirty minutes later a six foot one hundred eighty-five pound man walked toward her table. He sat in the seat opposite hers.

"Katie, don't worry. I made a call. Those guys must have given you quite a fright." He paused, taking stock of the panic in her face. Then he placed his right hand on her left shoulder, and continued. "You'll be alright, but it's important that you not stay at your place for a couple of days. I'll drive you home to pick up a change of clothes. You can crash at my place. I'll sleep on the couch."

She believed him. She had no one else to turn to, especially in this situation.

For two mornings Gary drove a grateful Katie to work. He had kept his word, but it's just like him, she thought. He was the consummate gentleman. He explained that he is engaged to be married. She felt so jealous, yet very safe with him. She wished he was in love with her.

"Here you go," he said, opening the passenger door for her on the second morning. As she stepped out of the car, he took her hands and looked down into her eyes. "Don't worry. It'll be safe for you to walk home today."

Katie removed her hands, looked up into his strong-featured face, placed her arms around his neck, and held him for a moment.

"Thank you, thank you, thank you," she murmured, then turned and walked up the front steps of her office building.

At the end of her work day, Katie walked home without incident. She collected her mail in the vestibule of the building and climbed two flights of stairs.

She had just entered her apartment when the telephone rang. It was Mary, her neighbor across the street. "I just want to make sure you heard."

"Heard what?"

"Heard about the big commotion in the neighborhood."

"What commotion?"

"Around 6 o'clock yesterday, just about the time you normally come home. A big pick up truck cut off a black van down the street. Several huge guys got out carrying sledge hammers and baseball bats, and smashed the van all over, breaking its windows and windshield, and putting big dents in it, all the while yelling over and over again, 'Stay away from the people in this neighborhood.' Neighbors sitting on their stoops were frightened. Somebody called 911."

Startled, Katie walked to the window, and looked out toward the street. "Did you see it?" she asked.

"No, some neighbors told me."

"And the police? Do they know who these guys are?"

"No, when the police arrived all they found was broken glass from the van. They're investigating."

The black van and the pick-up truck were never found. Did Gary, the U.S. Marshal, arrange this, she wondered. But how else would he know that she would now be safe. But sometimes, she thought, even the good guys play rough.

CHAPTER 55

The Scare Tactic Escalates

She felt like she could breathe for the first time in weeks. Crisp salty autumn air filled her nostrils. She had taken the last ferry on the Potomac River to its Washington Harbor destination in Georgetown—something she never did. It wasn't crowded tonight, and she was glad for the sense of space.

On the enclosed bottom deck, Katie bought a cup of hot chocolate, and left a small tip for the girl behind the food and beverage concession counter. A rough job, she thought, but to be on the water must be nice. On the top deck, she watched wispy clouds illuminated by a late October half-moon, barely visible in a portion of the night skyline.

In the distance beyond the ship's railing, artificial lights sparkled in a dark void, and grew slowly brighter. She took a deep breath and closed her eyes.

"Katie Manning?"

She spun quickly to see a tall dark figure approaching her from the left, and a shorter man from the right. She couldn't tell which one had spoken.

"Katie?"

She did not answer. There was nowhere to run.

"What do you want?" she shouted. "Here, take my purse!"

The shorter man slapped the bag out of her hand and grabbed her right arm, shoved her against the railing. She gasped as the metal bruised her back. She felt her feet leave the ground and she screamed.

"Why me?" she begged. The shorter man gave the taller one a signal, and they lowered her to the deck. Suddenly his face was pressed against her, and he whispered fiercely.

"This is a first and last warning. If you release any information that could hurt the future of Attorney Atmore, your life is over, do you understand?" The shorter man, eyes burrowing into hers, growled, "We're watching you, and if—" he pushed against her chest with a solid fist, "if any complaint is made against him you won't pleasantly walk home the next time we see you."

Unable to speak, Katie nodded. The men released her, and walked away.

Katie's heart was rushing, her blood pumping. Sweat poured from her scalp, staining her eyes. She pushed away from the railing and sat down on the deck floor, bringing her knees to her chest. She began to weep. Moments passed.

Still shaking, Katie raised herself from the deck, and looked around. The deck was desolate. She walked down the stairs to the auto cargo section of the ship, sat gingerly in her Mini Cooper, locked the door, and for the first time that Fall, she prayed.

CHAPTER 56

Kidnapped

It was just after dark on an unseasonably warm December afternoon, as Katie left the D.C. area for the Grievance Committee. She had concealed the letter that the grievance lawyer requested under the passenger seat. She checked her mirrors, placed her cell phone in the console holder, and turned up the volume on the radio. She hadn't noticed the dark colored Ford SUV following her. Tony kept the Mini Cooper in his sights. Ralph, riding shotgun and carrying one, would be tested.

Ralph's killing Katie accomplished two goals, Tony thought: she will be dead and no longer a threat to lawyer Robert Atmore. And by making the hit, Ralph will have passed his test for joining the organization. Tony heard that lawyer Atmore had promised a large sum of cash for the hit.

Two birds with one stone. After all, she had been warned on the ferry months ago. What did she expect? She was practically asking for it.

"You see her?" Tony barked into his cell phone.

"Got her," a female voice answered.

"When she stops, you bump her, and we'll be right behind."

"Got it."

Katie crossed a metal singing bridge and followed a desolate, two-lane paved road. She slowed the Mini Cooper as it approached a stop sign at the upcoming intersection.

Bang

Katie's head whipped back against the head rest. Her hands stiffened against the steering wheel. Within seconds a young dark-haired woman, clad in a jumpsuit, tapped on her window.

"Are you alright?" she mouthed.

Katie lowered her window. "I think so."

Shaken, Katie stepped out of her car and, with the young woman following, walked to the rear to inspect the damage.

"You ladies okay?" one of the two approaching guys asked.

"I think so," Katie answered, pointing to the back of her car and feeling a little dazed. "This lady's car just hit me."

As she bent down to examine the crumble in her rear fender, two strong arms closed around her from behind. Using the strength of her legs, she instinctively arched her back, trying to stand straight.

"What the hell?" Katie yelled, turning her head toward her assailant. The dark-haired woman slapped her hard, and within seconds, a small towel was wrapped around her head, stretched across her mouth, and a wet rag pressed against her nose. The taller man wrapped a climber's rope around her legs and arms, and the three of them lifted her small feet off the ground, and carried her toward the SUV. She blacked out before the vehicle had turned down an unfinished side road, and so she did not feel the hands all over her body.

The bumping of the SUV on uneven gravel woke Katie from her drug-induced sleep. She strained to raise her neck to look around. Tied down like a piece of luggage, ropes wrapped around her hands and feet, her arms crisscrossing her chest, she could hardly move. The back of her head surrendered to the truck bed, as her ears listened to the gravel rocks ricocheting off its undercarriage.

"She's kind of hot," a voice from the front of the SUV yelled. She recognized that voice. "We should take a little from her, you know. We can share, but I go first."

Katie whimpered in the dark.

"Hold on there," said the second male voice. "I need to concentrate now. We've got to make a clean delivery. Then we'll see. Keep your pants on, for Christ sake."

Moments later the SUV turned right, and Katie heard tree branches scraping the body and rear side windows. As the vehicle slowed to a stop, Katie felt herself slipping into a new kind of daze. She had never been this afraid.

The rear hatch lifted and the two men reached in, untied the ropes from the lateral posts, pulled her out and hoisted her to her feet. The ropes from around her chest were loosened, and she could see the shorter man looking at her chest. Gripping her upper arm, Ralph leaned into her right side and quickly ran his nostrils near her neck, sniffing her moisture, taking in some of her sweetness, letting it travel up his sensitive nostrils, almost tasting it and consciously implanting the memory of her for reliving when desired. But he wanted more than a scent memory. He bent down, and while removing the rope from her ankles, ran a finger across her skin, up her leg, slyly feeling her without her permission, and without giving Tony an excuse to rebuke him.

"Come on!" Tony barked, pushing her in the direction of a feeble light barely visible through wet tree limbs. The young woman in the jumpsuit led the way. She turned into an opening in the brush and landed on a rutted trail. They walked for several minutes, pushing aside small branches, and slapping at vines. Ahead, Katie saw a small wooden house with features more like a large shed, the wood weathered and faded. A small light dangled from a cord attached to an overhang near the front door.

A dark wooden door opened outward, and a man in his late twenties, wearing a black skull cap, faded blue workman's overalls, and a stern face, stepped out.

"What took you so long?" he asked in an irritated voice. "Been waiting here more than an hour."

Katie found the man's voice menacing, but his eyes sheepish. He kept darting them toward and away from her, as though embarrassed to look for long. The eyes of the young woman leading the group caught his.

"For God's sake, if you don't develop more patience, the boss will . . ." she stopped short.

The two guys pushed Katie forward into the doorway.

"Get outta the way," Tony demanded.

Skull Cap stepped aside as Katie was muscled into the small front room.

"Sit her over there," the still-nameless woman directed, pointing to a gray metal folding chair in the left corner next to two green cots lying on an unfinished plank floor. A lamp on a table near the cots gave Katie a better view of the person leading this mission—the same person who hit the back of her car, a large woman in her late twenties, hair pulled back in a bun, and a black scarf around her neck. No makeup.

"What do you want with me?" Katie pleaded as she was being tied to the chair. "I don't have any money."

"We don't want your money," the large woman assured her.

"You were warned," the older man said.

"What do you mean?" Katie asked, frowning with incredulous eyes.

"What do we mean? Come on. Robert Atmore and the ferry," he continued.

"What . . . but . . . but."

"No buts, Miss Katie," yelled the woman in the jump suit. "You were warned two months ago and this is what you asked for." She turned her back and looked at Skull Cap. "We delivered her. Our part of the contract is over. Now you finish her."

"I thought our buddy here with the shot gun was supposed to finish her off," Tony said.

"Orders changed. Plus burying her takes too much time. We gotta go right away," Jump Suit interrupted. "An emergency job just came up."

"My boys are on the way, anyhow," Skull Cap added.

"But I haven't said anything," Katie pleaded.

"If we'd let you drive ten more minutes, you would have," said the big woman, slapping Katie across her face, turning it hot. The woman pivoted and pointed her right index finger at Skull Cap. "And if anything goes wrong, the boss will take care of you, understand?"

Skull Cap, looking defensive, returned her stare, "Don't worry."

Katie had no choice. She screamed as loudly as she could.

"Shut the fuck up!" the big woman yelled, again slapping her, this time across the right side of her head. The force of the blow weakened Katie. Her screams turned into silent aches.

"I'm sick of you Little Miss Ivy Girl. Yeah, we know your background, and what you're up to," she yelled, pulling a small roll of duct tape from her jump suit pocket and wrapping it around Katie's mouth. "Now shut the hell up!"

Ralph winced, sensing he was going to miss his chance. "Maybe I can stay here and help until your boys arrive." He looked at Katie's ripped shirt.

"No, you come with us," Jump Suit ordered. "Boss wants it this way." Leaving the shack and Skull Cap behind, Jump Suit slammed the wooden door behind her.

Katie's eyes widened and she wiggled in the chair as Skull Cap reached toward her. He placed his left hand on the top of her head, grabbed the duct tape with his right, and pulled it off.

"Don't worry, you'll be alright," he announced in a relaxed tone.

It startled her. She had just separated her psyche from her body preparing for unimaginable afflictions.

"Don't ask, and don't get curious," he said, as he untied her legs. "Somebody called in a large debt to free you, and even I don't ask too many questions. The bosses at the top work it out."

Katie rubbed her wrists, and tongued her cheek. Her head ached, and she felt the whole world looking different.

Skull Cap assured Katie that he would safeguard her stay through the night, and she would go home in the morning.

At day break, a black sedan pulled up to the shed. The driver knocked on the shed door. Katie leaped into his arms.

"But how?" she asked.

"I'll explain on the way," Gary answered.

This mobster chit was his last.

CHAPTER 57

Return to Connecticut

Given the horrendous experience she had undergone, Katie could not get out of Washington, D.C. fast enough. She longed for the comfort and safety of her home.

The colors and sound of the Capitol City dissolved in Katie's weariness. Her parents kept their questions to a minimum, and though their curiosity bubbled, they saw signs of sadness in their daughter.

Waking up in on her own bed, far from D.C., far from the goblins that threatened and chased her, Katie pondered the options. Go to the police and face the questions? *Who are they? What do they look like? Where do they live? Where did this happen? Where are the witnesses?* Questions the police would ask. Questions to which she had few answers. She even doubted they would believe her.

Tell her parents? About being kidnapped? It would frighten them, and anger her father, possibly even expose them to danger too. She had only said that she missed them and wanted to come home for the weekend, though she knew they sensed more. Certainly she needed their emotional reaffirmation, and now she must figure out how to get the information to the Grievance Committee. The goons had failed to find the zip drive, hidden in her waistband for safekeeping, onto which she had placed a copy of the scanned report. She could mail it to the Grievance Committee.

Using her left hand—her right hand was still sore from the rough handling of her unnamed attackers—Katie lifted the top of her blankets, rolled her feet to the floor, and stood. God, she ached. Her back, her legs. She shuddered. She could feel their hands . . .

And now she was here. Nothing in her room had changed. Only the pale yellow paint on the walls looked new. Rudy, her teddy bear, stood guard by the rear window overlooking her mother's well-kept garden. Begonias, white chrysanthemums, red roses, and other assorted flowers favored this year by an unusually warm December unfocused her fear.

"Katie, telephone!" her mother yelled from the first floor.

"Thanks, Mom," she responded, while picking up the receiver on her desk.

"Are you okay?" a woman's voice asked. Katie hesitated.

"Oh, this is Olivia Reese . . . just calling to check up on you. I got your number from the National Child Guardian Center."

"Yeah, I'm fine," Katie answered, thinking it was odd to receive this call.

"I heard that you were in a little trouble recently, I'm just calling to make sure you're . . ."

"How did you know?" Katie interjected. Her heart was pounding now, and she was speaking in whispers.

"From your guardian angel."

"Guardian angel?" Katie repeated.

"Long story. We'll talk about it when you return to Washington."

Chapter 58

Olivia Reese

"What did I get myself into?" Katie blurted out, standing in the doorway to Olivia's apartment. She paused, then with a quizzical look, added "And how did you?"

"A guy from the U.S. Marshal's office. He said you'd know. I don't know how he found me, but those guys have some contacts. Look, as you know I'm the special assistant to the D.C. Child Protection Commissioner. Come on, lets go for a walk and talk," Olivia replied.

They strode down U Street into the old Chinatown section of D.C., passing highly adorned windows in tall glass-and-steel buildings bordering upscale boutique clothing and variety shops displaying dramatic colors of purple, bright red and turquoise hues. Mannequins stood at strange angles.

Katie explained her discoveries about Robert Atmore's connection to the missing money from the Merchant estate, and about her ordeal in the woods. Finding Olivia a wonderful listener, she said more than she meant to, taking advantage of the only opportunity she'd had to share the heavy burden of her secrets.

A shocked Olivia interrupted Katie several times by asking her to repeat portions of her story. As Katie linked it together, Olivia began to understand the remarkable scope and depth of what she had experienced.

"He's gone wild," Olivia said. "Not only is he fleecing this client, he's also having sex with an underage girl, the sister of his mentee. He is implicated in a kidnapping and attempted murder. My god, there is no end to his crimes."

Olivia pointed to a Starbucks. "I need to sit down to hear this again."

Finding an empty table, Katie glanced outside at the motley crowd of people briskly going here and there. She turned to notice Olivia standing confidently in line, back straight, head level. There was something solid and reliable about her, a quality Katie desired.

Returning with two filled cups, Olivia fixed her eyes on the young woman who had undergone such torture.

"Here's your French Roast," she said, lowering herself into her chair.

"Thanks for buying."

"Come on. The least I could do."

"Tell me more about the girl."

Katie started by looking down into her cup of coffee, hoping its soon refreshing taste would relieve some of her angst.

"Well, I became acquainted with Cheryl as a NCG volunteer in Juvenile Court." She stopped abruptly.

"What's the matter?" Olivia asked.

Katie raised her head to Olivia's eye level. "It's just that as a Court Appointed Special Advocate volunteer we are sworn to keep Juvenile Court information confidential."

Olivia cleared her throat and gave Katie a stern, concerned look.

"Listen, what you said earlier about the lawyer and Cheryl frees you of any confidentiality. You, and now I, since I am aware of it, have a duty to report it. It's a crime for a grown man to have sex with an underage girl. So please tell me."

Katie nodded and took another sip. "She was a Family with Service Needs case in Juvenile Court, you know, giving her mother a hard time—staying out late, smoking, not going to school—that sort of thing, almost beyond the control of her parent. So, as you know, the parent files the Service Needs Petition bringing the family and the child into court for court-ordered services, counseling for the child and family, parenting skills training, and court orders on the child. As the new National Child Guardian Program volunteer the case was assigned to me and that's how I got to know her."

"So when did you find out about this sex thing?" Olivia asked, crossing her legs under the table.

"About a week ago, I stopped by her house to get the latest information to prepare my final report for the court, such as her effort to improve her grades, how she and her mother are getting along . . . stuff like that. It was just after school and her mother wasn't home. She looked worried, so I asked her what was wrong."

"What did she say?"

"At first it was the typical teenager 'oh, nothing,' but I assured her that whatever it was I wasn't going to use it against her."

Katie glanced at the tables around her.

"Katie, it's okay," Olivia assured her, "no one is paying attention to our conversation."

Katie began. "We were sitting in the living room. She was in the recliner, and I was on the sofa. She started crying. She just clinched her face, pressed her eyelids together, and lowered her chin—the tears just flowed. After repeatedly asking her to tell me and reassuring her that I was there to help, she finally said it was Robert. He had hurt her.

"I asked her how and she answered by telling me he said that he and she were through. He told her this after she had given herself to him after he told her he loved and would protect her."

Olivia leaned across the table toward Katie. "Did she tell you what 'giving herself to him' meant?"

"Yes. In detail. Some of the things he did to her and got her to like are things none of my friends have ever experienced—or at least they haven't told me about."

"Sexual things, you mean?"

"Oh yes."

"And they involved touching, penetration?"

"Oh yes," Katie again answers. "And there is something else," Katie continued.

"What?"

"When I asked her whether there was anything else I should know, a shameful look crossed her face. Then she said that he gave her a disease."

"And the disease?"

"She said the doctor called it trichomoniasis, a minor case of STD. She later told me her mother is furious. She took her to the doctor, but the embarrassed girl refused to give the name of the guy that gave it to her."

The intense, bright mid-morning sunlight permeating the plate glass window of the coffee shop sharply contrasted with the foulness of lawyer Atmore's squalid deeds.

"We've got to convince her to report him," Olivia said, finishing the last few drops in her cup.

"But how, after I told her I wouldn't use the information to hurt her?" Olivia's face turned stern.

"You're not hurting her. You're empowering her to vindicate what that bastard did to her and will do to other young girls."

Then, as an aside, Olivia commented, "He likes them young—I wonder where that comes from?"

"Who do I report it to?"

"Report it to? Don't worry about that. I have friends in high places."

"What do I do in the meantime? I can't work at Swarthmore."

Olivia stared at her and said flatly, "Resign. Give your notice."

CHAPTER 59

Escape

"How did it go?" asked Sally, Ron's new foster mother.

"It's ok," Ron muttered, closing the apartment door behind him and tossing his bag on the living room couch.

"Pick up that bag and freshen up," Sally yelled, "dinner's ready in a few minutes."

"Yes, Ma'am," Ron answered, grabbing his bag. He was relieved to be home. The work day had been long. Mum throughout the dinner of canned soup and white rice, Ron asked to be excused and headed to his room earlier than usual. Although Ron's foster mother wondered why, her worries about whether she had enough money to put down for a rent-to-own big TV with income from only one foster child crowded out any empathy for her ward's stomach.

Ron sat in his room staring out of the window. He was worried that his foster mother would carry out her threat to have her boyfriend beat him if he stopped working the construction job. Also he was tired of her ups and downs, praising him for working, and other times severely criticizing him, calling him "dumb-ass," and saying "you won't amount to nothing, even your mama don't want you." Ron decided it was time to go.

The next day, Vinnie was the first to arrive at the demolition site. The weather man was right this time. No rain. Dark clouds surrendered to a crimson sunrise. Vinnie liked being first on the job. He parked his red pick up truck next to the ten story building, cut the engine, took a swig of coffee from his thermos, polished off a grape jelly donut, and grabbed his lunch box from the passenger seat. He pushed open the driver's door, stepped down onto the yard, and arching his shoulders toward his back, and pulling his arms wide, gave himself a good stretch. A quick yawn finished the job.

Energized, Vinnie walked through the open front door and surveyed the site. Demo was almost complete. The guys had done a pretty good job. Little debris was left. Leave it broom clean was the closing instruction. Pretty soon it will be on to the next demolition job in Kansas City.

Something at the end of the hallway caught his eye. It looked like what homeless people carry around. Vinnie pulled out his box cutter from his right pocket and walked toward the door adjacent to the large black plastic bag. He leaned over and opened it. Faded jeans, white t-shirts, sneakers, underwear.

He took a deep breath, knocked on the door and yelled, "Whoever is in there, you'd better come out. There's no trespassing in here. Come out now!" Vinnie flipped the switch on the overhead construction lights in the hallway and fingered the box cutter blade.

Moments later the door slowly opened, and a boy's light brown face emerged. "Ron?" Vinnie uttered.

Ron wiped his right hand across his face and stared up at his job supervisor.

"What are you doing here?"

"No place to stay," the boy answered.

Vinnie walked past Ron into the small room. "What do you mean, no place to stay, you must have a home, and this ain't it. The boss won't put up with this," Vinnie said, looking at the cardboard mat on the floor.

Ron lowered his head.

"You're just kidding, you got a home, right? Just kidding, huh?"

Ron shook his head.

Vinnie's eyes studied the boy. A twelve year old homeless. Two bags of clothes, one here, the other in the hallway. He looked tired, half-asleep, awakened too early from his troubles.

"Come outside with me. We need to talk. Have you had anything to eat?"

"No sir," Ron said as he stuffed his feet into his sneakers, and pressed his shirt tail under his belt into his jeans.

"You take the bag in here and I'll take the one in the hallway. We'll bring them to my truck."

Vinnie tossed the bags into the truck bed and secured them with tie downs. "Is this all you have?" he asked, not anticipating there would be any more, and there wasn't. "Get in, let's get you some food, I can be a little late today."

Looking across the table at the bright eyed but troubled youth stuffing his mouth with pancakes at the diner, Vinnie wondered how he can help his little leader of the boy demo crew who won't return to his foster home. Then he remembered. Ron had told him about an aunt in Kansas City whose husband had died. Maybe she can raise him. Their next demo job is in Kansas City. Maybe she could use a good boy around the house.

CHAPTER 60

Atmore's Arrest

Crossing the Potomac at mid-morning Lieutenant Lois Wilkins' dark blue Crown Victoria stayed well back of the Jaguar. She was sure they had the horse power in the police vehicle to keep pace with, if not outrun, the black cat carrying Robert Atmore. For now, she would wait. According to her sources at the elderly fraud unit, this day was payday for Robert and his lawyer.

But it was also payday for Lois and her driver partner, Alfred Cooke. Two arrests in a major investigation in one day—that equals front page.

"Let's not get ahead of ourselves," Lois told Alfred. "Stay focused and we'll get our names in the paper. You're a rookie anyway, your time will come. Not too close now. Keep him at least three cars ahead."

"I know, I know," Alfred said, easing off the gas. He looked at Lois out of the corner of his eye, and imagined that if she were in street clothes, and a little more relaxed, she might still turn heads. His eyes went back to the road just in time to see a sixteen-wheeler with a log load cut in front of them from the adjoining lane.

"Watch out!" Lois yelled.

"Jesus!"

"This guy's not looking where he's going. There're five lanes, for Chrissake, and he has to choose ours!"

Alfred tapped the brakes, muttered under his breath, steered the Crown Vic into the middle lane, and accelerating past the sixteen-wheeler at the perfect pace to not disrupt the SUV coming from behind, caught a glimpse of the black Jaguar just as the Interstate was bending to the left on its route to Arlington.

"Good maneuver!"

"Why thank you, Lieutenant."

"They train you well in the Academy, I guess."

"Nah. I was a New York City cab driver before I signed up."

They both grinned. It would not be the last time they smiled that day.

An hour later, sitting inside the restaurant, eating pasta and sipping white wine Robert and his new lawyer friend were surprised when a woman and a man pulled out chairs at their table, tossed a warrant toward them, slapped down badges hard enough to rattle the silverware, and announced that they were under arrest. The Lieutenant—Robert had learned to know ranks—in a blue denim jacket placed her right hand firmly on the table, and looked directly into Robert's eyes.

"Is all the money in the brief case?" she asked.

Robert nodded.

"Gentlemen, let's not make a scene."

Katie had told Gary everything about that Sunday she had snooped Atmore's files dealing with the Merchant estate and overhearing Atmore's phone conversation with an unknown person about which a considerable sum of money was to change hands at this restaurant at 5 pm today. Upon hearing Katie's story, U S Marshal Gary had notified the D.C. police.

CHAPTER 61

Atmore Exposed

"**Y**ou've got to be kidding."

"Robert Atmore has been arrested. You know I wouldn't—not about this. That's why I'm calling you."

Denise Hall, the new managing partner of Swarthmore, Jones and Smithtone, was shocked. Robert? It couldn't be.

"Do you have details?"

"None that I can share, but I thought you should know."

"You have to let me know what's at the center of the charge. Remember, Eric, we were on the ethics panel together. You can give me something."

Eric Wilkinson, head of the State Lawyer Grievance Office, sighed. "Yes. We have reliable evidence that Robert Atmore threatened the life of one of your interns."

"Threatened the life of an intern? Who?"

"Katie Manning."

"Katie! I don't believe it!"

"And that's not all."

"We also have reliable evidence that Robert Atmore has embezzled millions of dollars from one of your clients."

"What? Oh, this is too much! What client, Eric?"

"The last name's Merchant."

"Just give me a second," Denise asked, typing into an archive search engine. "There it is *Marie Merchant.* Yes, it's assigned to Robert. Which is unusual—because he generally doesn't handle probate matters."

"It's not the only thing that's unusual."

"Obviously."

CHAPTER 62

Katie's Testimony

Katie sat outside the Prosecutor's office, feeling terribly anxious about whether she will be up to telling the full story of her relationship with Robert Atmore.

The prosecutor's secretary greeted her and ushered her into his office. Introductory formalities were accomplished and Katie was warned that her testimony would be recorded.

"I had been suspicious that Cheryl, a young girl whom I'm mentoring, may have been having a sexual relationship with my boss. There were many signs, and she finally admitted it.

"Why did you think this?"

"He mentors Cheryl's younger brother, and Cheryl starting coming along with him. But now I'm pretty sure she started coming to the office alone. You know, just last week I saw her leaving his office after working hours. She is a minor, you know."

"Is he the kind of person who would—"

"I—" Katie began to shake.

"Katie? Are you okay?"

Katie regained her composure. "Yes. I think it's just—I also believe my boss has stolen from his clients. And about two months ago, I was threatened—two guys, on the ferry—they told me not to reveal anything that might harm him. I was so scared. I didn't know what to do." Katie was aware of the dramatic quiver in her voice, but could not control it. "I don't know their names. It was just this one night when I was coming back on the ferry two big guys picked me up and threatened to throw me overboard if I said or did anything that could harm my boss. Then a couple of nights ago, I was kidnapped, roughed up and threatened to be killed."

"And you don't know who did this? You don't have a clue?"

"No, I don't, I'm sorry. I'm so scared."

"You don't have to be. Robert Atmore has been arrested and he is telling the police everything about his criminal activities and naming names. The police are in the process of rounding up everyone involved. I would imagine they are running scared. They won't bother you anymore."

CHAPTER 63

Atmore's Conviction

All of the preparation by the prosecution went for naught. As his trial date neared, Robert Atmore realized he did not have a chance to beat the charges levied against him. To save himself the embarrassment of a public trial, he threw himself at the mercy of the court and pleaded guilty to all of the laundry list of charges: kidnapping, attempted murder, conspiring with members of organized crime, embezzlement, and having sex with a minor, to name a few. Showing him no mercy, the judge sentencing him to life in prison without parole. I imagine Robert Atmore will be able to continue his legal career as a jailhouse lawyer filling out the paperwork for appeals for his fellow inmates.

In an attempt to gain favor with authorities, Robert Atmore implicated Bruce Doyle and Charles Murphy as his contacts to getting in touch with mobsters. Doyle, as a result, lost his private investigator license and is awaiting trial on charges of conspiring to kidnap and commit murder. Charles Murphy, as a result of Atmore's testimony, suffered a major stroke and is totally incapacitated.

Tony and Ralph, through Doyle's testimony, have been arrested on charges of being members of organized crime, threatening, kidnapping, and attempted murder. There is no doubt they will be convicted and face long terms in prison where Ralph will be able to get all the sex he wants, although it may not be the variety he prefers. That is if the mob doesn't silence them first.

The dark-haired woman and Skull Cap have never been found and I doubt they ever will be. The mob has its own way of closing out investigations.

Oh, one more thing, his family no longer refers to him as Robert the Successful, in fact they no longer mention his name at all. It is as if he never existed. As for his ex-wives and children, they need another means of support.

As for me, I am shocked beyond belief by the Robert Atmore story. Robert Atmore was an outstanding lawyer, a pillar of the community, and a fine man when I knew him. I often ponder how Robert, my former law clerk and the one who sent me a warm thank you card each Christmas, could have committed all these crimes.

CHAPTER 64

The Warrant

Plain clothes officers escorted the Governor as he strolled from the Capitol Hill polling station at noon. The first microphone was in his face before he even saw the television crew. Before he knew it, a dozen reporters were shouting above each other, as heavy black cameras on shoulders pointed toward his face. For a moment, he thought they were guns.

"Governor, is there any truth to the rumor that there is a warrant for your arrest?"

"Governor, do you have any comment on the report that a warrant—"

Stunned momentarily, Mulvey quickly pulled out his charm. "Hey, if the Attorney General wants to see me, he can schedule a meeting with my staff. No need to arrest me!"

Typically this would have gathered at least a chuckle, but on this day, it fell on impatient reporters who knew enough to eschew sympathy. A crowd had now gathered. Mulvey's legs felt a little unsteady. He stumbled toward his waiting limo while his guards shoved reporters a little harder than necessary.

"Governor, there's a call for you," his driver said while Mulvey settled into the back seat of the black limo.

"Take a message, I'll return the call later."

"I'm sorry, sir—it's the Attorney General. Says he must talk with you right away."

Mulvey picks up the receiver. **"WHAT!?"**

"I regret to inform you Governor, but the State's Attorney has informed us that a warrant for your arrest has been issued by Judge Samuel Hughes—"

242

"On what grounds!"

"Corruption and risk of injury to minors."

Silence.

"Governor?"

Silence still.

"You have until 5:00 to surrender yourself to the State Police at—"

Mulvey hung up the phone.

CHAPTER 65

Governor Mulvey's Conviction

Soon after Mulvey was arrested, he resigned his governorship and pleaded guilty to depriving the public of honest service. He was sentenced to one year and a day to be served in federal prison. He made the following statement:

"Arrogance is very easy when you are put on a pedestal and start to believe your own press releases. It becomes all about me. You start to block out everything else around you. I found in my career that a lot of people will tell you how great you are, especially when you are the boss. But there will come a time when that career is over that it will come down to real faith, real family, and real friends, and I have too few."

The Mulvey political Sunday dinners are no more.

Chapter 66

Mementos

Sally Chandler used the new light blue Xerox machine to make copies of several photos and clippings from the packet of materials, which Beatrice and John Manning routinely provided at her quarterly visit to their home. It's 3:45 in the afternoon and Dorothy will be arriving soon for her little office visit. Returning to her desk, Sally inserted the copies into a white pocket file folder labeled *D & H Simmons*. Although it's against protocol and as a Supervisor she knew better, Sally felt an extraordinarily deep sorrow for Dorothy Simmons—so much so that she passed on copies of middle and high school report cards. Even photos of the girls as young children, teenagers, and young adults smiling and holding out their gifts at picnics and holiday get-togethers found their way into these white folders. And today would be no different. There was one prohibition—Dorothy could not contact the girls until Sally gave the okay.

At each office meeting Sally encouraged her to seek psychiatric counseling, and do the specific steps required to see her daughters. Dorothy always seemed so down when she came to these visits, but the photos seem to mollify her spirits. Gazing at them Dorothy wondered whether they were just mementos, or whether someday she would actually see her daughters.

CHAPTER 67

The Photo

Bouncing in his high chair, infant Terrance smiled broadly and emitted a joyous yelping squeal. "Cheerios don't go up your nose," Dorothy said, taking the cereal from Terrance's hand and placing it on the plastic spoon.

"I don't know who taught him that trick, but breakfast is no time to show it off," Henry said, grinning and tickling Terrance's chin. "Stop playing in your milk bowl, that's for the cereal," he added and then turned his attention to the golden brown sausage and creamy grits on his plate.

"I love these Saturday morning breakfasts, hon," he said, slurping from his cup.

Sitting at the table with her husband, and gazing at Terrance in the high chair playing with his spoon gave her some comfort. Yet Dorothy felt a longing, no an ache deep within her heart. She pushed her chair back and walked to the junk drawer next to the aluminum sink. She pulled it open, removed a file, and, returning to her seat, placed it on the table.

"Another white folder, I see. When did you see Miss Chandler?"

"Just the other day." She paused and took a sip of orange juice.

Henry removed the photos, and carefully examined each one. "My, my, they're like real grownups . . . I wish we could see them."

"We can't until we get Miss Chandler's permission, you know. Plus we don't have their address. It's somewhere in D.C."

Henry pulled one of the photos closer. He examined Katie's wide smile, and the word "home" on the placard Maria held in her hand, pointing to a building next to them. "Look here, hon, there's a street sign in the background, and a park. Hand me my bifocals."

Henry took the bifocals. He placed the bottom half of the right eyeglass lens on the photo and slowly moved it over the light green street sign. "Oh, I see."

CHAPTER 68

The Search

"Right here is fine."

"Here?"

"Yes. What's the charge?"

"Nine dollars."

She handed the cab driver a ten-dollar bill, told him to keep the change, and then stepped onto the sidewalk. "Come on," she said to her husband.

"Are you sure they live around here?"

"This is Constitution Avenue, right across from the park," she said. "Remember the street sign in the girls' photo said Constitution Avenue and it showed a park. We'll just stay right here until we see them," Dorothy said, looking intently at the faces of the women passing by and comparing them to the photos Sally Chandler gave her.

"Can we sit while we wait?"

"Bench right over there."

"How long do we have to wait?" Henry asked, while wiping his brow with a handkerchief from his pocket. "It's hot."

"Just a little while. Why don't you read the newspaper? I'll keep an eye out, and then we can take turns."

"Like we're on watch, huh?"

"Yeah, like that."

Henry opened his paper, but looked up after only a few moments. He parted his lips to speak. "We should have—," he started.

"Don't, Henry," she said sharply. "No looking back now." She paused. "No looking back now. No sir."

"I know."

"They turned out alright. That's what's important. Miss Chandler said they turned out alright."

"I should have gone to the counseling—"

"Stop it!" She looked at him intensely but without anger. "I've spent twenty years saying that. Now I'm saying something else. They turned out alright. They were where they should have been, Henry. No looking back now."

"Will they have us? It's been so long."

Dorothy did not answer, but sat beside Henry on the bench, feeling again the weariness of twenty years regret and now the new weight of expectation.

EPILOGUE

Yes, Dorothy and Henry saw their daughters but did not greet them in any way. That would come another day.

Denise Hall, the Managing Partner of the Swarthmore law firm recognized the vulnerability of the firm to law suits developing as a result of the Robert Atmore crimes and moved rapidly to quench the potentially ruinous publicity. She immediately restored the embezzled monies Atmore stole from the Marie Merchant estate by accessing the firm's errors and omissions insurance. Aunt Margaret received all the money bequeathed to her. Denise then contacted Katie and Cheryl's family and negotiated six figure settlements to both.

The money received by Cheryl allowed her mother to move to a more desirable neighborhood—away from the bad influences affecting both Frank and Cheryl. In addition, the money will underwrite both Frank's and Cheryl's education.

Katie returned to Connecticut, enrolled in and graduated from the Yale Law School while working part-time for the Child Protection Department (CPD) under the tutelage of Olivia Reese. She has been generous with the money she received from the Swarthmore law firm, giving an ample sum to Maria—who by the way has gotten married and is intent on raising a family—another sum to her foster parents, the Mannings, and, believe it or not, to her natural parents, Dorothy and Henry Simmons. It was through my intercession that Dorothy accepted the money. I told her it would guarantee Terrance's college education. If Terrance grows up anything like his father, I'm sure he'll become a student-athlete and win a scholarship. I'm also sure that Dorothy and Henry will meet up with their girls one of these days. After all, they will want to meet their brother.

Upon graduation Katie began working full time for CPD. Her work there has been notable for its quality and innovation. She was, as her co-workers would later joke, ubiquitous—everywhere speaking unwaveringly, passionately, as though she were carrying inside her more than one voice, the voice of thousands of children who had never been heard. She looked back on the web of grace, on the net of providence that had moved her from there to here. And she marveled at her good fortune.

Katie poured her heart and soul into her projects. It was so close to her because of personal exposure to how foster care can be a savior of lost children. She marshaled her unbridled enthusiasm and dedication to obtain grants from major foundations, which she used to fund a National Symposium on Guardians ad Litem. From that symposium, attended by representatives from a majority of states, Katie formed a National Committee that set out a list of best GAL practices, then distributed to all of the states by hard copy and made available on the Internet. A significant element of best practices focused on identifying, treating, and preventing injury from MSBP. The best practices became a national model, credited with preventing child abuse to thousands of children each year, and with improving the treatment of foster children. Unquestionably, I am certain that some future governor will select and appoint Katie to head the entire department and who knows that one day Katie could be part of some president's cabinet dealing with the nation's child safety issue.

Katie's work at the CPD was recognized by the new governor who awarded her Connecticut's highest award for Excellence in Public Service. Seated in the audience at the awards ceremony at the State Capitol were the Mannings, her sister Maria and her husband and, unbeknownst to her, two other sets of eyes. They were the eyes of two other persons who had slipped in and sat far back in the balcony, almost in the rafters, smiling, and wondering. Henry had seen the announcement in the newspaper.

Also unbeknownst to her was a man in the balcony with a gun, and an unobstructed view; however, not an assassin. Security officers cleared him after examining his credentials: Gary Maxwell, U.S. Marshal, her former boyfriend. His fiancée having left him, he anxiously wondered if Katie still cared.

When Katie received the award, the applause was louder than she expected. It seemed to come from every corner of the room. Katie stared out at the crowd but could only see the dim outline of members of the audience who had gathered for the ceremony, for the tears in her eyes were affecting her vision. And she definitely could not see the tears in the eyes of those near and dear to her who were filled with pride and joy.

Triumph indeed.

So that is the story of Triumph, and I guess this is The End, or is it The Beginning?

*   *   *

What happened to me? I thought you'd never ask. Well, I retired from the bench after spending more than twenty years as a trial judge. I am grateful for having had the opportunity through the Court to have spent so many years working with State Prosecutors, defense lawyers, lawyers for children and their parents, guardians ad litem, social workers for the Department of Children and Families, as well as having access to the resources of the Department itself, in attending to significant legal, parenting and social issues affecting the lives of multiple hundreds of children and their parents.

POSTLUDE

FYI

Child Protection

The Child Protection Department (CPD) has four mandated areas of activity: Child Welfare, Children's Behavioral Health, Juvenile Services, and Prevention. The Department facilities include several schools and a psychiatric center. The CPD also has a central office located in the State Capitol City and 14 area offices organized in five regions of which the Elm City is one.

At any point in time, the Department yearly serves thousands of children and families across its program and mandate areas, its central focus being to work with families and communities to improve safety, ensure that more children have permanent families and advance the overall well-being of children.

The CPD's areas of concern include 1.) Adolescent and Transitional services to assist youth under the care of the Department to make the transition from out of home care to a self-sufficient, productive life as an adult in the community; 2.) Juvenile services to develop competency, accountability, and responsibility in all programs and services with the ultimate goal of each child achieving success in the community; 3.) Medical/Health Services to assure that children in the care and custody of the Department receive optimal health care; 4.) Prevention services to enable children and families to thrive independently in their communities and to apply best evidence-based and best practice prevention approaches at strategic points in the Department's continuum of care.

On average 513,000 children in the United States are in foster care, with ages ranging from less than a year to 20 years. The median age of these children is 10.6. Twenty-four percent of the children are in relative foster family homes; forty-eight percent are in non-relative foster homes; eight percent are in group homes; and ten percent are in institutions. Only four percent are in pre-adoptive homes. One hundred fourteen thousand are waiting to be adopted.

CPSIA information can be obtained at www.ICGtesting.com
Printed in the USA
LVOW11s1655240315

431691LV00001B/3/P